The Battle of St. Bartholomew's

by

Caitlyn Callery

A Rotherton Romance

The Battle of St. Bartholomew's

Cover Art by *Tina Lynn Stout*

The Wild Rose Press, Inc.
PO Box 708
Adams Basin, NY 14410-0708
Visit us at www.thewildrosepress.com

Publishing History
First Edition, 2026
Trade Paperback Print ISBN 978-1-5092-6454-4
Digital ISBN 978-1-5092-6455-1

A Rotherton Romance
Published in the United States of America

Dedication

Dedicated to the memory of my sister, Molly.
Defender of those who could not defend themselves,
no bully was safe when you were around.
You are missed.

Chapter One

May 1818

"Come on, Addams."

Diana Villiers stood on the steps of her father's house and waited, impatiently, for the door to open. She had knocked four times now, and there was still no sign of anyone coming. If she stood here much longer, the neighbors would notice. Not only that, but she was hot and bothered. Her shift stuck to her back, her skin felt grimy, and her scalp itched. She needed a bath.

That was hardly surprising. After all, she'd spent the last two days in an airless, cramped public coach with a variety of other passengers, some not as sweet-smelling as they might be, and many of them encroaching upon her space. There'd been no respite from the discomfort: if one person left the coach, another took their seat, and invariably they pressed against her until she was squeezed tightly into the corner, making herself as small as possible to minimize contact.

There'd been no comfort to be had at the brief stops along the way, either. Whenever they stopped to change horses, the coachman warned that he wouldn't wait for stragglers, so they'd best be quick. There was barely time to use the necessary, much less take a drink and assuage her thirst. Eating was definitely not possible. By the time the food she'd ordered—and paid for—arrived, the coach was ready to go. The innkeepers did not look sympathetic as they took the meals back to their kitchens, no doubt to resell to passengers on the next coach. It was, she decided after the second inn, a lucrative trade, and she'd stopped ordering meals at that point.

By the time she arrived at La Belle Sauvage Inn at Ludgate Hill, she was starving, and looked forward to whatever Cook had on hand as she put the whole experience behind her. From now on, she vowed, she would only travel in Papa's private vehicle.

Some of the discomfort of the journey was her own fault. Diana acknowledged that. Had the innkeepers known they were dealing with Miss Diana Villiers, daughter of Sir Charles Villiers, respected businessman, and shipping-line owner with interests and properties across the world, they might have been more circumspect.

Alas, that hadn't been something she could admit, not without creating a scandal to blight the Season she so looked forward to. That Season was several years later than it should have been, thanks to the travelling she'd done with Papa. It would also be shorter than normal; most of the other debutantes had been in Town for over a month already. However, it was her Season, and she was determined to have it.

Preferably without damaging gossip. Bad enough that the *ton* would be whispering about the size of her dowry, and that Papa would inevitably have to weed out the fortune hunters before allowing any genuine suitors to come near. She would not have her name dragged through the mud as well.

Which was why, when it became obvious that she must travel to London by public transport, unchaperoned, she had adopted a false name and persona. Miss Villiers, heiress, might not take such a journey, but Miss Wilde, impoverished young woman on her way to become a governess, could do so.

Diana had been proud of her plan at the time. She grinned now, self-deprecatingly, at her own naïveté. If she'd known then what she knew now…well, there was never any use in regretting one's actions. All one could do was learn from them and do better next time.

Still, she'd thought her disguise clever. She'd found a shabby, outmoded dress in Aunt Mathilda's attic, and a very unbecoming bonnet, then tried to give the impression that she must be careful, that every penny counted. For the duration of this journey, that had been true, actually, since the only coin she had until she reached London was the remainder of this quarter's pin money. That, in itself, had been an eye-opening lesson into what life was like for those born without the privileges she'd always taken for granted. She didn't think she would soon forget it.

To her way of thinking, of course, she'd been left with little choice. Papa had decreed that she would remain at Aunt Mathilda's home, and that was something she could not, would not, do. She had, therefore, decided to come here, confront him, and remind him she was not an old cloak he could put into a garderobe and forget. She refused to be consigned to the backwaters of Norfolk and ignored.

Papa had sent her there, rather abruptly, a few days after their return from Boston. He'd said he had business he couldn't put off, business she could not be involved in, and promised to bring her home in time for the Season. Since Diana expected Aunt Mathilda to be her chaperone, she hadn't minded going to the lady's house. They could get to know one another before the hustle and bustle began.

But then Papa hadn't brought them back to London. In fact, far from bringing her home, he'd ordered her to stay where she was!

It wouldn't have been so bad if it hadn't been so...boring. Norfolk was pretty enough, she supposed, with its fens and waterways, but the part of it in which Aunt Mathilda resided was quiet and staid and completely lacking in Society. On top of which, her aunt, a lady of a certain age, was set in her ways. A lively young woman like Diana could not hope to thrive in her home. Not when she knew that London was awash with young ladies she could befriend, and gallant gentlemen to take her driving in Hyde Park, and invitations for balls and musicales, soirees and At-Homes, picnics and garden parties, trips to the theatres, to Vauxhall Gardens, and Greenwich, and goodness knew what else.

She had, therefore, no choice but to defy her father's wishes, make the journey, and force him to honor his commitments.

Since he'd forbidden her return to London, there was no possibility Papa would send his coach to collect her, and Aunt Mathilda didn't possess one. Even if she had, her aunt would never have allowed Diana to come, knowing Papa did not approve. Diana wouldn't have put it past the widow to lock her niece in her bedchamber, if she got wind of Diana's plan.

All of which left her only one choice. She'd adopted her false identity, left in the middle of the night, and taken the public coach.

Two days later, she'd arrived, gratefully, in London,

and used the last of her money to pay the cab fare to Mayfair.

As the cab drove away after depositing her on the pavement outside her home, she flexed her shoulders, trying to rid herself of the tight ache between them. She closed her eyes and imagined the bath she would order when she got inside. It would be hot, heavily scented with soothing lavender oils, and followed by a long sleep in her soft bed. After which, she and Papa would have words. He needed reminding that she was not a child any more. She would not be sent away and forgotten.

Of course, none of that could happen until Addams let her in!

Worried she might be attracting the attention of her neighbors, who would certainly make something of Miss Villiers being left to stew on her own doorstep, she looked around, ready to smile and talk, and act as if this was the most natural thing in the world. Thankfully, none of her neighbors seemed to be around. The only person in sight was a man in a shabby coat and misshapen hat. He leaned against the railings bounding the park at the center of the square.

There was something about him that made her wary. For one thing, his rundown clothes and indolent manner did not suit the surroundings. This was a street filled with large, well-cared-for houses, populated by well-to-do families. The gentlemen here wore well-tailored coats and mirror-shined Hessians, not patched clothes. When they left their homes, they strode with purpose. They did not lollygag about the place, shoulders resting on the railings and hands thrust into their pockets.

Diana frowned. Papa had warned her, from an early age, that being in possession of a fortune changed the way people saw you.

"Some resent you," he'd said. "They want nothing to do with you. They withdraw friendship and goodwill toward you. It's as if they believe your money will taint them somehow. But they are few and far between.

"More common are those who wish to use you to enrich themselves. Some hope to marry for it. More than one widow has thrown herself into my path, and you must also learn to discern between gentlemen who like you and those who like your money. Someone as pretty as you will attract plenty of the former, but once you are out, you'll have to learn to tell the difference.

"Then there are those who look for opportunities to take it. In many ways, they are the more honest villains, for they don't simper and bow and steal from you with soft compliments. They simply break in and take your valuables.

"But whichever camp the villain falls into, you, my darling daughter, must be aware that they are there, lurking, ready to pounce."

Did this man, leaning on the railings, plan to rob one, or more, of the homes on the square?

Diana took note of his appearance, and committed to memory details that might prove useful to the authorities in the event that a robbery occurred.

He was not a tall man, not much more than her own five feet five inches in height. His waist was thick and his stomach round, his face red in a way that suggested a propensity to drink. His hair was dark, and uncombed, and his beard was not trimmed and well cared for.

Not much to go on. Her description of him wouldn't be of much help to the constables. But it was better than nothing, and if it came to it, she could identify him after he was apprehended.

The man suddenly seemed to realize Diana was watching him. He straightened and took a step forward, his hands out of his pockets now. For a moment, she feared he would approach her, and she stiffened, unnerved by the thought of him trying to talk to her. She turned back to the door and knocked again, as hard as she could, then glanced over her shoulder at the man.

Rather than come nearer to her, though, he turned and fled along the street, not slowing, even as he approached the corner. Diana watched, astounded, as he slid around it, and disappeared from sight.

She would mention it to Papa. If she ever gained admittance, that was. She began to wonder if Papa truly had had business to attend. Had he gone away and neglected to remove the knocker from his door? Diana prayed not, for if he'd left London, she wasn't sure what she would do. She knew nobody else who might take her in, and she didn't have money to go to a hotel. She didn't even have the coin to take a cab to Papa's man of business and enlist his help.

Just as the panic set in, the door finally opened.

For a moment, Addams stared at Diana, dumbfounded. Then, he collected himself, opened the door wider and ushered her inside. He peered out at the street, looking to right and left before he closed the door, and locked it. Diana's eyes widened. She'd never known the front door locked during the daytime before.

"Did anybody see you arrive, miss?" he asked, urgently.

Before Diana could answer him, her father bellowed along the corridor. "What the devil are you doing here?"

She stood, open-mouthed in shock. Papa had never

shouted at her before. He'd scolded her a few times, of course, but it had always been a gentle chiding. Now, his face was dark with fury, his eyebrows low over narrowed eyes, and his whole body stiff with his rage.

"Get in here!" he ordered, gesturing to the library, which also acted as his study. He said it soothed him to be surrounded by all these books while he worked.

He didn't seem very soothed at the moment.

Diana stepped into the room where she'd spent so many hours while growing up. She'd sat in the corner, drawing, writing letters, completing schoolroom exercises, while Papa worked to build his business. When her governess came looking for her, she climbed the shelf ladder to the top of the bookcases and lay in the gap between the top of the shelves and the ceiling, hidden from sight. Not once had Papa given her away. He'd sent the pinch-lipped governess away, looking for her charge in other parts of the house and gardens. Diana had suffered the tongue lashings later, but oh! it had been worth it to spend the hours in company of her beloved father.

Papa didn't look as if he wanted her company now. "You'd better bring tea," he said to Addams. "Have you eaten, girl?" He sighed and shook his head. "Of course you haven't. Addams, bring bread and cheese, if there's any in the pantry."

Bread and cheese? Cook would have a conniption at the very idea of serving only that. And why was Addams being sent for the tea tray, anyway? That was a job for a lower servant.

As that thought came, she noticed the unnatural stillness of the house. There was no lower servant to fetch the tea. There was nobody else here at all. That couldn't be right. Even when Papa was away, he kept a skeleton staff of six people. When he was in residence, that number trebled. And yet…

"Where is everyone?" she asked, at the same moment Papa said, "I told you not to come."

He rubbed his hand across his face, agitated. "Why couldn't you obey me? A daughter should obey her father." He paced to the window, looked out at the garden, then turned and paced back to his desk.

A dreadful thought struck Diana. Something she wouldn't have believed possible. And yet… She swallowed, and asked, voice trembling, "Have you lost your money, Papa?"

"Would that I had," he murmured. He blew out a deep breath and pasted on a smile that did nothing more than bare his teeth. "I needed you to stay with your aunt until I sent for you. You must return to her at once."

"Papa, I don't—"

"Do as you're told, Diana!" His shout made her rear back in shock and horror. He shook his head, lips pursed. "I have indulged you too much," he said. "You need to learn obedience."

"My Season—" she began, then stopped as the door opened and Addams brought in a tray with tea things, and a plate containing a hunk of bread and a lump of mature-smelling cheese. After two days on the road with nothing to eat, the cheese made Diana's mouth water.

"Thank you," said Papa. He looked up, horrified, at the sound of the front door knocker.

"The door is secured soundly, sir," said Addams, the ever-unflappable butler.

"Do not open it."

"No, sir."

"The back of the house?"

"I will see to it now." Addams gave a short bow and left the room as if nothing untoward was happening at all. The pounding at the front door continued, louder.

What on earth was going on?

"Papa?"

Her father took a deep breath. It seemed to calm him. "Your Season can wait. It's not as if you're out of time. You're only twenty two, nowhere near to becoming an ape-leader yet. I didn't marry your mother until she was almost thirty. I always believed we were happier for the wait."

"Yes, Papa, but—"

He fixed her with a stern stare. "I'll brook no argument, girl," he said. "It has to be this way." His face crumpled, the sternness replaced by a fear so strong, there were tears in his eyes.

The pounding stopped. The silence which followed had a ringing aftereffect that sang on the air and tightened the tension until Diana could scarcely breathe.

Glass smashed. Something large—a window? Papa startled. His fear infected Diana, and her heart jumped and skittered, while her muscles tensed to the point of snapping.

"Hide," he said. He looked frantically around the room. "Where you used to hide from your governess. Quickly. Go!" He pushed her to the shelf ladder, and held it steady while she climbed. She was shaking so much she could barely pull her legs up, and her hands, still encased in cotton gloves, slipped on the narrow rungs.

There was no sensible explanation for any of this. It was madness. Beyond madness. It couldn't be real. Any moment now, Diana would awaken in her bed at Aunt

Mathilda's home and find she'd had a nightmare. She willed herself to wake. Now.

The nightmare continued. She obeyed Papa's demands.

At the top of the ladder, the dusty roof of the bookcase was surrounded by a decorative molding, tall enough to hide her from the view of anyone below. There was about eighteen inches between the top of the bookshelf and the ceiling. As a child, she'd had plenty of room, able to move to her heart's content. More than once she'd lain on her stomach, propped up on her elbows, and read a book while she hid. It had been a cozy nook.

Now, though, it seemed horribly confining. Once she was up here, there'd be no room to change her position. She'd be trapped, unable to move until it was time to come out again. That thought caused her stomach to swoop and her pulse to speed. Her breath caught in her throat and she fought an urge to cry. For a moment, coherent thought escaped her.

Uncertainly, she looked down at Papa, hoping against hope that he would call her down. He didn't. Instead, he gestured that she should complete her climb. The desperation on his face increased the panic within her. It took everything she had to tamp it down.

There has to be a reason for this. Of course there was a reason. A good one. Papa wouldn't be like this otherwise. So she'd do what he said, for now, and later he would explain everything.

Later. Not now. Now, she would do as he asked.

She lay, flat on her stomach, on the bookcase roof. At Papa's hissed instruction, she pulled her skirts closer to her legs so they wouldn't show over the ornate edging.

"You stay there," he commanded in an urgent whisper. "Whatever you hear. Whatever happens. Do not show yourself. Do not make a sound. Promise me."

Somebody was running in the corridor outside.

Papa pleaded. "Promise me!"

"I promise, Papa."

The library door slammed open.

Chapter Two

Lord Tristan Leonard, the fifth Baron Leonard, sat at his desk in the study of St. Bartholomew's vicarage in Rotherton and checked the column in the ledger once more. Satisfied his figures were correct, he closed the book with a dusty thud. The accounts were what he would call healthy. Strong and in good order, able to support the estate and the people who relied upon it for another year.

It was a pity they weren't *his* figures, pertaining to *his* estate.

The way things stood, the figures for the Leonard estate would never look good again. Not in his lifetime anyway. Most of the assets had been sold, leaving only one entailed property, and the only reason that was not sinking further into a financial quagmire was because he'd let it to a tenant willing to pay a high rent. With no farm lands left, that rent was the property's only source of income, but at least it covered the costs of the place, and paid the pensions of the family's retired staff.

He was grateful there were no actual debts to be paid off. The wealth of the barony may be gone, their possessions lost, but at least there were no duns at the door. His brother, the fourth baron, had settled his debts of honor before his ignominious end, and Tristan had paid off the tradesmen and anyone else with a claim when he took up the mantle. Broke he may be, but he was in no danger of debtor's prison.

If only things had been different. If he'd been here, he could have encouraged his brother to husband the family resources in a more prudent way. Steered him past the gaming houses and the race tracks, the gentlemen who goaded him to wager more than he could afford to lose, and the Captain Sharks who lured him into deals he'd never stood a chance of profiting by...

He shook his head. He couldn't have helped, even if he'd been here to try. Lancelot had been stubborn to a fault. He was in charge, and there was no gainsaying him. He certainly wouldn't have taken kindly to any interference from his younger brother, and Tristan's well-meant advice and gentle admonishments might well have made the problem worse.

Tristan hadn't known what Lancelot was doing. He'd been on the continent, chasing the last of Napoleon's men and helping to build the fragile peace that followed Waterloo into something more robust. He'd only discovered the depths of the disaster at home when Lancelot's death forced him to sell his commission and come back to take up the title.

He sighed, impatient with his moment of self-pity. There was no use to cry over spilt milk, after all. He could only do his best going forward, and be thankful that David—Lord Rotherton—had provided him and Cassie with a home and then given Tristan a face-saving way to earn the money they needed to live on.

Cassie was Tristan's only real regret. She deserved so much more than life had thrown at her, and he would love to have spared her this. Not that his sister ever complained. She stoically accepted the loss of her dowry and, with it, her future hopes. Thanks to Lancelot's fecklessness, she would never have a Season and would probably never marry. Instead, she—

"Tristan, are you going to Rotherton Hall today?" Cassie pushed open the door and came into the study. She held a large packet, tied with string and addressed in her neat, steady handwriting. "Do you think Lord Rotherton would send this for me?"

It was a rhetorical question. David never refused to send her mail. He never charged for the postage, either. Not only that, but Tristan had no doubt Rotherton knew exactly what the packet contained and would never judge her for it. Apart from Tristan and the man who received the packets, David was the only person who knew her secret: Cassie wrote stories for publication in a popular periodical.

Tristan was proud of her talent. He'd like to admit her penmanship openly, but acknowledging that hers was the mind behind the compelling adventures of Death-or-Glory Rory, banished earl's son and honorable pirate, would only cause more scandal for the family.

More than wishing he could publicly acknowledge her cleverness, though, Tristan wished Cassie could indulge her passion for writing because she wanted to do so, not because it bolstered their income. Sometimes, her writing was the difference between a good cut of meat and a bad one, and that shamed him.

His feelings must have showed on his face, because Cassie rolled her eyes and clicked her tongue at him. "It is in no way a reflection upon you that I do this," she said, just as she had said a dozen times before. "I enjoy doing it. And I enjoy being paid for it."

"You shouldn't have to."

"Pish! If I wasn't paying the butcher with the

money, I'd be paying a haberdasher with it. I know you'd give me an allowance if you could, but it's far more satisfying when the money is the fruit of my own labor."

"I'm sure it is. That doesn't make me feel... Never mind. I'm sure Rotherton will send it for you." He held out his hand to take the packet from her. She passed it to him, together with a look of sympathy. Yet again something he saw on her face regularly and always hated.

"It isn't your fault, Tris," she said, softly. "And don't tell me you should have prevented it. Don't say you should've known. How could you have? You were a soldier, not a magician. You didn't have one of those crystal balls fortune tellers have at the fair. So you couldn't have known."

The fact that she was correct did not ease his conscience.

"Anyway, even if you had known, you could have done nothing to stop it. Lancelot was...Lancelot. He went his own way."

That was true, too. Lancelot very much went his own way. He went his own way right through the barony's two unentailed estates, the townhouse, and a modest but adequate fortune, to say nothing of Tristan's portion as the younger son, and Cassie's dowry. All within a year of inheriting. Then, once there was nothing left, he walked into the townhouse he'd just lost, and blew his brains out, leaving Tristan to come home and try to put the family back on its feet.

He hadn't known what to do when he saw the extent of the damage. If it hadn't been for David... Rotherton had remembered Tristan from school, although he'd actually been in Lancelot's year. He'd come to see

Tristan and, without fanfare, given him a chance at survival. It was the one debt Tristan could never hope to repay. Although he'd spend his life trying.

Now, he took Cassie's packet and the ledgers, stashed them into the footwell of the pony cart that came with the tenancy of the vicarage, and left for Rotherton Hall.

He was admitted through the front door by David's butler, Johnson, who put the ledgers on the hall table before taking Tristan's coat and hat.

"I'll take the books to the office for you, my lord," said Johnson. "Lord Rotherton thought you might call today. He asked that you attend him in the blue salon."

Tristan frowned. It wasn't unheard of for David to invite him to share a drink, but it was usually informal, unrehearsed. This invitation sounded much more deliberate. He wondered if David had something important to discuss with him.

"His lordship has other guests," explained Johnson.

That explained the formal invitation, but it also made Tristan uncomfortable. A nobleman he might be, but he was not thought of as good *ton*, and he didn't want to cause David any awkwardness with his presence. "I can return," he said, reaching to take back his hat.

Johnson deftly pulled it out of his reach. "No, my lord," he said, politely but firmly. "You are expected."

Tristan sighed. "All right, then," he said. "The blue salon it is." He followed Johnson along the corridor that led from the wide entrance hall with its polished, dark wood floor and wood-paneled walls, past the wide wooden stairs and to the salon at the back of the house.

Rotherton Hall was built in the reign of Elizabeth I, in the classic E shape of that time. It was larger than many homes of the period, presumably because whichever Earl of Rotherton had been in situ then wanted to impress the world with his status. It was rumored locally that Queen Elizabeth had stayed here, although since there was no record the earldom had ever suffered bankruptcy, Tristan was inclined to take the story with a large pinch of salt.

Successive earls had redecorated the house, replacing the Tudor wood-paneling in many of the rooms with wall hangings in pale colored silks, making them lighter and giving an illusion of more space, but the basic architecture remained untouched. Presumably, the large number of rooms in the original building had negated the need to extend, and the thick stone walls were sturdy enough to need minimal reworking. Now covered in ivy, they, along with the myriad mullioned windows, had held firm for more than two hundred years and likely would do so for another two hundred.

The blue salon had been refurbished in recent years. The windows were original, not large, but kept clear of the encroaching ivy, allowing the maximum amount of daylight. The walls were covered in sky-blue silk, on which were painted delicate gold flowers which gleamed in the sunlight. A blue rug covered the middle of the floor, its edges picked out with gold, while blue armchairs and sofas were dotted about in an informal way. Occasional tables stood near several chairs, and a huge fireplace took up most of one wall. Its Elizabethan stone surround stood out against the opulent furnishings of more recent vintage.

David crossed the room to greet Tristan. They shook hands warmly before the earl introduced him to his guests.

He already knew the first of them. Lord Fremont had visited Rotherton several times over the past year. His last visit was to attend the wedding of Miss Ashton, now Baroness Abberley, but it was rumored he'd also been involved in clearing up some of the less savory goings-on in the neighborhood. Tristan wasn't party to the details, other than that there had been some sort of criminal plot a few months back. Fremont, David, and others had foiled it, and during the fight, Viscount Hadlow had been killed. He'd been given a hero's burial and the neighborhood eagerly awaited the arrival of his successor, who didn't seem in any hurry to get here. Tristan couldn't blame him. From what he'd seen and heard, the Hadlow estate was as much a millstone as the Leonard estate. Both were broke, liabilities that would suck the life and joy from any man tasked with looking after them.

"Of course, you've met Fremont," said David. Tristan bowed and Fremont bowed back. The man's manners were impeccable, but there was a coolness about him that was less than friendly, and he eyed Tristan with suspicion.

Since Tristan had not, to his knowledge, offended the man, he assumed Fremont's coolness was rooted in the Leonard family's recent losses. He wouldn't be the only member of the *ton* who would equate Tristan's worth as a man with the size of his fortune. To Tristan, such an attitude diminished Fremont far more than it upset him, so he chose to ignore it.

David introduced his second guest, a clergyman, Daniel Fielding, who had arrived to take over the three vacant parishes: St. Bartholomew's in Rotherton, St. Simon and St. Jude's in Crompton Hadlow, and St.

Denys's in Frantham. He was dressed in the simple black garb of his profession, the only color about him the white of his clerical collar. Slightly shorter than Tristan's own six feet three inches, he was slender but not thin, and he held himself in a certain way: broad shoulders back, chest out but not puffed. It reminded Tristan of soldiers he'd known. He wondered if Mr. Fielding had once been a military man.

More importantly, he wondered what sort of cleric he'd be. The previous incumbent had been a decent man who made efforts to secure the souls of his parishioners. His legacy, however, had been tainted by the actions of his sister, who was, in Tristan's opinion, quite mad.

Tristan's wariness over Mr. Fielding was not solely as a result of his predecessor's sister, though. It was, to his shame, far more personal than that.

The previous curate, Mr. Burgess, had resided in the Curate's Cottage at Crompton Hadlow. Miss Burgess, the curate's sister, had complained bitterly at that, saying Tristan and Cassie should quit the larger, grander vicarage in favor of her and her brother. David had resisted all her entreaties, but would he do the same now? Or would they be asked to move out to make room for Mr. Fielding?

The question was pertinent, especially in light of the third of David's guests, the beguiling young woman sitting on the sofa, elegantly pouring tea into china cups. Fremont had no wife, so Tristan knew she wasn't Lady Fremont. Nor, as far as he was aware, did the viscount have a sister. Which meant the lady must be here with the curate.

She didn't look like Mr. Fielding's sister—there was no familial resemblance whatsoever. She was as fair as the Reverend was dark, with honey-blonde hair that shone like spun silk, and cornflower-blue eyes so deep a man could dive into them and never re-emerge. Her skin made him think of summer, of golden peaches and fresh cream, while her lips were the color of strawberries. There was a playfulness about her properly polite half-smile that drew him, and encouraged him to know her better.

He blinked. What was the matter with him? He was waxing lyrical about a woman he didn't know! A woman who might be another man's wife. A *clergyman's* wife!

Although, to be honest, she didn't look like a clergyman's wife, with her trim waist and high, pert breasts and the hint of long, slender legs tucked against her chair. Even her plain, homespun gown could not disguise the sensuous figure and pulling allure of this woman.

No. She didn't look like a clergyman's wife at all.

But then, Tristan supposed he did not look too much like a baron these days.

If she *was* Mrs. Fielding, there might be, now or in the near future, some little Fieldings to be catered for. Which meant the Curate's Cottage would most definitely not be suitable for them, and the vicarage would be needed.

Was that why David had asked Tristan to join them? Was he about to be asked to vacate the property in favor of the Reverend and his divine wife? Where would they go? Could he prevail upon his friend to help them find somewhere else, at a rent they could afford?

"Lord Tristan Leonard," said David, cutting into Tristan's thoughts, "may I make known to you Miss Diana Wilde?"

Not the curate's wife, then. Not anybody's wife. Tristan smiled, and told himself the relief he felt was merely because the curate, being a single man, was unlikely to need the vicarage. It had nothing to do with the fact that the delectable Miss Wilde was also unmarried. That mattered not a jot to him. Why would it?

She was not for him. Put simply, he had nothing to offer her—or any lady, for that matter. Tristan couldn't support a wife. And by the time he could, *if* he ever could, someone like Miss Wilde would have been snapped up by somebody else. Somebody far more worthy of her. Still, a man could look, and dream, could he not?

"Miss Wilde is an old school friend of Ella Forbes-Smythe. She's come to stay with her at Amberley Place."

Tristan knew Ella, of course. A spinster, determined to stay that way, she was unusual in that she managed her own estates, which she'd inherited free of oversight by the men in her family. She was forthright in her opinions and happy to castigate her neighbors if she felt they weren't doing their best for their tenants and workers. The late Lord Hadlow, who'd known her from childhood, had received more than one set-down from her.

The demure Miss Wilde looked as far removed from Ella as it was possible to be. Then again, did they not say opposites attract? Perhaps that applied to friendships as well as to love.

Or it could simply be that Ella desired to help an old school friend who'd fallen on hard times. For although she was clearly a lady, Miss Wilde's dress suggested she was not well off. If she'd had to retrench, it would be just like Ella to invite her to stay.

"Lord Fremont did us a great kindness," said Mr. Fielding, as Miss Wilde handed Tristan a cup of tea. Her hand brushed against his as he took the cup, and a strange sensation tingled in his fingers, not unlike the feeling in the air just before a thunderstorm. The look of bewilderment in her eyes left him wondering if she'd felt it too.

He swallowed, and nodded his thanks. She looked away.

"A great kindness indeed," continued Mr. Fielding. He nodded, sagely.

"I was travelling here anyway," said Fremont, with a shrug of indifference. "It would have been churlish of me to keep my carriage to myself while you and Miss Wilde endured the public stage."

"You should not belittle your deeds, my lord, for they were well and gratefully received on earth, and, no doubt, in heaven, too. For, as it says in the Book of Proverbs, '*He that hath pity upon the poor lendeth unto the Lord; and that which he hath given will He pay him again.*' "

Fremont smiled and nodded, and managed not to look too discomfited.

Tristan fought the urge to groan. He had no objection to any man, especially a clergyman, living by Biblical tenets, but he did hope the man wouldn't quote the Good Book *ad nauseam*. It would not endear him to his flock: the previous curate's sister had done precisely that, emphasizing her piety and service to God at every opportunity. She had, however, turned out to hold some very strange ideas about what that service to God should mean, and exactly what actions constituted Christian charity. From what Tristan could gather, it had left local people with a suspicion of what he'd heard some call, "God-botherers."

Over tea, David explained to Mr. Fielding that he could take up residence at the Curate's Cottage at his earliest convenience. "It's vacant, and has been kept in readiness for you," he said as he picked an imaginary piece of lint from his pristine trouser leg. "I realize some might think the vicarage in Rotherton more suitable but, I regret, it is not available. It is let on a long-term lease to my good friend Lord Leonard and his family. I'd be loath to see them quit it." His smile was charming and softened the words, but his tone brooked no opposition.

Fremont's sniff was quiet, but it left Tristan in no doubt as to the viscount's view of David's decision. Tristan looked over and found Fremont watching him, his expression a mixture of suspicion and disapproval. Why? Did he think Tristan was taking advantage of David's generosity? That he and Cassie were, somehow, cheating Rotherton?

Wondering, yet again, what he'd done to so offend Fremont, Tristan told himself that the man's opinion of him didn't matter. David knew the truth of their situation, and his was the only opinion that counted. Everybody else could think what they liked.

Even so, the unfairness of Fremont's harsh judgment rankled. Tristan turned away and hoped the look on his own face told Fremont that his contempt was reciprocated.

Unlike the viscount, Mr. Fielding saw nothing wrong with the Leonards continuing to occupy the vicarage. "I would not have Lord Leonard and his family inconvenienced for my sake," he said, with a smile that looked genuine. "I saw it as we drove through the village, and it seems a large house. Far too large for a single man." He chuckled. "Were I married with a dozen children, it might be a different matter, of course, but as things stand, the cottage you have described would suit my needs far better." He sipped his tea before continuing, "I will, however, need a housekeeper, and a cook, as well as a man and a girl for more menial tasks. I hope, my lord, that you can quickly put me in the way of suitable persons for those positions?"

David said he would put his man on it and, until the staff was in place, the reverend must stay at the Hall.

"Your lordship is too kind," said Mr. Fielding. "Your efforts on my behalf are appreciated."

David waved a languid hand through the air. "No effort involved, old chap," he said. "Not on my part. Rest assured, if I were required to do the work myself, I wouldn't have invited you."

Mr. Fielding frowned, clearly not used to such candor.

"Fortunately," David went on, "I have staff, who I pay to do things I don't wish to do. Which, you'll soon discover, is everything. For the most part, I live a life of carefree indolence."

Tristan raised his eyebrows and gave David a sidelong look. His friend's words were far from truthful. However he might pretend otherwise, David took his role as the area's ranking nobleman very seriously and, unless Mr. Fielding was a fool, he would soon realize that.

He shook his head, silently admonishing the earl for lying to a clergyman, then drank his tea and reached for one of the delicious shortbread biscuits on the tea tray.

Chapter Three

Diana sat in the blue salon and willed Lord Fremont to announce it was time for them to leave so he could escort her to Amberley Place, where she would be staying for the foreseeable future. Then, perhaps, the discomfort she felt would subside.

She hated lying to people. But since that day last month when she arrived unannounced at Papa's home, it seemed that lying was all she'd done. The only person with whom she'd been completely truthful was Lord Fremont, a man she'd met on her twelfth birthday, when Papa said he trusted him with his life and, if she ever found herself in need of help, she could turn to him.

Lord Fremont had lived up to Papa's promises. He'd taken her in and hidden her, shielding her from both the villains who sought her and the investigators on their trail. He'd arranged everything necessary to keep her safe.

Thanks to him, she was no longer Diana Villiers, heiress, but Diana Wilde, penniless schoolfriend of Ella Forbes-Smythe, a woman she had, in fact, never met. Lord Fremont said he trusted Ella, and that Diana would be safe with her while he worked to bring the criminals to justice. She was, he warned, to trust nobody else. Nobody at all. It was far too dangerous.

If only Diana had known of that danger before she left Aunt Mathilda's home! Had she known why Papa had sent her there, it might have made all the difference. Doubtless, she'd still have wished herself in the thick of the London Season, but her exile would have been easier to bear, and she would have stayed.

She hadn't known. And in her ignorance, she'd brought the world crashing down.

That was something she could not allow herself to think of. If she did, she'd cry, and that must not happen. Not in public. Nobody could know there was anything wrong. Nobody could be trusted.

Not even a man of God, it seemed. Though a clergyman was surely bound by his office to keep secrets and divulge them to nobody but God, Lord Fremont had not taken the Reverend Mr. Fielding into his confidence. If he would not trust a clergyman…

"The villain we want has a very long reach," Fremont had explained to her. They'd been in the parlor of his townhouse, where he'd explained his plan to spirit her away from London until the danger was past. "Many people work for him. Many more daren't defy him. He's powerful. Very powerful."

"You know who he is. Can you not arrest him?" she'd asked.

He grimaced. "It's not that simple. Men like Milton Percival know how to protect themselves. All we'd do in arresting him would be to warn him that we are aware of his involvement. We must wait until we're ready." He moved to the fireplace, leaned on the mantelshelf, and rested one foot on the low rail surrounding the hearth, staring into the cold grate as if it held the secrets of the world. "You must trust nobody, Diana," he continued. "Nobody—and I do mean nobody—must know who you are. Not even Ella. Not just for your sake, but for theirs.

Not only is it possible that anyone you encounter may be in Percival's pocket, it's also possible that, though they be innocent, knowledge of your story may put people in danger, too."

Fear for the safety of other people as well as herself was enough to make her agree with Fremont's plan. As per his instruction, she'd left everything that identified her behind and taken on a new identity. The only thing she'd kept from her old life was the false name she'd adopted on the journey from Norfolk. Fremont had agreed it would be easier than learning to respond to yet another name.

He hadn't wanted to take the curate up in his carriage for the journey to Rotherton, but once asked to do so, there was no plausible reason to refuse. Thankfully, Mr. Fielding had seen nothing suspicious in her story and had accepted Diana for what he thought she was.

Not everyone seemed as easy to fool, though. Lord Rotherton eyed her with skepticism when they were introduced, and he watched her carefully, as if his piercing blue eyes could cut a hole in the mask she'd donned and lead him to the secrets underneath. It was unnerving, to say the least.

Then there was Lord Leonard. Younger than Rotherton and Fremont, he'd captured her attention just by walking into the room. She didn't understand why that should be. Since Mama's death, Diana had spent much of her time travelling with Papa. She'd entertained his colleagues and business contacts and been introduced to countless gentlemen all over the world. Most of them were charming and likeable and carried themselves with the confidence of success and a warmth of personality that drew people to them. Yet she didn't remember any of them affecting her the way Lord Leonard had, garnering all her attention just by being here.

He exuded confidence. Then, he was a peer; self-assurance seemed to come naturally to titled people. It set them apart from others and marked them as leaders, entitled to respect. The only other men in whom she'd seen such innate confidence were army officers. But since most officers were drawn from the ranks of the nobility...it was a circular argument.

When it came to Lord Leonard, though, it was more than the confidence of rank. Diana couldn't explain it, even to herself. She couldn't say why, even in a room filled with other noblemen, he stood out.

It wasn't his beauty. He was good-looking, but she'd seen more striking men. There was nothing extraordinary about him. His features were pleasant, his cheekbones high, nose straight, chin firm. He was tall, over six feet, but then, so were both Fremont and Rotherton. Like him, they had broad shoulders, wide chests and flat stomachs. Yet there was something about Lord Leonard that drew her eye, where the others did not.

That something was not in the way he dressed. No dandy he, covered in fine silks and lace. He was modestly dressed, in a style she would expect from the gentry rather than the nobility. Although his clothes were of good quality, they were not new. His hands were calloused, the hands of a man who worked. Which was commendable. Hadn't Papa said so, many times? Usually as he rolled his sleeves up and prepared to dirty his own hands.

"If a man wishes to take the spoils, he must be prepared to do the laboring."

The voice in her head was so real she had to hide her gasp and fight the urge to look and see if Papa was in the room. She tamped down the renewed urge to cry, distracting herself with further contemplation about Lord Leonard and why he so attracted her attention.

His hair was brown. Not a dark brown, and not light enough to be called blond, but somewhere in between. On anyone else, it would be called nondescript. A curl flopped over his forehead, boyishly, and the crinkles at the edges of his eyes suggested he was a man of good and ready humor, although there was a seriousness about him that also hinted at sadness and strife.

Those eyes, though. They were—compelling. They were a dark, dark brown, the color of the coffee Papa had drunk at breakfast, rich and deep, almost black.

The thought of Papa savoring the drink he'd loved was enough to make her cry again. She lowered her eyes, sipped her tea, and pressed down her emotions, trying to distract herself from the memories.

Which was why she now contemplated Fremont's reaction to the arrival of Lord Leonard. He'd made no attempt to hide his dislike of the man. He hadn't been rude, exactly. He hadn't cut him. But he had been decidedly cool.

There was, as far as Diana could discern, nothing objectionable about Lord Leonard. He was well-mannered and hadn't behaved in any way that might give offense. Indeed, she'd discerned an honor about him that was not always present in a man. He seemed pleasant and unexceptionable, and kind.

Then again, she'd proved herself to be no judge of character. After all, she'd been largely unconcerned about the man loitering across the road from Papa's house. His name, she'd later learned, was Mickey Hicks. She'd thought him a thief, a would-be burglar, but she hadn't been as alarmed by his presence as she should have been.

Not that it would have helped her if she had been. By the time she saw him, it was already too late.

Fremont had men looking for Hicks, but he'd gone to ground. Nobody had seen him in any of his usual haunts, or if they had, they weren't saying. Fremont's men had come close to catching him near Aunt Mathilda's home. One of those men had been killed in the effort, and Hicks had escaped, along with his brother, Simon. Aunt Mathilda was, thankfully, safe.

Unable to go to her aunt, there were very few places where Diana could find sanctuary. Most of her friends lived abroad, and she had no desire to put the few who lived in England in any danger. It was one of the reasons Fremont had brought her here. Diana had no connections whatsoever to Rotherton, or even to Sussex in general. She knew nobody here, and there was no reason for anyone to look for her in this area.

Besides which, Fremont trusted Ella Forbes-Smythe. Since Diana knew he did not easily trust many people, his high opinion of the woman meant Diana was willing to come to her.

As if her thoughts had silently communicated themselves to him, Fremont now stood.

"My thanks for the tea, Rotherton," he said, affably. "And for putting me up for a few days. If you don't mind, I will escort Miss Wilde to her friend's home now, before the day grows too late. I'll be back for dinner. I take it you keep country hours?" By which he meant that dinner would be served several hours earlier than would be expected in London.

"We do," said Rotherton, "but we'll hold back until you are able to join us. Don't feel you need to rush."

Minutes later, Fremont's carriage moved down the drive, Fremont and Diana safely inside.

They sat in silence for a while. Diana thought she should ask about her hostess, but she could think of no questions. She would soon get to know the woman for herself. Her hope was that they would quickly become friends in truth. Come to that, she hoped her other new neighbors would be welcoming as well. It would make her stay here more bearable if they were.

Which brought one new neighbor back to mind.

"You don't like Lord Leonard," she said. It was a statement rather than a question.

"I don't know him well," replied Fremont. He looked out of the window at the parkland that separated Rotherton Hall from the road.

Diana looked out, too. Deer grazed on the grass. Buttercups shone, bright yellow dots against the rich green. They were interspersed by clusters of dandelion clocks, little balls of white offering themselves to the breeze. A few trees dotted the park, and bushes almost hid the stone wall surrounding it.

"You didn't know Mr. Fielding at all until he joined us this morning," she pointed out. "Yet you did not treat him the way you treated Lord Leonard."

He grimaced. "It's been a long day," he said, "and I am tired. If my fatigue made me rude to Leonard, I will, of course, apologize to him. Thank you for bringing it to my attention."

Which felt more like a set-down than an actual scolding might have done. She answered in a way she hoped was truthful, yet conciliatory. "You weren't rude to him, my lord. Indeed, I cannot image you ever being rude to anyone."

He grinned. "It has been known."

"Not in this instance. I wouldn't have called your behavior toward him rude, exactly. A trifle cool, perhaps. As if he was not somebody whose company you relished. Then again, if you're tired, that will explain it."

They drove into Rotherton village. It was a large village, with a fine variety of shops for such a rural place. In just a cursory glance as they made their way along the High Street, Diana noted a haberdasher, a milliner, a book shop, and an apothecary, as well as the more normal butcher, baker and greengrocer. There was a large church which, she surmised, must be St. Bartholomew's. The impressive-looking vicarage next to it was, apparently, Lord Leonard's home. She wondered why he was a tenant of Rotherton's. Would it not be more usual for a peer to live in his own property?

It was none of her business. She really ought to put the gentleman from her mind.

Outside the coaching inn, The Golden Goose, a group of men had gathered, most of them holding tankards. A few of them were dressed as laborers, in smocks and floppy-brimmed hats. Others looked like seamen, though the town was some miles from the coast. One or two men wore more fashionable coats, though they were not of the highest quality, and their boots were worn down at the heels, the leather dull and creased. Other people, going about their business in the village, seemed to avoid the men, even crossing the street to pass them.

Diana shuddered. She had seen groups of such men

in the less exclusive areas of larger towns, both in England and in other countries where she'd gone with Papa on business. They always unnerved her, though there wasn't always an obvious reason for that. Sometimes, there was a perfectly good excuse for them to gather. Near the coast, they might be newly returned from longer voyages and enjoying spending their wages before signing on to a new ship and setting off again. Sometimes, they were honest workers idling away a rare day of leisure.

But sometimes, they truly were ne'er-do-wells, gathered in the hope of getting rich quickly without too much effort, and happy to start trouble if it aided them in that quest. Something about these men made her suspect they fell into this category. Or were her recent experiences making her see evil where none existed?

One of the men stared at them as they drove past. Nothing unusual in that, she thought. A smart private coach would attract attention in a place where, doubtless, most vehicles were farm carts and pony traps. But there was something about the man that frightened her. He was tall and thin, with shoulder-length dark hair. He wore a shabby coat, a floppy brimmed hat, and worn-down boots. He looked exactly as she imagined a pirate might look.

She looked squarely at him and met his eyes, and realized what had made her wary of him. He had not turned to meet her gaze. She had turned to meet his. Because he hadn't been watching the carriage as a whole. He'd been watching her.

She pulled back from the window and out of his sight. It was probably nothing. Any man, given the chance, would look at a young woman passing by. It meant nothing.

Even so, when Fremont touched her arm, she jumped.

"I'm sorry," she said, her voice breathless. "I didn't mean… I just… I'm sorry."

Fremont smiled. "I'm not the only one who's had a long day, am I?" His voice was kind, understanding. "After a difficult few weeks. Rest easy, my dear. All will be well. When you reach Amberley, I make no doubt Ella, who has never been one to insist on pretentions and proprieties, will insist you have a hot bath, a good supper and a long sleep. She will say there'll be time enough for you to meet each other properly on the morrow."

They turned off the road onto Ella's private drive. Diana put aside all thoughts of the impertinently curious man and prepared to meet her new "old schoolfriend."

Chapter Four

Tristan was almost at the vicarage when he remembered his promise to his sister. He'd handed her package to Johnson along with the ledgers. It wasn't obvious that it needed franking—Tristan had tucked it between the ledgers for safekeeping, so it was probably languishing on his desk in the tiny office on the side of the library. It was a perfect workroom for him, close to the vast shelves of books, including all manner of information about the estate, so it was to hand should he need to reference anything, yet secluded enough for discretion. Neither Tristan nor David felt the need to broadcast the fact that he was employed by the earl. If too many people knew, what little remained of Tristan's standing in Society would be gone, along with whatever faint hopes Cassie had of a good marriage. People knew he was penniless. They accepted that. Working for a living, though, was a step too far for most of them.

Unfortunately, everything Johnson had put onto Tristan's desk was now ensconced in an office that nobody else would visit, and would, therefore, lie undisturbed for another week. Cassie couldn't wait that long for her manuscript to be posted. And Tristan had promised her.

On a sigh, he turned his vehicle around and headed back to Rotherton Hall. He would retrieve the package and put it where David would see it. If he saw the earl,

Tristan would, of course, mention it, though there was no real need. David had told Cassie he was always happy to frank her post.

On his way back, Tristan thought about why the package had slipped his mind. Learning that David had guests, Tristan had known he couldn't discuss business with him today, though he'd still planned to mention Cassie's packet at a discreet moment.

Renewing his acquaintance with Fremont hadn't been enough to make him forget, nor had his introduction to the new curate. Meeting Miss Wilde, on the other hand...

The woman was stunning. Her looks were guaranteed to make a man look twice. More than twice. They'd garnered his whole attention and driven every other consideration from his head. Tristan wondered if that was why she sat so quietly, her eyes lowered, pose demure, as if she tried not to bring attention on herself. Perhaps she was tired of gentlemen acting like brainless twits in her presence and had hoped they wouldn't notice her today.

He grinned at that. There was no chance whatsoever that that woman would slip past a man's notice. Not unless he was dead.

It was more than her looks. She'd barely spoken and had done nothing to make her character shine, but even so, there had been something about her, something that would not be ignored. Tristan barely remembered details about anybody else in the room with her. He doubted he could recount much of their conversation.

One thing he did recall, though. She was a schoolfriend of Ella Forbes-Smythe. He frowned at that now, as he'd done when he first heard it. It didn't ring true. Not because he didn't think it possible the two women had attended the same school: they were both ladies, of similar class, if not of like fortune. But Ella was considerably older. Tristan believed she was in her mid-twenties. Miss Wilde was much younger. If he had to guess, Tristan would say she was, at most, one-and-twenty. While it was possible their times at the school had overlapped, it was unlikely they would have been bosom bows with that age difference.

Then again, why would Miss Wilde lie? And what business was it of Tristan's anyway? He had better things to think about than dubious claims of friendship made by a penniless woman he'd never met before and would probably meet infrequently in the future, if at all.

He pulled around to the side of the Hall, intending to enter through the servants' entrance rather than knocking at the front door. As he turned the corner, he had to pull on the reins sharply to avoid hitting the young lad who emerged from the kitchen door, his shirt stuffed, adding strangely shaped bulk to his frame. A frame which, Tristan knew, was actually thin to the point of emaciation. The lad had long gangly limbs and a sharp-featured face that needed fleshing out. His clothes were ragged and old, his boots worn, and his hair grew in clumps, as if he'd cut it himself without benefit of a mirror. Which he probably had.

"Ned!" Tristan called, exasperated at the boy's carelessness. "I might have run you down."

Ned grinned, unbothered.

Tristan narrowed his eyes, suspicious. "What have you got there?"

The lad pulled his arms tighter around himself, shielding his hoard.

"Does Cook know you've been in her larder?"

Tristan fought to keep a straight face. Of course David's cook didn't know. If she had known, she'd be out here now, chasing the feral boy with a skillet held like a club, ready to brain him. Not that she'd catch him; Ned Fellowes could run like the devil was on his tail if he'd a mind to. At which, the woman would take her grievances to the housekeeper, who would be forced to listen to her opinions on "half-wit thieves who should be strung up as an example to others," before she demanded the release of funds to replenish the provisions. Funds the housekeeper would release without demur because David preferred to turn a blind eye to Ned's thievery, as long as it didn't get out of hand.

"I could have him arrested," he'd told Tristan once. "But then, as magistrate, I'd have to deal with him. What would I do with him? It would be cruel to put somebody like Ned Fellowes into a jail, where he'd be at the mercy of heartless villains. And even more cruel to lock him in an asylum. So I'd have to think up something else as a punishment, and I'd rather not, because it's such damned hard work for me."

That was something David said often. Everything was, "such damned hard work" for him. Usually, he said it when trying to persuade somebody not to do something foolish. Often, the flippant comment was enough to defuse a dangerous situation, so that nobody was hurt or arrested, and people had the opportunity to calm down before there were lasting consequences. If some people thought David indolent because of his attitude, so be it. David didn't care.

Ned cocked his head to one side and yipped at Tristan in an accurate imitation of a puppy, then turned

39

and ran into the woods and out of sight. Tristan shook his head. He would warn the housekeeper about the shortfall in the larder before he left.

He made his way up the steep and narrow back stairs and let himself into the office next to the library. He put the ledgers onto the shelves where they belonged, then decided that, as he was here, he might as well finish the last pieces of work on his desk before he took Cassie's package to David. He'd barely sat down when he heard the library door open.

"She's a friend of Ella's, you say?" asked David.

"From school," answered Fremont. "They were happy to be reunited. It was touching. Good for the heart to see."

David laughed. "That, I do not believe. You don't have a heart. Here's the book I promised to lend you." There was a rustle of paper and the slight thud of a book losing its support and falling against another on the shelf. "What brings you here anyway? I can't believe it's merely to deliver Miss Wilde as a favor to Ella."

"I'm always happy to do a favor for Ella. But I do have business here myself."

"I was afraid of that. Is it likely to involve effort on my part?" David sighed, wearily. Tristan grinned at the image he had of his friend's pained expression.

"Could do." Fremont was unapologetic.

David groaned. "You, my friend, create chaos wherever you go. And I'm the one who has to deal with it. It's always work, work, work, whenever you've been in the vicinity."

Tristan gave a silent chuckle at David's protest. As Fremont spoke again, Tristan looked down at his work, intent on concentrating on it and not eavesdropping.

"The smugglers are active in this area once more," said the viscount.

Tristan looked up sharply. That was not good news. Men had fought and died to bring the villains to justice. It would be dreadful if their blood had spilled for nothing.

He wasn't supposed to be hearing this. Fremont was talking to David in confidence, giving information that wasn't to be bandied about. Which meant Tristan should make his presence known now, apologize, then leave.

Fremont already viewed him with suspicion and contempt. If he thought Tristan had been listening—worse, if he thought the eavesdropping was deliberate—the man's opinion of him would plummet even more. He might even accuse Tristan of being a spy. Fremont worked for the Home Office, and he probably saw spies in every corner. Tristan wasn't certain what the man did for the government, but he suspected he could make life difficult for anybody he suspected of being in league with criminals. Since Tristan had no wish to discover those difficulties first hand, he stayed still, kept quiet, and waited for the men to leave so he could make good his own escape.

He heard the swishing, rustling sounds of pages being flipped through, then the soft click as books were replaced on the shelf.

"I thought we were rid of them," said David, in answer to Fremont's announcement.

"I thought so too," said Fremont. "And, to an extent, we are. These villains are not Bonapartists. Hopefully, we've snuffed out that particular breed of miscreant." More pages were flicked through. "May I borrow this one, as well? The smugglers we're dealing with now are just that. Smugglers. Motivated by nothing more than greed. Which is good, in some respects. I'd prefer a greedy man looking for profit to a zealot. If his motive is financial, his instinct for survival is strong, and he's less likely to stand and fight, which means my men are less likely to be hurt. On the other hand, any man might be tempted by money. There are far fewer suspects when one is seeking men willing to fight and die for a cause."

"Damn!" muttered David. "I hope none of my people are caught up in it."

"It's inevitable, I'm afraid." Now it was Fremont's turn to sigh. "I'm not an unreasonable man, Rotherton. I would hope you know that. I don't expect you to hang every last man in the area."

"Glad to hear it." David sounded wry.

"I couldn't care less about the odd casket of brandy, or a few ounces of tea here and there. If that were all it is, I'd leave it alone."

"But it's bigger than that?"

"Big enough the government has to take notice. And that is simply not on."

"I'll keep my eyes and ears open for you."

"Thank you. Have a care, though. The gang we're looking for is vicious. They left two revenue officers dead last month, and a third one missing. I don't hold much hope for him."

Tristan stiffened. Smuggling was fairly widespread in coastal areas, and it often spread a few miles inland. Most of the poorer people in this area involved themselves in one way or another. Hardly surprising, when a tubman—a person who carried the illicit goods from the beach to wherever they were stored prior to sale—could make more money in one night than he'd make in six months working a legitimate job. Plus, the prices in shops and warehouses were high because of the duties the government slapped on any goods imported legally. Smuggled goods could be sold at half the price, or less, and still net a decent profit. No wonder everybody turned a blind eye.

But a vicious gang murdering officers? Nobody condoned that. Should Tristan come across those men, he, like David, would make Fremont aware of it.

"Unfortunately, there'll be some not-so-guilty men caught in the net," continued Fremont. "In fact, the…I won't say innocent, exactly, because, in law, they're not, but the foot soldiers, if you will…are more likely to face the noose, or transportation, than are the truly guilty ones."

"You just said you'd turn a blind eye to the odd casket," objected David. His voice did not raise. Those who didn't know him would not notice any change to his indifferent drawl. But Tristan knew him well enough to hear the tightness in his tone. These were his people and, while he would do his duty, he would also protect them if he could. David knew the difference between the law and justice, and he sometimes bent the former to deliver the latter.

"The foot soldiers I refer to aren't bringing in the odd casket," said Fremont. "This gang's smart. They've taken their recruiting tactics from the Royal Navy. Press gangs."

David swore. Silently, so did Tristan.

"Quite. Forcing local men to join their network, whether they are willing or not, serves two purposes. One, they have the men they need for the job, and two, nobody will talk to us about it because, to do so would be to condemn their own loved ones."

"Clever," said David.

"Too clever. Whoever is running this gang is a little more capable than the average, when it comes to planning and logistics. It wouldn't surprise me to learn they have military leadership experience." There was the briefest pause before Fremont went on, "how long has Leonard been living in your vicarage?"

Tristan frowned. What was Fremont implying?

"About a year. Why?" David's tone was defensive.

More book pages rustled. "I don't trust him."

Even though Tristan already knew that, it still rankled to have the man's feelings voiced so openly.

"Why not?" asked David.

Fremont sniffed. "The man's virtually bankrupt. One can never trust somebody who is in dire need of money."

Tristan's shoulders stiffened and his chest felt tight. How dare the viscount question his integrity? He knew nothing about Tristan, and he had no business making such sweeping and generalized statements. Not everybody who was short of funds was also short of honesty, and if Fremont was half the judge of character he obviously thought he was, he would know that.

"Being broke's a common complaint," said David. "If you were to suspect every peer with pockets to let, you'd never finish your interrogations. And that's before you add in all the suspects you'd have from the general population."

His gentle but firm set-down of his guest helped rein in Tristan's temper.

"True," conceded Fremont.

"I'd say Leonard's more honest than most," David

went on. Tristan swallowed, grateful for a loyal friend. It wasn't something he took for granted. Too many others would have agreed with Fremont's assessment. "He's done nothing to hide his penury," David pointed out. "Or are you saying that retrenching and working to put right one's affairs are somehow less honest than ignoring the problem and hoping it will go away? Perhaps you feel he should have proclaimed undying love to some whey-faced chit with more hair than wit but a healthy dowry to cover her shortcomings?"

"You're being provocative."

"And you are barking at the wrong tree. Tristan Leonard's a good man. It will take a lot for you to convince me that he can be corrupted in any way. Let alone enough to lead a gang of murderers."

"Perhaps." There was a small thud. Tristan guessed that a pile of books had been deposited on one of the occasional tables dotted around the library. "But I have to consider him."

In all fairness, Tristan could understand Fremont's point. He wouldn't be doing his job if he didn't count everyone a suspect until proven otherwise. It still hurt, though.

"After all," Fremont continued, "the previous Lord Leonard was not what you'd call scrupulously honest in all his dealings, was he?"

Tristan frowned and turned his head, as if he might see the viscount through the office wall and gauge his meaning. Was this another example of his provocative pronouncements? Lancelot had been reckless and selfish, yes. He'd gone through the family fortune in a dizzyingly short amount of time, seemingly with no thought as to how anyone else would be affected. But this was the first time Tristan had heard him accused of anything more than inconsiderate stupidity.

David must have given Fremont a look that said this was news to him, too, because Fremont elaborated. "There are whispers, credible whispers, that Lancelot Leonard was doing deals with the devil. A particularly nasty devil, to be precise. He was caught up with a notorious gangster in London. Milton Percival. I see you've heard of him."

"I most certainly have."

So had Tristan. One could not spend time in London and not hear that name mentioned. An East End gang boss he might be, but even in the hallowed halls of Mayfair, Percival's name was whispered with dread. If Lancelot had fallen into his clutches…

"We aren't so far from town here," David carried on. "And, rumor has it, Percival's trying to muscle his way into the underbelly of Brighton. Which puts Rotherton in the pinch between his finger and his thumb, so to speak."

"London. Brighton. He even chanced his arm at the port in Dover last year, though it came to nothing. That time. I make no doubt he'll try again. The man is nothing if not ambitious. And he has more than one lordly puppet dangling from his strings."

Lordly puppets such as Lancelot? Tristan was sickened by the thought. How could his brother have been so foolish? He wasn't an imbecile. He must have seen a man like Percival for the villain he was. What on earth would have induced him to involve himself with such a person?

"There are those who believe that, had the fourth Baron Leonard not shot himself, he would either have ended on the gallows or he'd have been found floating in the Thames, depending on which side got to him first."

Tristan's eyes burned and his vision blurred. It was bad enough to have lost a brother, especially by Lancelot's own hand, the grief and bewilderment over his death mixed with the shame and guilt of a suicide. Now, to have his name dragged through the mud, to hear allegations and accusations he was no longer here to defend against...Tristan wanted to storm out, grab Fremont by the throat and make him eat his nasty words. He wanted to silence any and all speculation, to insist that those who defamed his brother should prove it. He dared not, because part of him suspected the proof would be there, irrefutable, ready to blacken still further his brother's name. Tristan was not ready to face that. He probably never would be.

"Tristan is not Lancelot," said David, his tone adamant. There was a pause before he went on to ask, "Have you found all the books you want to read?"

Jarred from his regret-filled musings, Tristan wiped the tears from his eyes and tried to pull himself together as quietly as he could. What was done was done. Wishing it different would not make it so.

"I could spend fifty years in here and never finish finding books I want to read," replied Fremont, his voice much lighter now, his tone carrying the hint of a smile. "But these three will do for the moment."

"Good. Because you owe me the chance to thrash you at billiards." The two men walked across the room, their boots loud on the polished wood of the floor. "No business talk while we're playing. No distractions at all. Let's keep it fair and square."

Fremont chuckled. "I wouldn't have it any other way."

The library door closed and Tristan was left alone once more. It was a long time before he felt able to resume his work.

Chapter Five

Diana stepped tentatively into the breakfast room. Even after three days, she still felt very much a guest at Amberley, although Ella had done all she could to make her feel welcome. She gave her a tour of the house and a potted history of the estate, asked for her meal preferences, and provided her with a personal maid, something Diana had missed.

But Ella did not know the truth, and that made Diana uneasy. She thought Ella had every right to know who was staying in her home, and why. Fremont had disagreed. He believed the fewer people who knew the full story, the better. He hadn't even told Rotherton, and he was the area's magistrate.

In some ways, Diana had to admit, her adopted persona was freeing. She knew it had worried Papa that she would be the target of every fortune hunter in England, and it would be impossible to discern the true motive behind anyone's befriending of her. As a spinster of moderate means, that problem disappeared. If a gentleman showed interest in her now, it must be because he found her attractive and wished to court her rather than her inheritance.

An image came to mind of Lord Leonard. That wasn't, of itself, startling. In the last three days, he had been frequently in her thoughts. He was nothing like she might have envisaged a baron to be. He was a peer of the realm, but he didn't have that air of entitlement so many lords wore like a second skin. Even Fremont, who was usually down-to-earth and easy to get along with, expected to get his way as a matter of course: if he ordered something, he was genuinely surprised if it wasn't done immediately and without demur. Lord Leonard was not like that, and Diana found that refreshing, if a little disconcerting.

At first, she wondered if it was because of the way he'd been dressed. Unlike both Fremont and Rotherton, Lord Leonard's clothes were not of the highest order. They were well made, but his coats were older, worn, lived-in. His manner was humbler, too—the manner of a man who worked for his living rather than one who enjoyed a life of leisure. That was confirmed by the callouses on his hands, and a slight tan to his face spoke of time spent outdoors, unshielded from the sun.

His manner toward her had been polite, yet distant, but she thought he had not been indifferent to her. She had seen the surreptitious glances he threw her way. Diana was not experienced at all when it came to such things, but she believed—hoped—he'd found her attractive.

Not that his attraction to her would cause him to seek her out, of course. Titled gentlemen did not court girls of less than stellar fortune at the best of times, and this man was clearly down on his luck himself. He would needs marry a woman of means, and no other consideration would enter into it. So, although Diana Wilde may well catch his eye, it was Diana Villiers who would receive his attention. That saddened her, but it was the way of the world. There was nothing to be done about it.

"Lord Leonard," said Ella, bringing Diana out of her musings. Startled, she wondered if she'd said his name aloud. A mortified heat crept over her cheeks. "At least he's honest about his lack of funds," continued Ella. She popped a piece of jam-covered toast into her mouth. "Don't misunderstand me. He doesn't stand on the street, wringing his hands and bemoaning his lot in life, but he doesn't live beyond his means, either. That is to be commended."

Diana's blush subsided as she realized Ella's comment was not in answer to anything she'd said. Although why Ella had mentioned him was anybody's guess. Guiltily, Diana bit her lip and waited silently, hoping for a clue to the context of the conversation.

"That's where Bertie fell down," Ella went on.

Diana nodded. Bertie, she'd learned, was the recently deceased Lord Hadlow. He'd died a hero, stopping a gang of treasonous villains who worshiped Bonaparte, but before that, he'd apparently been a feckless gambler, a rake living far beyond his means and never attempting to pay his debts. In fact, the reason he'd been here to take on the Bonapartists in the first place was because he'd left London to avoid being dunned.

"I loved him dearly, and I miss him," said Ella. "But if he were alive now, I'd strangle him. Just as I'm likely to strangle the new Viscount Hadlow if he doesn't come to take up his duties soon. His workers and tenants—and the whole Hadlow estate, for that matter—need him *now,* not whenever he finally deigns to make an appearance."

"I see." It was all Diana could think of to say.

"The situation is dire. After breakfast, let's ride over there in my trap. Then you can see for yourself the sorry state of the place. I'm sure you'll appreciate the urgency, once you've seen it." She grimaced. "If the dratted man doesn't come soon, I may be compelled to take matters into my own hands and become that most despised of creatures, a managing and interfering female."

Diana grinned. She'd only known Ella a few days, but she didn't think the woman would be too regretful if managing and interfering in Lord Hadlow's business became a necessity. Ella did what needed to be done, and hang what anyone else had to say to the matter.

Half an hour later, Diana held onto the side of the trap as Ella bowled along the roads crisscrossing her estate at a fast clip. She pointed in one direction and told her that was where her land marched alongside Rotherton's, then in the opposite direction, where she had a boundary with land owned by Mr. Potter, who'd bought his estate recently and built a house to his wife's exacting specifications, and why not? If he had the money to spend, said Ella, he should get precisely what he wanted for it. She then pointed to a narrow lane on the edge of her land, which led toward the river, and to somewhere called Marshy Meadow.

"Probably best not to go there," she advised. "It's a swamp at the best of times. But, if you follow the road that way," she pointed in the other direction, "it leads through the village of Crompton Hadlow, and into Rotherton. And there, straight ahead, is the Hadlow estate. If we head over there—whoa!"

She pulled hard on the reins, and the trap swerved violently to the side as the pony shied at the alarming suddenness of the command. Diana clung to the rail with both hands, terrified of being thrown from the vehicle and breaking her head on the hard earth below.

Ahead of them, a boy stood in the middle of the

road. He looked as if he'd already met with misfortune. His clothes were ragged and dirty and too short for his long, thin frame. His skeletal face was topped by carelessly chopped hair, and his bare shins and hands were covered in scratches.

"Ned Fellowes, what are you about?" scolded Ella. Fear at the near-miss sharpened her tone.

The boy hung his head, sheepishly. He said nothing.

"Don't look at me like that," Ella said. "I might have killed you." The front of his shirt moved, and he cradled it. "What have you got there?"

The boy quacked like a duck, then drooped one shoulder as if that arm was useless to him.

"Can you fix it?"

He grinned, and quacked again.

Ella rolled her eyes. "Be on your way. And look before you run across the road in future."

He barked like a small dog, then scrambled over the wall that bounded Ella's property and disappeared along the road. Diana gaped, scarcely believing what she'd just seen. His animal impressions had been remarkable in their accuracy, but...

"He might have said sorry for almost upending us," she decided, shifting in her seat to regain her position.

"Ned doesn't speak," said Ella. "Not with words, anyway."

"Oh." Now Diana felt awkward. "I didn't mean...I meant no offense."

"None taken. He's too busy with his wounded duck to worry about us."

"His...wounded duck?" Diana blinked.

"Tucked into his shirt. It had a broken wing." Ella grinned at Diana's confusion. "He doesn't use words, but he can make himself understood. Ned has an affinity with all of God's creatures. If he finds one in need, he'll do what he can. It doesn't endear him to some of the neighbors when he nurses a fox, or rescues the bird they've caught for dinner."

"You think that duck was somebody's dinner?"

"Indubitably. But he'll take it home and care for it, while they have to make do with bread and cheese. They won't be pleased about that, I daresay. Which is why it's probably best if we tell nobody we saw him. Or the duck."

"I didn't. See the duck."

Ella laughed, righted the position of her trap, and moved on.

They crossed the boundary from Ella's estate to Lord Hadlow's. At first, the difference between the two was not obvious. The woodland straddling the border was lush and well-kept, the trees in good health, the brambles and bracken around them thick and lush. Bluebells waved shyly from the shade, misty violet clouds in the deep green grass. Along the verges, cow parsley grew, their lacy cream flowers bending softly in the breeze. Marguerite daisies stood tall, and occasional poppies splashed red over the scene.

Then they left the woodland, and the neglect became clear. Where Ella's fields were tended nicely, crops growing in some, animals grazing in others, Hadlow's fields were unkempt. Some small strips looked to have been worked but, for the most part, the land was overgrown with nettles and dock leaves, thorny suckers and thistles, and all manner of other weeds. The houses they passed were in a poor state as well, with patches on the walls where damp showed, while doors sagged on their hinges. Thatched roofs looked flat and old, tiled ones showed gaps. In a narrow road with a rutted surface, children played, jumping back and forth over a narrow stream that smelled foul.

"Oh, my word," whispered Diana. She'd seen poverty before. It would have been impossible to travel with Papa and not see that some people's living conditions were not as good as they should be, but this seemed worse, because it was deliberate, careless neglect, overlaid with an air of hopelessness and defeat. It wasn't hard to see that most of these people had simply given up.

"I can see why you want the new viscount to come," she said.

"Yes." Ella sighed. "Although, if I'm honest, I don't think it'll make much difference."

"You think he'll be as uncaring as the previous Lord Hadlow?"

"He must be or he'd have been here by now, don't you think? But that isn't the real problem. Even Bertie wouldn't have been this neglectful of his property if he'd had the money for it." She looked around her, a grim expression on her face. "Until his last day on earth, Bertie had no money. So he had no means of making repairs. Without making the repairs, he couldn't generate income. No income, no money, no repairs. A vicious circle. Plus, Bertie..." She smiled, sadly. "Any money he put his hands on went into his gambling stakes, not his land. Some men cannot resist the lure of the dice, and the cards."

"My father said that," agreed Diana. "He warned me never to marry a man with gambling debts." Then, conscious that she'd said more than she should, she shut up.

It was too late. Ella shot her a sidelong look. "Men like that look for plump dowries."

Diana's cheeks heated.

"You don't have to tell me anything," continued Ella. "Philip—Fremont—is invested in your welfare, and that's all I need to know." She looked around at the rundown cottages again. "On the day he died, Bertie finally won a jackpot. He would have squandered it again, given the chance. As it is, it went to pay some of his debts. Barely made a dent in them." She shook her head. "Not a penny of it was available for this. And now…" She straightened, her expression suggesting she had made up her mind. "I believe it may be better to ask the new viscount for forgiveness rather than permission. What do you think?"

"I'm not sure I follow."

"If I arrange for some of the more necessary repairs to be done, *before* his lordship arrives, what can he do about it? He can hardly tear the new materials away."

That sounded a dangerous strategy. "He may be angry. Men have their pride."

"Pish! Angry men don't frighten me. I've encountered them before."

That, Diana believed.

Ella turned the trap around and headed back to Amberley. As she drove, she listed the things she planned to do for those of her neighbor's tenants most urgently in need.

They were almost home when she slowed again, drawing to a stop beside an elderly woman in a patched dress and a shapeless bonnet. The woman's back was bent with age and infirmity, and she walked with a limp, a roughly made walking stick helping her to keep her balance.

"Mrs. Carter?" Ella called. The woman turned, ready to defend herself, then relaxed when she saw who it was. Her eyes were puffy and red, her cheeks chafed. She must have been crying for a long time for them to be so sore. Ella jumped down from the trap.

"They took my boy," Mrs. Carter hiccupped. "They took my John."

With a pained expression, Ella hugged the woman, who sobbed loudly into her shoulder. Then, when she calmed down enough to be coherent, she poured out her tale.

Her son, who she repeatedly insisted was, "a good boy, never in trouble," had been arrested and taken to jail, where he would be kept until his trial. Then he would be hung. Or transported, which was, to his mother, just as bad. She was on her way home from appealing to Lord Rotherton, who had, apparently, been very nice about it, even as he'd said there was nothing he could do.

"They're not coming up before him, you see. They've been taken to Haywards Heath, and they'll be tried at the Assizes. And the judge there will hang him." She sobbed again.

Ella helped the woman up onto the trap's seat, squeezed beside her, then took her home to her cottage. It was a pretty building, its walls whitewashed and clean, windows gleaming. The garden was neat and tidy, filled with many-colored flowers, bean canes and rows of carrots.

They followed Mrs. Carter inside. Downstairs was one room, about ten feet square. One wall was taken up with a huge fireplace, where Ella set to, building a fire.

Diana watched her, impressed. She wouldn't have known how to do that chore, yet Ella made it look simple.

Mrs. Carter bade Diana sit. Diana took one of the ladder-backed chairs at the tiny table, while Ella encouraged Mrs. Carter to sit in the rocking chair, refusing to take it for herself, even though the woman insisted. A dresser stood against another wall, its shelves holding plates, bowls, cups and cooking pots. A narrow staircase climbed up a third wall and, presumably, led to bedrooms. The flagstone floor was slightly sunken, but it was clean and smooth, with no cracks.

"I cannot say for certain," Ella told the woman after she'd got the fire going, "but I'd be surprised if Lord Rotherton did not intend to speak up for John. He knows he's usually a law-abiding man. Rest assured, I will certainly ask his lordship to do that."

Mrs. Carter looked more hopeful.

"I cannot promise he will," Ella added. "And if he does, I cannot guarantee his word will have any sway. But we'll do what we can. Now, tell me exactly what happened."

It seemed that John Carter, "the good boy, never in trouble," had been waiting with a cart in Rotherfield, a village a few miles from here. He'd been ready to collect run—smuggled—goods, brought from the coast by tubmen. The revenue men had waited, in hiding, while each man unloaded his burden onto the cart. Unknown to John, as each tubman left, he'd been arrested, out of sight, so as not to give the others any warning of what was to come.

When the cart was full, John drove it away and was ambushed. The goods had been unloaded at the jailhouse in Rotherfield, a sturdy, stone building where they would be held until they could be taken to the Customs House in Dover, to be used as evidence. John's was one of three loaded carts that had been intercepted. The drivers, tubmen, and others who'd been caught had been marched away in chains to Haywards Heath prison, where they would languish until their trial. Two Customs men had been set to guard the goods at Rotherfield.

Having assured Mrs. Carter she would speak to Lord Rotherton, Ella led Diana from the cottage, and they drove home.

"Can you do anything to help?" asked Diana as they headed toward Amberley. The sandstone walls of the house gleamed in the early evening sun, which made the windows shine orange, so that it looked as if the house was on fire.

"Doubtful," Ella admitted. "I shall try. But three carts full of run goods speaks to a large operation. The authorities won't wish to be lenient in such a case." She muttered something under her breath that sounded like a curse. "I'm sorry. That wasn't very ladylike of me."

"It isn't a ladylike situation." Diana smiled encouragement at Ella. "I feel for Mrs. Carter. But her son surely knew the risks before he took the job? One cannot break the law and then cry foul when one is caught."

"That's what I don't understand. John Carter *is* a good man. An honest one. There are several men whose involvement with a smuggling operation would not surprise me in the least. Carter is not one of them." She pulled the trap up at her front door, and a groom came running to take care of it.

"I will write to Rotherton and invite him to dinner.

Perhaps we can put our heads together, and come up with something useful."

Chapter Six

On the last day of June, David paid Tristan. As soon as he could, Tristan walked into Rotherton to pay the traders what he owed, as he did every month. He had vowed that, while he was head of this family, not one invoice would be left outstanding, not one bill marked overdue. As always, he was thankful for the simpler, cheaper life he'd grown accustomed to in the army. There, apart from his Mess bills and a few minor expenses, there'd been no need for profligacy. It had taught him well, and made him ready for the life he now led.

He paid the butcher and the baker, and was on his way to the chandler when he heard the jeers. They came from a group of men gathered at the front of the Golden Goose, in the center of the High Street. The men, most wearing the rough clothes of laborers, called out lewd comments at a woman, who crossed the street to pass them. She kept her head down and clutched her shopping bag tightly.

A quick glance along the road told Tristan the woman was not the only person intimidated by the men. Nobody walked on that side of the road. Very few walked on the other side, either; unusual in the normally busy village. The apothecary's doors were closed, and the greengrocer was taking in his displayed boxes of vegetables, something he usually didn't do until closing time.

As well as being a tavern, the Golden Goose acted as a tea and coffee house. As such, it was often used by local ladies, who met in the private parlor after they'd finished their shopping. Tristan hoped no ladies were in there now, because those men did not look as if they would respect the wellborn any more than they'd respected the woman who now scurried into the greengrocer's. The shopkeeper looked warily up and down the road, then closed his door behind her.

Tristan wondered that Seth Fayers had allowed this to happen. Ordinarily, the landlord of the Goose ran a tight ship. He was proud of his establishment, proud that respectable people frequented it, and Tristan would have expected him to move the rabble-rousers on before they reached this stage of rowdiness. He didn't tolerate trouble, especially if it might interfere with his profit.

Even as Tristan thought that, Seth came out and approached the men. But, to Tristan's astonishment, he didn't remonstrate with them, or ask them to leave. Instead, he replenished their tankards, left the half-filled jug of beer on the bench they'd congregated around, and turned to go back inside. As he did so, he glanced at Tristan. He, too, did not seem himself. Gone was the self-assured, assertive man who ruled his domain with a rod of iron, and in his place was a meek, almost obsequious man.

That Seth had served the group himself was concerning. Usually, one, or both, of Seth's two serving wenches would be out here, flirting, displaying as much of themselves as public decency permitted, and setting up their chances of earning an extra penny or two later. They, or their boss, had clearly decided that, in this instance, the extra pennies were not worth it.

Perhaps Seth needed help. As well as his serving girls and his cook, he employed an ostler, who was as old as Methuselah, and a young stable lad. Neither would be much help against this group of miscreants.

Tristan, however, might be. Not only was he a gentleman—and working men were often wary of fighting with a gentleman because hitting one's "betters" carried stiff penalties, but he had experience of situations like this. In the army, he'd had to deal with men looking for trouble. Perhaps he could do the same here.

When he took a step forward, though, Seth shook his head. The movement was small, almost imperceptible, but Tristan took it for what it was: a plea not to interfere.

Who were these men, that they could terrorize a big, burly man like Seth? And if they were working men, as their clothes suggested, why were they here, idling the day away, instead of doing their jobs? Today was not a holiday.

The sound of a vehicle distracted him: the brisk hooves of one horse, together with the swish of wheels on the road surface and the creak of the wooden cab. He looked away from the men, then groaned inwardly, when he saw Ella Forbes-Smythe driving her pony trap toward him, Diana Wilde on the bench seat beside her.

Both ladies were well turned out. Ella wore a pelisse in emerald green, a matching hat with three very flamboyant green ostrich feathers perched on her bright blonde hair. Not for Ella the quiet pastels of a debutante, or the staid, dark colors of a country spinster. Confident and assured, she always stood out. Normally, Tristan applauded her for that. Today, with these men watching, he would rather she wasn't so noticeable.

Not that it would have helped if she had been more conservatively dressed, if her companion was anything to go by. Diana's plain dress was a dark shade of lavender, and over it, she wore a spencer which was slightly darker, as was her bonnet, a plain hat, devoid of all adornments.

For all that her appearance was quieter than Ella's, Diana Wilde drew the eye. Something about her stood out and made a man take notice, even though she tried to make herself invisible, a drab sparrow hiding behind the spectacle of her more brightly plumed friend.

The men at the inn threw catcalls at them as they drove by. The pony shied at the unfamiliar noises, but Ella held him expertly and soon had him back on track. Neither lady so much as glanced at the Goose, or its noisy patrons. It was a sensible choice: having provoked no reaction from them, the men quickly tired of baiting them and turned back to their drinks.

All except one. A man with shoulder-length hair watched them drive by. He was dressed in a shabby coat and a floppy brimmed hat, and boots that had seen better days, and he held a clay pipe in one hand, his drinking tankard in the other. His stare was intense and unwavering, and Tristan braced himself, ready to step in should the man make a move to do anything more.

He hoped nothing would come of it. He was under no illusion that he could win if a fight began, since the man's friends would, doubtless, join in. With the best will in the world, six against one was not good odds, and these six did not seem the sort to observe the rules of Gentleman Jackson's Pugilistic Club. If it came to it, though, he would try. Before he went down, he would give Ella and Diana enough time to make their escape.

Ella steered the trap into the stable at the end of the High Street. The man stared in their direction for a moment more, then turned back to his friends. Twice more, he glanced at the stable. Finally, he turned his back decisively, and fully immersed himself in the revelry.

Tristan turned on his heel and walked back along the High Street, toward the stable. The spacious barn sat next to a farrier's workshop, shut up and unused now, since the last blacksmith had been arrested at the same time Hadlow had been killed.

He stepped out of the sunshine bathing the High Street, into the cool darkness of the stable. And found himself threatened by the tines of a vicious-looking pitchfork.

****

Diana jumped from the seat before the trap rolled to a stop in the dimly lit stables. Nobody was in here, and Ella's pony was the only animal, although fresh straw had been laid on the floor of at least one of the stalls and the place had a sweet, clean feel rather than the stale smell of neglect and disuse that emanated from the forge next door.

As they'd driven along the High Street, Diana had been thankful for the bruising pace Ella set. When they drove across Amberley park land, the speed Ella liked seemed reckless, foolhardy. Diana held fast to the side rail and prayed they would reach their destination without breaking any limbs, or necks. But today, Ella's speed took them past the Golden Goose before any of the men outside could try to stop them, or even slow them down.

Not that Diana thought most of them would do anything of the sort. They looked happy with their drinking and carousing, speaking too loudly, laughing raucously, and doing little else. Four of them had been outside the inn the last couple of times she'd come into town with Ella. Diana had wondered at that. How could they make their livings when they spent all day drinking?

They were clearly a nuisance as far as Mr. Fayers was concerned, and people in the village were intimidated by their presence. But, as far as Diana could tell, the four men had caused no actual trouble. All they seemed to do was shout and jeer. Nuisances, yes, but harmless ones.

They certainly didn't seem especially interested in her or Ella. Oh, they'd looked up as the trap passed by, just as they had on the other days. They'd grinned, called out, laughed, and made what she suspected were lewd gestures. But when they got no reaction from either lady, they'd turned back to their conversation.

Today though, the four had been joined by two other men, and one, in particular, had frightened Diana.

She'd seen him before, on her way to Ella's home with Fremont. The man had stared at her then, just as he'd done today, watching her closely, showing far too much interest. It was as if he knew her, knew who she truly was, although Diana was certain she did not know him. She would have remembered him, had they met before.

Then again, who could say he hadn't seen her from a distance? She'd visited many a seaport, ship, and warehouse, with Papa. Lots of men worked in those places, men she'd had no cause to meet. Any of them could have seen her then and known her now.

But Diana didn't think she was immediately recognizable to most people. Her clothes were now plain, the drabness of them draining the vitality she'd had in abundance when she wore more vibrant colors. Her bonnet was old and misshapen, which changed the shape of her whole face. Her hair was well hidden under it, and the gown she wore was too big for her, because she'd lost weight since the day she'd arrived home from Norfolk. In short, in her own opinion, she looked different enough that a passing acquaintance would not know her.

And yet…

The man stared at her as if committing every last detail to memory. She shuddered and willed him to look away.

"He's staring at you," Ella had said, low enough that only Diana would hear. "Do you know him?" She drove past the inn, on to the stables. They'd planned to leave the pony and trap in the cool building while they joined Mrs. Bell for her monthly At-Home.

"All the ladies in the area will be there," Ella had explained at breakfast. "And some gentlemen. It will be a good place to introduce you to them."

Diana had looked down at her dove grey dress. "I'm hardly an exciting addition to the neighborhood." She hoped, anyway.

"Fustian!" Ella replied. "They will love you. And it'll do you the world of good to make yourself known to them." She narrowed her eyes. "I have come to know you over the past few days, Diana, and it is my considered opinion that you've been deprived of decent company for far longer than you should have been."

That, in itself, was true. Diana had arrived in London from Papa's latest business voyage expecting to begin preparations for her Season, only to be hurriedly packed off to Aunt Mathilda's isolated home. She had seen no one, met nobody.

"No more excuses," decided Ella. "We will go to Mrs. Bell's, and you can meet people."

Now, with the long-haired man watching her intently, Diana wished she'd argued more strongly against this outing.

They drove into the stable, but she still felt his eyes upon her. It was as if he could see through the weathered wooden walls and pick her out as easily as if she stood in the middle of the street. Her stomach roiled at the thought of him, and her throat felt as if her heart had lodged itself there. If he came after her...

She didn't know that he would do so. He'd made no attempt to follow Fremont's coach, so there was no reason to suppose he would come after Ella's trap. But if he did...Diana was determined to defend herself. She'd sworn she would never again lie in hiding, defenseless, helpless, at the mercy of villains.

Someone had left a pitchfork propped against the wall of a stall. Diana grabbed it and held it out, ready to fend off any attacker. Although they'd discussed no plan, it seemed Ella was of like mind, because she gathered her skirts, jumped from her seat, picked up a manure shovel, then rushed to stand, hidden and ready, in the darkness just behind the door.

Footsteps sounded on the hard ground outside; a man's boots, steady and heavy in their stride. He stood in the doorway, blocking the light and, for a moment, Diana saw nothing but the silhouette of a tall man with broad shoulders. Frightened, but determined not to show it, she gripped the handle of the pitchfork tighter, ready to thrust it at him, to make him retreat.

The man came farther into the stable...

At the last moment, she saw who he was. She relaxed her hold on the pitchfork and lowered it, reducing the threat, while he took one step back, his hands raised in surrender, his body rigid with the shock.

Unfortunately, it was too late for Ella to abort her action, and the wide pan of the shovel came down hard across his shoulders. He grunted and stumbled forward, only just missing impaling himself on the pitchfork tines as he fell to his knees.

Ella raised the shovel again.

"No!" shouted Diana. At least, she tried to shout, but it came out as more of a terrified squeak. Thankfully, it was enough to stop Ella before the shovel arced forward in a second attack.

Lord Leonard was on all fours at Diana's feet. He glared up at her, then over his shoulder at Ella, who grinned, sheepishly, at him. He did not grin back.

"Sorry," she said, sounding completely unrepentant. "I thought you were someone else."

Lord Leonard used the trap's wheel to pull himself upright. He grunted again as he stretched his back and rolled his shoulders. "I suppose I should be grateful I'm taller than you could reach," he muttered. "Or I might find my head missing."

Diana bit her bottom lip, and wondered if she should add her apology to Ella's. Although she hadn't actually attacked him, she couldn't help feeling responsible for what had happened. If it weren't for her...

"You can't blame us for being careful," argued Ella. "Here we are, two defenseless females—"

"Defenseless?" His laugh was short, and devoid of humor.

"I'm sorry, my lord," said Diana, hoping to defuse the situation before he and Ella started to argue, which would make everything worse.

Lord Leonard gave her an angry look. "If you're worried about the long-haired man, don't be. He's still at the Goose with his friends. He made no move to follow you."

"Then you saw how he—"

"I saw him watching you." Lord Leonard nodded. "I came to see if you needed assistance. Being, as you are, two *defenseless* females." He glanced meaningfully at Ella, who blushed, her face darkening noticeably even in the dim light of the stables.

"Did I hurt you?" she asked.

"I'll live." He rolled his shoulders once more, then brushed straw dust from the knees of his breeches and the tails of his coat, before he turned back to Diana. "Do you know the man?"

She shook her head.

"He seemed to know you. Or, if he doesn't, he would like to."

Diana swallowed, hard. That was not what she wanted to hear. For two pins, she would run out of here now, back to Amberley Place to wait for Fremont to return and take her somewhere else, somewhere safer, where there was no danger of anyone recognizing her. Although, where that might be, she had no idea. Papa's business had taken them all over the country. All over the world.

Lord Leonard reached for the pitchfork from her, gently pulling it out of her hands. He stood it against the barn wall, and Ella placed the shovel beside it.

"Where is the ostler?" he asked, looking into the

dark stillness of the place.

"There isn't one," said Ella. "When we get a new farrier, it will be part of his duties to see to this place. Meanwhile, Seth Fayers sends his lad down once a day to keep it clean. He uses it as extra stabling if he gets a large number of people at the inn. And I can't swear to it, but I think he's also claimed it as a cold harbor when there's a mill or a cock fight nearby."

A cold harbor was a space, such as a stable, where travelers without the price of a proper room could bed down for a penny. It was basic accommodation—out of the wind and rain, but with no other comforts. While Mr. Fayers could, and probably did, offer space in his own stables for the purpose, he was not actually permitted to use this place in that way.

Not that anyone was likely to stop him. Diana doubted that Lord Rotherton would bother with Mr. Fayers' opportunistic moneymaking, as long as it didn't get out of hand.

Lord Leonard nodded at Ella's words, and stroked the pony's neck. His touch was gentle and soothing, and the pony shivered his pleasure. Diana had the strangest sensation, a longing almost, for him to touch her in the same way.

Startled, eyes wide, she swallowed, and pushed the absurd and inappropriate thought away. Clearly, the tension of the moment had created a temporary madness within her. She blinked, then looked quickly at her companions, and was relieved that neither seemed to have noticed anything strange about her.

"Did you have a specific destination in mind today?" Lord Leonard asked. His deep, low voice seemed to make the air vibrate. The citrusy tang of his cologne mixed with the sweet, fresh straw, and the flat, damp musk of ancient wood. His boots were dusty, and there was a smudge of grime on his knee, dark against the light color of his pantalons. His leather gloves gleamed dully in the scant light coming through the door.

"We were for Mrs. Bell's gathering," said Ella.

Yes. We were.

Diana swallowed and brought herself back into focus. Mrs. Bell's gathering. Where she was to meet the neighbors. That was why they were here. The only reason they were here. It had nothing to do with meeting broad-shouldered barons who stood too close for comfort.

She took a step away. She was glad to put some distance between them. Truly, she was. This man took up far too much room in the stables.

"Allow me to accompany you to Mrs. Bell's home," he said with a short bow. "And when your visit is done, I will happily see you both safely back to Amberley."

No! That would not do at all. They needed to move away from this disturbing man, not bring him along with them! He must have things of his own to do, things they were distracting him from. Diana would thank him, refuse his offer, and have nothing more to do with him.

"That would be wonderful of you, my lord," said Ella.

A moment later, he held out both his arms so they could take one each. Ella took his right arm, slipping her hand into the crook of his elbow with a winning smile. More reluctantly, Diana put her hand through his left arm. A shot of warmth seemed to flow into her at his touch, an electricity that straightened her back and made the hairs on the nape of her neck stand to attention. He tensed. Did that mean he had felt it, too?

She swallowed, hard. He glanced at her, then turned to Ella.

"Shall we go?" he asked. Was it Diana's imagination, or did his voice sound a little husky?

If Ella noticed, she didn't think it worthy of a reaction. She simply smiled her usual bright smile, then walked beside him, out of the stable and toward Mrs. Bell's home.

Chapter Seven

Tristan took his place on a sofa in Mrs. Bell's drawing room and accepted a cup of tea from Miss Julia Bell. The young lady smiled demurely at him, then sat down on a chair across the room. He knew she was not yet out in Society—since her older sister, the recently married Amelia, was only eighteen years old, Julia could not be more than seventeen, hardly old enough to contemplate such a thing. Yet she had a poise and a confidence many older ladies would envy, together with a classically beautiful face and an alluring figure. She would, doubtless, be crowned a Diamond of the Season when she did make her debut.

"Of course, now that Amelia is Mrs. Summersby," said Mrs. Bell, proudly, "we plan to launch Julia next year."

Julia's eyes flickered for an instant, and Tristan thought he saw annoyance there. Did she not wish for a Season? He thought every young lady wanted one. Cassie had certainly been disappointed to learn hers was forfeit to the family's finances.

Moments later, he realized it wasn't the idea of her Season that upset Miss Bell, so much as the way her mother used it to goad others.

"You had a Season, didn't you, Miss Forbes-Smythe?" asked Mrs. Bell, her voice far too sweet, while her smile reminded Tristan of a cat in the seconds before it pounced on a bird. "Did you enjoy it?"

"I had several," replied Ella, seemingly unbothered by the implication that she hadn't been a success. To have come through several Seasons and still be unmarried made her an abject failure. "And I enjoyed each and every one of them." Ella's smile did not dim. Nor did it look forced. Tristan wanted to cheer. She clearly had the measure of her hostess.

"Yet you did not find a husband?" Mrs. Bell's newest question was full of practiced sympathy. Tristan gritted his teeth. Diana looked up, aghast, and Julia closed her eyes, shame and embarrassment on her face.

Ella, however, shrugged, nonchalantly. "True," she said. "But never fear, madam. I'm sure that, by the time Julia makes her come-out, the quality of the available gentlemen will have improved. I had the choice of remaining unwed or settling for second best. There have been thin pickings in recent years."

"There have?" Mrs. Bell looked nonplussed.

"You see the same thing with horses. A thoroughbred is all well and good, but the lineage can be too pure."

Mrs. Bell's eyes widened. Diana raised her eyebrows, then studied her hands in her lap. Julia bit down on a smile, as did Tristan.

A few seconds passed. Then Mrs. Bell swallowed, turned pointedly from Ella and pinned her false smile firmly back into place, her narrow-eyed gaze settled on Diana. "And what of you, Miss Wilde?" she asked. "Did you also find the gentlemen of your Season not up to your exacting standards?"

Diana blushed. "I did not have a Season," she said, quietly.

Mrs. Bell's smile became triumphant, scenting her prey. "Oh? And why was that?"

There was a moment of hesitation before Diana answered, "Circumstances prevented it." She lowered her eyes, but not before Tristan saw the pain within them. Whatever had brought her to this point had been difficult for her. He remembered how she'd sat in Rotherton's salon, saying nothing while the conversation went on around her. She'd looked then as if she wanted to shrink into the sofa and disappear. She had the same look now. Tristan wanted to shield her, to take her hand and tell her all would be well. He would protect her.

Inwardly, he groaned at his own folly. Protect her from what? Mrs. Bell might be a bit of a dragon, but she hardly needed a knight in armor to keep her at bay.

"Circumstances?" prodded Mrs. Bell.

Tristan felt his jaw tighten as anger rose within him. Anybody could see Diana was uncomfortable with the woman's questions. Nobody should be forced to divulge information simply to satisfy another's thirst for new gossip. Whatever the circumstances that had destroyed Diana's hopes of a Season, they were no business of Mrs. Bell's. Or any of the other avid listeners in this room. He stiffened and leaned forward in his seat, prepared to interrupt, to change the subject.

Ella beat him to it. "Goodness! Is that the time?" She made a show of looking at the ormolu clock on the mantelshelf before she stood. "I thank you for your kind hospitality, Mrs. Bell. As usual, your cook has surpassed herself. I wonder if she would share the receipt for those delicious cakes with my cook? Alas, though, we must now leave."

"So soon?" Mrs. Bell did not look pleased.

Ella's smile was regretful. "I'm afraid so. Lord Leonard has kindly offered to escort us home, and we do not want to detain him too late into the evening, do we?"

"I—suppose not. But—"

"I do look forward to seeing you at the Assembly next week. Come, Diana. We don't want to inconvenience his lordship when he's been so kind. We are ready when you are, my lord."

Minutes later, Tristan followed Ella and Diana out onto the pavement, leaving a clearly frustrated Mrs. Bell to ponder over the mystery of Miss Wilde and her lack of a Season.

"You don't have to escort us home, my lord," Diana declared, as they walked back to the stable. The sun made its way down through the western sky, tinging the edges of tiny white clouds with pink-orange and giving the landscape a soft, golden glow. Most of the businesses along the High Street looked to have closed, and the Golden Goose was quiet. Whether that meant the men had left the inn, or had simply moved into the taproom, Tristan couldn't say. If they had left, they could be anywhere by now, their skins full of beer and minds full of mischief. Considering the sinister interest the long-haired man had shown in Diana earlier, Tristan was not about to leave her to travel unescorted. Not even when the journey was less than a mile.

"I will ride with you." He made sure that his tone brooked no argument.

"Your company is appreciated, my lord," said Ella. "My companion may be fearless and intrepid, but I am not. I will feel better with you beside us." She turned to Diana. "Please forgive me for being so milk-livered, but I truly would feel better if Lord Leonard came with us."

"Of course." Diana nodded and followed Ella into the stable.

Tristan smiled to himself. It was a pity women could not be diplomats, because Ella Forbes-Smythe would have been perfect. She'd managed to keep Diana safe without making her feel small and helpless. The way in which she'd handled Mrs. Bell had been masterful too, assured and confident, firm but never rude. She was a very accomplished lady.

Two hours later, he had escorted the ladies to Amberley, returned to the vicarage, changed, and joined Cassie in the dining room. Built for a clerical family, it was plainly painted in a light blue, with darker blue curtains at the windows, and a bare wooden floor. As well as a table large enough to seat a dozen people, there was a sideboard, on which were stands for chafing dishes, a large epergne which they had never used, and two pewter candelabras which matched the one in the middle of the table. Although it was still daylight, the candles were lit, and they brightened the room while throwing long shadows against the walls. A painting of the three crosses at Golgotha hung on the wall over the sideboard. It was the only artwork in the room.

Cassie sipped her mushroom soup, then looked at her brother, a small grin playing on her lips. "I hear you went to Mrs. Bell's At-Home," she said.

"I did," he replied.

"Why on earth would you do that?"

For some reason, he was reluctant to tell his sister about Diana and his suspicion that she was in danger, much less the need he'd felt to protect her. He certainly was not about to tell her how he'd been ambushed in the stable by two self-proclaimed defenseless women. He'd never hear the last of it from her.

So he shrugged and said, "I was told the lady measures her success by the number of families represented at her gathering. It seemed that I should represent ours, since you were not there to do so."

"Lord, no." She pulled a face, then took another spoonful of soup. "I consider I've been well-behaved this month, so I had no need to do penance."

Their manservant, who had brought in the wine as she spoke, chuckled, then hid it behind a discreet cough. Tristan raised his eyebrows at Cassie, who had the grace to look contrite. Neither of them spoke again until the manservant left the room.

"A little circumspection, Cassie," Tristan warned.

Cassie pouted. "You can't tell me you enjoyed it."

"There was no need to be rude about it."

"Don't be such a stick-in-the-mud. It isn't as if I said it to her friends. And anyway, it's the truth. Mrs. Bell holds court once a month so she can feel she's somehow superior to the rest of us. The only time it's at all enjoyable is when Mrs. Potter is also there, and the two ladies vie to see which of them can outdo the other. I had it on good authority that the Potter family had gone to Tunbridge Wells today, so that delight was not on offer."

"Tunbridge Wells?" Tristan took a bread roll to eat with what remained of his soup. The spa town was a few miles from Rotherton, so an outing there would have taken all day. "That seems a lot of trouble to go to, simply to avoid Mrs. Bell's At-Home."

"They weren't just avoiding the Bells' At-Home, you ninnyhammer." He pulled a face of mock offense, and she laughed. "Caroline Potter had some fittings with a modiste there." Cassie grinned and waggled her eyebrows. "I know. There is a perfectly good dressmaker in Rotherton, who is easier to reach, and probably better value. Even if her French accent does slip every now and then." She sipped her wine. "Madame Charlet is as French as I am. There's more Birmingham than Bourbon about her. But we forgive her little subterfuge because she's very good at what she does. Just not good enough for the Potters. Because Caroline is making her come-out next Season, don't you know? And therefore, she must have something...more. Tunbridge Wells is not quite Bond Street, you understand, but it will do until the family reaches Town, and finds something more exclusive."

Tristan shook his head. He would never understand the logic of people like the Potters. To him, a dress was a dress. He had no reason to think a skilled dressmaker in a country village would create something inferior simply because of her location.

"It's a shame they have gone to all the expense of kitting her out," continued Cassie. "Caroline Potter is so shy. She's not in the least interested in being a debutante, but her mama is adamant. The girl has a good dowry, and her ambitious parent hopes it will buy her a title." She finished her soup. "Unfortunately for you, Mrs. Potter is after something higher than a baron, more's the pity. Caroline's a sweet young lady who will make a lovely and biddable wife. You could do worse."

"Stop it, Cassie."

"I'm just saying. Her dowry would restore the Leonard family fortunes at a stroke. You'd be free of cares. We could live in our own property. You wouldn't have to work for Rotherton."

"Cassie," he warned.

"Julia Bell comes with a fortune, too. Although, now that Amelia has snared the heir to a viscountcy, I doubt Mrs. Bell will settle for anything less than that for her younger daughters. Especially since Julia is counted a beauty."

He couldn't argue with that. Julia Bell was uncommonly pretty. She was also fresh from the schoolroom, and did not deserve the speculation Cassie was making, any more than Caroline Potter did.

"But you are a baron," Cassie went on. "That has to count for something. And you do have to marry, eventually."

"I said, stop it." Tristan glared at his sister. He was well aware that, as a titled gentleman, he was expected by Society to marry and create an heir. Although, considering the burden he found the title and its responsibilities to be, he wasn't sure his heir would thank him for it.

Society's expectations were one thing. They didn't matter. He could keep his distance from the tabbies and their designs on his future. He didn't have to listen to them, or take note of them in any way. His sister, on the other hand, was not so easily avoided.

"If you don't want Mrs. Potter or Mrs. Bell as your mother-in-law, and frankly, who could blame you for that?" she continued, seemingly oblivious to his souring mood, "there are other, more palatable alternatives. Ella Forbes-Smythe is as rich as Croesus. It's all her own money, too. She's of age, so free to make her own decisions, and her father has died, so you wouldn't have to woo him to get to her. She does have a brother, but from what I can gather, he has no influence on her, whatsoever." She laughed. "He'd like to have, of course.

Or at least, he'd like some influence over her money."

Enough was enough. He put down his glass so hard, it was a wonder it didn't break. The wine sloshed up the sides but, thankfully, did not spill onto the table cover. "Once and for all, Cassandra Leonard," he said, "get it into your feather-filled head— I. Am. Not. In the market for a wife! And if I were, I would choose a lady with whom I could be happy! Good God, woman! I'm not yet thirty. I could have another fifty years to live. Would you have me shackled for that long to a woman who made me miserable? And whom I would make miserable in return?"

Cassie ran her fingertip around the top edge of her glass and avoided meeting his eyes. "Poverty makes one miserable," she pointed out, quietly. It took the anger right out of him.

Because she was right. Worrying over money destroyed peace of mind and robbed a man of sleep. It filled his every thought, took away his reason, and ruined his life.

Tristan was a man with no fortune. No money at all. He barely survived from day to day. It was a life he'd come to terms with, but it pained him to know Cassie must endure it, too, and he could do nothing to prevent that.

Cassie's only way out was to marry a man who could give her the life she'd been raised to expect. Without a dowry, though, her chances of any man even considering her were slender to none. Unless and until he turned the family fortunes around, she was as trapped here as he was.

As for himself...as plain Mr. Leonard, he'd expected to love the woman he married. As the baron, he still wanted that. He couldn't stomach the idea of selling himself to the highest bidder.

But if he married for love, without any thought to the practicalities, he would consign his wife to a life of anxiety and dread. Over time, the worry would eat at her beauty and good nature until it destroyed her, along with any feelings she might once have had for him.

And yet...he thought of Diana Wilde. By Cassie's logic—and he knew his sister was right—Diana was the one woman in the area that he could not marry. She had no dowry to save him and his estate, and no family to stand behind him in times of trouble. The fact that she was staying with an old schoolfriend told him she was no eligible lady, for who but an impoverished orphan needed to rely on the generosity of others?

If he'd any doubt as to the parlous state of her finances, he need only look at the way she dressed. Her clothes were well made and respectable, but they were not expensive garments. Her bonnet was shapeless and her pelisse shiny with age. Helping her into Ella's trap earlier, he'd noticed her half boots were worn, too, the leather creased, the heel edges rounded unevenly.

Not that the rundown clothes could detract from her beauty. They couldn't hide her delicate heart-shaped face, nor the honey-blonde softness of her hair. Today, that hair had been pinned up in a tight bun, with not a single curl escaping. It should have looked severe and uninviting, yet it had been captivating. Her eyes were arresting, a stunning cornflower blue. But looking closer, one could see they were filled with sadness, wariness, and mistrust. She had the air of a deer in the glade—a timid creature, ready to run at an instant's notice.

What had made her that way? What had put such

fear into her?

Had her family abandoned her when her parents died? She would not be the first young woman to be cast out by people who should have looked after her, but were unwilling to shoulder the burden of her keep.

If that *was* what had befallen her, then thank God for Ella Forbes-Smythe. Ella had happily taken her in. It was clear she intended to look after Diana, and would see she was comfortable and provided for.

Which was more than Tristan could do. He could offer her nothing but a life of hardship and pain, and she had the look of somebody who'd already endured more than her share of those.

His musings were shattered by a loud pounding at the front door. Cassie's eyes widened, and she turned to Tristan as if to ask who could possibly be calling on them at this hour, and in so urgent a manner. Tristan shrugged an I-don't-know at her, then stood to go and find out, but stopped when two men came into the dining room, followed by the agitated manservant.

"I'm sorry, my lord. They insisted," he said.

"It's all right, Henry," Tristan assured him. The servant made a grateful retreat.

The two men, a lieutenant and an ensign, made perfunctory bows, first at Cassie, whose pardon they begged, and then at Tristan. Both were dressed in the uniform of the local militia—a short red coat, with a double row of brass buttons running down the front, and a high collar pulled around a dark stock, dove-grey pantalons, and black boots that presently bore evidence that they'd ridden hard to get here. Both men carried chapeau-bras under their arms. Neither wore a sword, which indicated that, although they were commissioned officers, they were not from well-to-do families. Exactly the type of officers the army would send for the less than glamorous job of patrolling the coast, holding back the second sons of noblemen for more prestigious tasks.

"What can I do for you, gentlemen?" Tristan asked.

"We are sorry to intrude on your dinner, my lord," said the lieutenant. "I am Lieutenant Paisley, at your service. This is Ensign Roberts."

"Pleased to make your acquaintance. How can I help?"

"Lord Rotherton is not at home, and we have a…situation." Lieutenant Paisley glanced at Cassie, who stood up.

"Don't mind me, gentlemen. I'll leave you to it." She walked from the room. The soldiers waited until the door closed behind her, then turned to Tristan, their faces grim.

"The jailhouse at Rotherfield was attacked this evening," said Paisley. "They took the run goods that were being stored there."

Tristan frowned. "The goods were still there?" That made no sense. "They were confiscated two weeks ago. Why were they not in Dover?"

"My question exactly, my lord," said Roberts, his irritation coloring his voice. "We are told there was an oversight."

"I'm sure it will be investigated," added Paisley, throwing Roberts a warning look. "In the meantime, though, the goods are gone, and the guards are dead."

Tristan groaned and closed his eyes. It was never good to hear of men who'd fallen in the line of duty. Especially when it should have been preventable. "How many guards?"

"Two."

He rubbed his hand across his jaw and clenched his teeth, angrily. This attack had not only been preventable, it was predictable. There'd been a sizeable haul stored in that jailhouse. With just two guards. Guards who were probably local volunteers rather than regular soldiers. In all likelihood, they wouldn't even have been properly trained, and their weapons would have been whatever the authorities felt they could spare. With a large enough group of men, the smugglers would have known the raid could succeed.

Tristan would wager the attack was deliberately timed, as well. Lords Fremont and Rotherton, both of whom could have commanded reinforcements from the garrison at Winchelsea, had left for London yesterday. Tristan did not expect David back for at least a week. The only other nobleman in the area was Lord Frantham, who was elderly and frail and, like Tristan, held no authority to summon the militia. Which meant, for now, they were on their own.

How many times had that happened to him during his military career? He sighed wearily. "Give me two minutes," he said. "I'll saddle my horse."

Rotherfield's main street was lit by dozens of torches, some held aloft by locals trying to see what had happened, some by soldiers keeping them at bay. Men spoke at each other, some loud and knowing, others in shocked whispers and appalled mutters. Women clutched shawls tightly around themselves. Older men gathered outside the Catts Inn, holding beer tankards and puffing on clay pipes. The soldiers stood, nervous, with tight grips on their muskets as their eyes darted back and forth, looking for trouble.

Which, if Tristan was any judge, would likely find them before the night was out.

"There are too many people here, Lieutenant," he said softly as they dismounted outside the squat, stone building. The oak door hung skewwhiff on its massive iron hinges, the lock broken, the wood scarred from the shots fired at it. A dead customs man lay in the doorway, a cloak draped over him.

"Yes, my lord," said the Lieutenant. "Ensign, see these people go home."

"Persuade them, Ensign," added Tristan. "Don't use force unless you absolutely have to. We don't want more bloodshed." *Not unless it's the blood of those who did this.*

Roberts, who looked no more than eighteen, led half a dozen soldiers toward the crowd. The people grumbled at his order, but most dispersed. The older men ambled back into the pub.

"This did not happen in a few seconds," said Tristan, peering at the damaged door. "Somebody must have seen or heard something." Not that he regretted sending the people away. Such a large number of them, together with soldiers on high alert, was a recipe for disaster. Nobody would offer information in front of their neighbors anyway. Better to conduct a quieter investigation tomorrow, when things had calmed and people could speak anonymously.

"I have heard a rumor," said Paisley as he led Tristan into the jailhouse. The door to the large cell had suffered in the attack, and scuff marks on the stained and sunken flagstones indicated something had been dragged across them.

The second guard sat in the corner of the cell,

propped between two walls, one leg stretched in front of him, the other bent, his arms hanging at his side and his head lolling forward. He would have looked as if he slept if not for the large dark stain on his chest.

"A rumor, sir?" asked Tristan.

Paisley's face was grim, his jaw set. "There's talk that the gang brought in a couple of big guns from London. Two brothers with quite the reputation in the stews, Simon and Mickey Hicks. This is the sort of thing they'd do. They'd want to show their strength. Establish themselves as not to be trifled with."

"From London?" That didn't bode well.

"Smuggling is a lucrative business, my lord. Far more profitable than burglary and thieving."

"More dangerous, too. In London, they can hide. There are crowds, and dark alleys to disappear into. Here? A couple of men from the rookeries are going to be as exposed as scarecrows in a field."

Paisley shrugged. "It's just a rumor. But if it is them, we're in for trouble. The Hicks brothers are vicious. They used to work for a gang boss as two of his chief enforcers." He sniffed. "Might still be working for him, for all I know. He's been trying to muscle in on the coast—Brighton, Eastbourne, Hastings."

Alarms sounded in Tristan's head. He recalled the conversation he'd overheard between David and Fremont. "A gang boss? What's his name?"

He was dismayed, but not surprised, when Paisley said, "Milton Percival."

Chapter Eight

The sun streamed through the window of the morning room at Amberley. It bounced off the wide stripes in the cream-and-gold wallpaper and enhanced the rich blue velveteen covering the chairs. The face of the mantel clock reflected the light into the room, making it impossible to see the time, although Diana thought it must be around noon. She held an embroidery hoop in her hand, a piece of cotton stretched taut within it, and had traced out the shape of three roses, with their stems and leaves, onto the cotton, but she had set few stitches in the time she had been here today.

Sitting at the table, Ella busied herself attaching, then detaching a wide ribbon to a bonnet which showed signs of distress under her constant changes of mind and plan. Strewn across the table were silk petals in various colors, thin modelling wire, and leaf-shaped pieces of cotton.

Ella pulled the ribbon off the bonnet yet again, then threw the hat down in disgust. "Daft thing!" she said. "I cannot get it to go right."

Diana put her embroidery onto the occasional table next to her chair. "Would you like me to have a go?"

"No." Ella grinned. "I don't need to see you do it beautifully to know I have no talent for it." She picked up the hat and turned it this way and that. "It's beyond saving. The only thing this is good for now is the cat's bed." Her grin widened. "You can argue, or you can tell the truth, but you cannot do both. Which will it be?"

Diana eyed the ruined bonnet, and said nothing.

Ella nodded at Diana's embroidery. "It looks like I'm not the only one making no progress. You had three leaves done on that when you started. You still have three leaves done."

"My mind is not on it today," Diana admitted.

"Why is that?"

"I don't know." It was a lie. Diana knew exactly why she couldn't concentrate on her embroidery.

It seemed Ella knew, too. "Perhaps your head is filled with a certain beguiling baron?"

Diana's cheeks heated. She knew her blush was deep.

Ella laughed. "You cannot deny it. Not when your face gives you away so easily. In your defense, he is a fine figure of a man. Very handsome." She leaned forward, elbows resting on her knees. "I think he likes you, too. I saw how he looked at you when he thought no-one could see."

Diana lowered her gaze, unsure how to answer that. On the one hand, the idea that Tristan liked her was…gratifying. Any woman would be flattered by the attention of such a man. And since he had no idea who she was, or how much she was worth, his regard was all the sweeter. For the first time in her life, she could truly know a person liked her for herself. She had learned early that Papa's money attracted friends and admirers who otherwise would not have given her the time of day. But Tristan Leonard thought she was penniless. He liked Diana Wilde, orphaned schoolfriend, not Diana Villiers, heiress.

The thought made her smile, and her heart did a strange pit-a-pat. She wanted to hum a lively tune and dance around the room.

But there were two sides to every coin. Tristan's ignorance of her identity was as a result of her lying to him. And those lies meant nothing could come of any attraction between them. The light feeling within her grew darker and heavier, erasing the smile that had played on her lips a second before.

"What's the matter?" asked Ella. She sat beside Diana on the tiny sofa. "Let me guess." She patted Diana's hand. "It's because you're not who he thinks you are, isn't it?"

Diana looked up, sharply.

"Don't worry. I'm not going to tell anybody your secret. To be fair, I can't. Because, although I worked out for myself your name is not Diana Wilde, I don't actually know what it is. Not that it matters. You can call yourself the Empress Josephine for all I care. It's your business."

Diana studied her friend for a moment, sorely tempted to tell her everything. She knew Fremont wanted her to tell no one, but she trusted Ella. The woman was keeping her safe, giving her a roof over her head. Did she not deserve to know?

"I don't want you to tell me, either," continued Ella, as if she'd read Diana's thoughts. "Philip—Fremont, that is—has obviously told you to say nothing, and you must do as he says. And I'm happy to know you, whatever you call yourself."

"Thank you," whispered Diana. To know this woman would take her at face value and help her without asking anything in return was a priceless gift indeed.

"And," Ella went on, "I'm certain that Lord Leonard will feel the same way."

For a moment, Diana allowed herself to hope. But... "He may feel I have deceived him."

"He'll forgive you." Ella grinned, and nudged Diana with her shoulder. "If the man has feelings for you, he will forgive you anything."

Diana hoped that was true.

"Now, with the disaster that is my bonnet, and your obvious reluctance to embroider, I think we should..." Ella stopped mid-sentence and looked up as her butler opened the door.

"Pardon me, miss," Carlton began, then stumbled as he was pushed aside by a portly gentleman wearing a coat that was too tight across his shoulders, and which would never meet over his stomach. His cravat was intricately tied above a brocade waistcoat. The jowls on the sides of his face pulled down the corners of his lips, giving him a sour expression.

"There you are, Eleanor," he said in a voice that seemed to come from behind his nose.

"Robin." Ella was, Diana thought, put out by the man's arrival. "What are you doing here?"

"You know what they say. If the hill will not come to Mahomet, Mahomet will go to the hill."

Ella stood and greeted him with a quick kiss on his cheek, then turned back to Diana. The genuine smile of moments before was now replaced by a social one, teeth bared, and no warmth. "Diana," she said. "May I make known to you my brother, Mr. Robin Forbes-Smythe? Robin, this is my friend, Miss Diana Wilde."

"Charmed," Robin said, automatically. He didn't bow. Not even an inclination of his head.

"Good day to you, sir," said Diana.

He threw himself into the armchair nearest the hearth. His expression told Diana he'd already forgotten her name. Ella rang for more tea.

"Marianne sends her regards," he said, leaning back into the chair and stretching his legs. "Tell your cook some of her cakes would be welcome. I've ridden here. I am famished."

"Of course."

Diana could see this would likely be a tense interview between the siblings. Robin displayed no warmth toward his sister, and Ella's greeting had been just the polite side of icy. On top of which, Robin now glared at Diana as if he wondered how she had the effrontery to be in his sister's house at all.

So she stood, and gave them both a curtsy. "Do excuse me," she said. "I am sure you have much to discuss, and I've been meaning to take the air while the weather is nice. I am honored to have met you, sir."

Robin gave a grunt of dismissal. Ella's smile was both grateful and apologetic.

As Diana closed the door behind her, she heard Robin say, "Another of your waifs and strays, Eleanor? You really are too generous. They take advantage. If you would only consent to come and live with me and Marianne…"

Diana gritted her teeth. *Waifs and strays!* The man had no right to make such an assumption. Although, in all fairness, it was a natural mistake for him to have made. It was likely the conclusion others would have come to. In the clothes she now wore—chosen by Fremont for their drab plainness—she did look like a poor relation, and she couldn't deny she'd felt as lost as any stray, ever since the day when…

No! She would not think of that! If she did, she'd dissolve into a puddle of tears, not just of grief, but of guilt. For, without her impetuosity, her reckless disobedience, none of what had happened would have taken place, and Papa would be…she covered her mouth to hold in the sob and blinked back her tears.

It took a moment to push away the abject hopelessness. It had taken longer to recover at the time.

Lord Fremont had helped. She'd run to him as soon as it was safe to leave her hiding place, praying with every step she took, from shadow to shadow through London's streets, that he would be at home. If he hadn't been there, she didn't know where else she could have turned.

He'd taken her in and assumed control of the situation. He'd hidden her and let the world think Papa had died in a tragic fire, while he set men to investigate the villains who had killed him. Then, he'd soothed and reassured Diana when she'd taken the blame upon herself.

"You are in no way to blame for this, my dear," he'd said. "This is the work of that blackguard Percival and his nasties. They did this, and I will prove it." He clenched his jaw and his eyes hardened. "And then, I will watch him swing."

"But if I hadn't come—"

He shook his head. "They would have moved against your papa anyway, sooner or later. Percival is not a man of infinite patience. I'm surprised he waited this long, to be honest. I can only surmise your father's wealth made him cautious." Fremont sighed, deeply. "The man seldom encounters anybody more powerful than he is. He usually just takes what he wants and gets away with it. But with your father…he was more cautious. But he was having him watched."

"Yes. I saw the man across the road." More tears spilled onto Diana's cheeks. Fremont gave her his handkerchief, and she dabbed at her face. "And the man saw me."

"That made no difference," insisted Fremont. "They were preparing to attack. Perhaps your presence brought it forward, but only by a day or two." He smiled, and his voice brightened. "What you did do was make sure they didn't win." She frowned in confusion, so he explained, "If you hadn't come to London, the attack would still have taken place, and then, having found your aunt's direction, they would have gone to Norfolk, looking for you. You would have been oblivious to the danger until it was too late. Now…" He gritted his teeth, determined. "He will not win. I *will* bring him to justice."

Then he had held her for a long time while she sobbed.

"He will not win." Diana now repeated Fremont's vow. It strengthened her somehow. She straightened her shoulders and stiffened her spine, and set off for her walk.

It was a pretty day. Tiny white clouds deepened the blue of the sky, and the bright sunlight picked out the colors of the landscape, making them look like jewels. There were the flowers: delicate pinks and bright whites, deep reds and yellows, lilacs and creams. They wafted on the breeze, nestled against a backdrop of myriad greens, from the emerald of the formal lawns near the house to the almost black of the yew growing against a grey stone wall; the deep, shiny waxiness of new holly leaves; the matte of nettles growing next to dock leaves; the many shades in the wood; the lighter bracken growing under the trees. The leaves of those tree branches spread toward each other, thick and abundant, almost hiding from sight the narrow path that wound between the trunks, quietly inviting her to explore.

Diana didn't know the names of the trees and flowers, but that didn't spoil her enjoyment of them as she followed the trail through the wood. She stopped only when she saw a fox, sniffing at a fallen trunk. The creature froze, and watched her carefully. She stared back. For several moments they stood still, each taking the measure of the other. Then, perceiving her to be no threat, the fox trotted away to forage elsewhere. Only when it had gone completely from sight did she resume her walk.

On the far side of the wood, she stepped over a verge of long grass. The road on the other side of the verge was familiar; it led from Ella's estate to Rotherton. If she walked along it, she could re-enter Ella's grounds through the main gates and walk up the drive, giving a satisfyingly long walk. If she was lucky, Ella's brother would be gone by the time she got back.

As she made to move, she heard a stone skitter across the road's surface. Startled, she turned and her eyes widened in shock and fear. Behind her, half crouched as if he'd just jumped over the wall on the far side of the road, was the long-haired man.

He stared at her. She swallowed, hard, and a shiver went through her. Her breath caught in her throat, while the muscles in her stomach tightened. Inside her gloves, her palms felt clammy and hot. She glanced quickly to the side, to the trees. They were on Ella's land. He couldn't follow her there. Not without trespassing.

Would he care that he was trespassing?

Then again, did she need to run from him? The last two times she'd seen him, he'd done nothing more than stare, just as he was doing now. Yesterday, he could have followed her into the stable. She'd feared he might, but he'd made no effort to do so.

Perhaps he was harmless. Even so, she wanted to distance herself from him. She took a step toward the verge.

The man grinned. His top front teeth were missing, and some of his other teeth were grey with decay. He moved toward her. Her heartbeat sped up. She could feel the flutter of the pulse at her neck.

He took another step closer. "Morning, miss," he said. The voice was mocking.

Diana glanced at the trees once more. A step onto the verge, a hop over the ditch, and she would be on Ella's land. But would she be safe?

"I know someone who says he'd like to meet you."

She ran.

The man cursed. She raced past the first trees and into the semi-light of the wood. Behind her, she heard a twig crack and leaves rustle as he gave chase. Diana pushed on, running as fast as she could, swerving between the tree trunks, ducking under low branches, hurdling over brambles that snaked across the woodland floor. She scrambled up a sharp rise and down a craggy slope, slipped on a patch of mud and grabbed a tree to keep herself upright. Twigs and stones and broken plants dug into the soles of her boots. Long-fingered branches snatched at her hair, and snagged her pelisse. She lost her bonnet.

And still he came after her. She could hear his footfall. It was slower and more lumbering than her own, but it didn't seem to become more distant, the gap between them never widening. His breathing was heavy and labored enough to carry through the wood. He was clearly struggling. She prayed he'd have to stop. That he couldn't keep up the pace. That she could outlast him and escape.

She must be nearly at the park. Surely, she could outrun him there, on open land? Perhaps one of Ella's gardeners would be nearby. They would stop him.

Tears filled her eyes, making it difficult to see. Her breaths were short and shallow, and her chest felt as if her corset was too tight. Her head spun, light, out of focus. Trees blurred past, adding to the dizziness she felt.

Just another few steps.

A shadow jumped out in front of her. She squealed and reared back in alarm, almost falling down with the sudden change in her momentum. Had he managed to get in front of her, somehow? Panic ratcheted her heartbeat up to impossible levels, battering her ribs until she thought she must explode. It filled her ears, momentarily blocking out all other sound.

She pushed down the panic as her senses returned. She smelled the sweet dampness of mulched leaves, the freshness of green plants, the earthiness of the mud. The silhouette in front of her changed from a shape to a person, with features and details and color. He growled like a threatened dog. Which was when she recognized him. Ned. The boy who did not speak.

The last fuzziness cleared from her mind, as she realized Ned was not growling at her, but at something he could see behind her. His eyes narrowed, and his teeth bared, just like the dog he mimicked. His shoulders hunched and his knees bent, ready to spring.

There was a thud behind her. She turned and saw the man. He leaned against a tree trunk, his chest heaving, his breath whistling. His face was scarlet, and a muscle jumped in his cheek. His hair, which had been in a long queue, now hung loose around his face. He glared at her.

Seconds passed. They felt like years. Nothing moved. Not him. Not her. Not Ned. Even the breeze died, the leaves still and silent.

The man took a step forward. It broke the spell. Birds called in the trees, which shushed them. A fox barked. In the distance, she heard sheep, bleating.

Ned growled. He pushed past Diana, and stood between her and her pursuer. A voice inside her screamed that she should run. Find help. But that meant leaving Ned here, alone with a man twice his size.

She could not abandon him. Not when the danger he faced was because of her. She must help. Diana looked around frantically for something to use as a weapon. There were no hefty, loose branches. The only fallen branches were soft and decaying, their rotting wood no good for anything but splinters. The ones that had not rotted were too small to do any damage.

Then, everything happened in a blur. She wasn't sure if the man attacked Ned or if Ned went for the man, but suddenly they were fighting. The man lashed out. Ned ducked under his fists, avoiding what would have been crushing blows. He darted to the side, chopping at the man's ribs as he danced by him, scratching at his face and neck, leaving small bloody marks on his skin, kicking deftly at his legs.

The man's face darkened from scarlet to puce. His

eyes glittered with growing rage, and he roared at Ned. Ned growled back.

Taking another glance around for a weapon, Diana saw the pile of stones. Tumbled together in a rain-made groove on the slope, they'd caught on a lip where the land hadn't been completely washed away. They were only pebbles, but some of them were big enough, heavy enough, to make a mark. If she could throw them straight, that was. If she could hit the man... and not hit Ned...

They were better than nothing.

She picked up the three biggest. They were round and solid. Thrown with enough force, they would certainly hurt. Would they be enough to stop the man's advance? Or would they make his anger worse?

The man kicked out, a side kick which caught Ned squarely in the stomach. The boy doubled over, his breath whooshing from him, and his attacker followed through with a vicious punch to Ned's head. The boy went down. The man raised his foot, his teeth bared in a snarl as he made to stomp on Ned's face.

"No!" yelled Diana. She threw the first stone, putting all her weight behind it. It hit the man in the back, between his shoulder blades. It didn't do much damage, but it was enough, coupled with his one-footed stance, to knock him off balance. His raised foot came down, harmlessly, beside Ned. The boy rolled away, though he was clearly in pain, and more than a little groggy.

The man turned to Diana. His eyes were narrowed into slits, his lip curled. Ned forgotten, he moved toward her. She threw the second stone. From this distance, she could not miss, and it caught his cheek, below his eye.

He yelled and put his hand to his face.

Diana ran. A moment later, she heard him give chase once more.

Chapter Nine

Tristan spent the day at Rotherfield where, together with the officers, he questioned people about the attack on the jail. If the reports they'd collected were to be believed, the attackers had come into the village on silent horses, pulling wagons with muffled wheels. They shot at the jail with guns that discharged soundlessly, quietly tore the doors from their hinges, loaded their wagons with nary a thud, and sneaked away again. Not one person had heard a thing.

Since nobody had seen anything, either, the smugglers must have been invisible. Either that or there'd been a thick fog.

Some people had been defiant as they denied all knowledge. Others were frightened. Tristan had tried to reassure them, promised to protect them. To no avail.

Frustrated beyond endurance, he didn't take the main road back to Rotherton. Instead, he tried to shake the fidgets from both himself and his horse by riding through less used country lanes that added at least an hour to his journey.

It was worth it. Apollo, the horse David had given him to use, had needed a long run, and was now much more settled, while Tristan himself felt better for the ride. His face was warm, glowing with the wind he'd galloped through, while his muscles held that combination of invigoration and relaxation that always followed exercise. His head was clearer, and he'd been able to sort his thoughts somewhat.

That the smugglers held sway was in no doubt. The people were frightened, not only into silence about what they were doing, but into actively helping them do it. If he was to find the ones who'd murdered the customs men, he would have to break through that fear.

It was concerning that they'd enlisted the help of London thugs. Tristan was unfamiliar with the name of the brothers Paisley had mentioned last night, but he had heard of the man they'd worked for. Milton Percival was spoken of in awed whispers across London, even in the gentlemen's clubs in St. James'. It didn't matter how rich and powerful they were, nobody was keen to cross him or incur his wrath.

But, if Fremont was right, Tristan's brother had had dealings with the man. *"There are whispers, credible whispers, that Lancelot was doing deals with the devil."* Fremont had implied that Lancelot had been Percival's "lordly puppet."

The rumor had all but destroyed the reputation of the whole family, if Fremont's reaction to Tristan was anything to go by. Whatever his brother might have done, Tristan had always tried to behave with honor and integrity, yet he was now held in suspicion and contempt, guilty by association.

And now, it seemed, Percival was moving in on the criminal elements in Rotherton.

It stuck in Tristan's throat that men like Percival and the Hicks brothers could come into the area, terrorize the locals, and set a gang to murder two men in cold blood. He wanted justice. To his mind, that meant arresting not just the men who'd pulled the triggers, but the men who commanded them, too. He would do all he could to make that happen.

And perhaps, if he accomplished it, he could also make up for any perfidy of Lancelot's.

Having decided *what* must be done, he pondered *how* to do it as he rode.

He passed the Hadlow estate, with its overgrown fields and sagging houses, and Hadlow Hall itself, shuttered and locked, and carrying an air of sorrowful neglect.

The estate was bordered to the east by Crompton Hadlow, the village for which Lord Hadlow was nominally responsible, although David had taken over many of the duties in recent years.

To the west, the estate marched alongside Amberley, which was, by contrast, run very efficiently by Ella Forbes-Smythe.

Thinking of Ella brought to mind an image of her houseguest, Diana Wilde. The two women could not be more different. There was a stubborn independence about Ella that Diana did not have—although Diana was not pliable and meek. She'd been ready to stand her ground yesterday against the men at the Golden Goose and, Tristan would wager, she would not blithely accept her fate if it made her unhappy. Not that that should be a surprise: he doubted Ella would claim friendship with a milk-and-water miss. It was just that Diana's was a quieter confidence than Ella's, a less obvious refusal to bow to other people's demands.

If she'd had a dowry, even a modest one, she would have been the Diamond of her Season. Instead, she'd been denied the opportunity and reduced to relying on the generosity of friends.

Life was just not fair.

As if his thoughts had conjured her, the lady burst from the woods that bordered Ella's estate, running as if the devil himself was on her tail. She almost collided with Apollo, making him shy. It took Tristan several seconds to bring him under control, by which time, Diana had taken off along the road at an impressive speed, her gown's hem held at her knees.

There was more crashing in the trees, and the long-haired man fell onto the road. Apollo reared back, his hooves narrowly missing the man, who looked as if he'd already fought a battle: his face was covered in shallow scratches, and there was a bruised swelling under one eye. His hair hung in rats' tails, and his clothes were snagged and pulled, the seam at the shoulder of his coat torn open.

And he was chasing Diana.

Tristan spurred Apollo forward, blocking the man from following her. The man staggered back, but did not fall. He looked up, his eyes full of venom. Then, with a snarl of frustration, he turned and ran in the opposite direction.

For half a second, Tristan debated chasing after him and demanding an explanation. But what explanation could there be? It seemed crystal clear: an undesirable lout had taken a fancy to a pretty lady and tried to force his attentions on her.

If he had hurt her...a red haze descended as Tristan imagined the horrors she might have suffered. He would see the man hang if he'd laid a single finger upon her.

Still, it did not appear as if the man had done more than frighten her, yet. Yes, her bonnet was gone, and her hair hung down. Yes, she was clearly terrified. But her dress was still intact, and she didn't seem...

The bastard could wait. Diana's well-being was paramount. He went after her.

Already she was several hundred yards along the road, with no sign of stopping or slowing down. Tristan spurred Apollo, caught up and jumped down into her path. She swerved, trying to get around him, blind panic on her face. He reached out, touched her arm. She hit him, with all the force she could muster. The blow to his chest didn't hurt, though it was strong enough to make him step back.

"Miss Wilde," he said.

She hit him again. Her eyes were filled with frightened tears, her breaths coming in sobs.

"Miss Wilde. Diana! It's me. Tristan Leonard. I'm not going to hurt you. Diana!"

His insistent voice finally penetrated her terror. With one last sob, she stopped struggling, although her body stayed rigid and he could see she was still ready to run. She blinked. The tears fell, clearing her vision. She looked around, frantic, scared.

"He's gone. He ran off." Tristan gestured with his head to indicate the man had run in the other direction.

Diana breathed out a huge sigh and slumped in relief. Tristan pulled her into his arms and held her against him. Even through the layers of clothes, he could feel her heart beating impossibly fast.

"He's gone," he repeated. "You're safe."

"He chased me...I thought...what if he comes back?"

"I'll set men to watch for him." It was a vow he would not break. He *would* find that man and make him pay for distressing her.

Her breathing evened as panic subsided. "Thank you," she whispered. She made no attempt to pull away. Rather, she seemed to nestle into him, her body against his. She trembled a little, and her arms went around his waist. Her head rested against his shoulder. Her hair hung loose down her back and over his arm, tickling his wrist where it was exposed between his sleeve and his glove. She smelled of lavender, and fresh air.

"Thank you," she whispered again, and she looked up at him. Her deep blue eyes sparkled. The tears clung to her lashes, making them dark and long. Her face softened, and her lips parted.

She was…beautiful. Stunning. Her skin was flawless; cream, tinged with rose. Her lips tempted him to lean toward her, to touch his own lips to them, to taste them. Her eyelids fluttered, half closing, inviting him. All thought of anything else fled from him. The world narrowed to just the two of them.

He wasn't certain if she moved closer to him, or if he moved to her. All he knew was that her lips were nearer to his, so near now he felt the warmth of her breath on his face, smelled the mint of her toothpowder, mixed with the sweet tang of the tea she'd drunk earlier. He heard her sigh, quiet and gentle. She closed her eyes slowly, inviting him.

Their lips met. It was the lightest of touches. Barely there. She tasted of tea and sugary biscuits, sunshine and summer-fresh air. He kissed her once more, a little deeper, a little firmer. His arms tightened around her, drawing her closer, her lush, full breasts pressing against the hard planes of his chest. Her arms were around his waist, her hands beneath his coat. He felt the warmth of them through his shirt. His pantalons tightened.

She gave a tiny moan, her lips parting on the sound, and he slipped inside, his tongue savoring the feel of hers. She gasped, then sighed, and relaxed into him, one hand caressing his back. Her touch, like her kiss, was inexpert, untutored, and more alluring than the most rehearsed touch of any courtesan.

Triumph surged through him. This was all his. He could tell. Nobody else had ever...

Tristan froze. *What the hell was he doing?* He stood in the middle of a public road, kissing an innocent woman. An innocent woman who had just been threatened by a brute, panicking her into running for her virtue, if not her very life.

Virtue Tristan was now putting at risk himself!

What kind of man was he, to take advantage of her vulnerability like this? He was no better than the villain he'd just seen off! This was, without a doubt, conduct most unbecoming. If he was still in the army, he would have been flogged for it. And he would have deserved every lash.

It took effort and willpower, but he pulled away from her. Shame filled him. He couldn't meet her eyes. He should apologize. He *would* apologize, at least for his behavior. Not for the kiss itself, though. He could never regret that. He would be a liar and a hypocrite to pretend otherwise, even for form's sake.

"I..." He cleared his throat. "That was wrong of me. I should not have..." He swallowed. "I apologize for my behavior, Miss Wilde. Please forgive me."

He should now assure her that it wouldn't happen again. But he couldn't promise that. He wouldn't lie. If the chance arose again, he would take it. Whether he should or no.

Diana colored, her cheeks darkening to a fiery red, and she lowered her gaze. "Nothing to forgive," she mumbled. She glanced around her, at the road, at the trees on one side of it, and the drystone wall on the other. She looked over at Apollo, chomping at the grass on the verge. She looked at anything, it seemed, but Tristan.

"I must have lost my way," she said, after a moment. "I thought I was headed to the park, not the road."

"It's easy to do." His voice sounded raspy. He cleared his throat again. "Easy to do," he repeated.

"I thought he would…hurt me. He hurt…" Her eyes grew wide and round and her mouth formed an O. "He hurt Ned," she breathed. "Oh, Lord! We must see to Ned!" She raced back along the road to where she'd emerged from the trees.

"Ned?" Tristan frowned and followed her. "Ned Fellowes?" Apollo snorted and shook his head, then walked after them.

"He tried to save me. He was hurt." She gave a cry of distress. "I left him! How could I just leave him?"

Tristan touched her arm, trying to reassure her. "You did what you must."

She shook off his touch. "But he—"

"You had to save yourself before you could help him."

Diana bit her lip, clearly unconvinced.

"Where is he?" he asked. "Let's find him."

"I hope I can," she answered. "I got lost." She stepped into the wood and looked around, as if to get her bearings.

It took several minutes of searching, calling Ned's name, but eventually they found him. His face was bruised and his lip bloodied, and he couldn't stand straight. It was plain to see his ribs hurt, but when Tristan stepped toward him, he backed away, as skittish as a wild deer.

Tristan held up his hands. "I want to help you, Ned. I won't hurt you."

Ned narrowed his eyes in suspicion.

"Please, let us help you," begged Diana.

The boy glanced from Tristan to Diana, and back.

"You helped me," she continued. "I need to know you're all right."

Finally, Ned gave a curt nod and limped away through the wood, in the direction of the park. Diana and Tristan followed, careful to maintain their distance from him, so they didn't frighten him, and Apollo followed them.

Ella's cook was horrified to see the state of Ned. She ushered him into the kitchen, promising to clean his wounds and tend to him. The word, "clean," made Ned rear back in horror, and the shock of the movement made him hiss through his teeth, but a reassurance that he would not be forced into a bath, and he'd be given a slap-up meal afterward, convinced him to cooperate.

When he was settled, Diana and Tristan went up to the family part of the house.

"I should warn you," said Diana as they went through the door that separated servants' quarters from the residence proper, " Ella's brother was here."

"Hmm." Tristan had met Robin Forbes-Smythe once, when he'd arrived at the same time Tristan and David had called. Ella's brother had not impressed either of them. He prayed the man was gone now.

His prayers were answered. They entered the morning room to find Ella alone, although from the way she slumped in her chair, looking both tired and relieved, he hadn't been gone long.

"It's all right," she said, grinning as Diana pushed the door open, tentatively. "He's not here. You escaped him. I wish I could—what happened to you?" Her grin fell and she stood as she took in Diana's disheveled appearance, then settled her glare on Tristan, from whom she seemed to expect an explanation.

Thoughts of the kiss he and Diana had shared flooded his mind and he could not, in all honesty, defend himself against Ella's suspicions. He hadn't caused Diana's distress, and he was not responsible for her rumpled appearance—mostly—but he couldn't say he hadn't touched her, and he couldn't claim that he'd behaved appropriately.

Diana rushed over to Ella and grabbed her hands firmly. "It was that man," she said. "The long-haired man from the Golden Goose. He chased me. Lord Leonard saved me. Ned Fellowes helped, as well." Her voice cracked. "He was hurt, Ella. Ned was hurt."

Quickly, she told Ella all that had happened. Tristan sat and listened, seething as he learned the details of what she had suffered.

"I will find him," he promised, mentally adding the man to the list of people he needed to bring to justice. "He will pay for this."

Ella called for a bath to be prepared for Diana, telling her she'd feel much better after a soak in scented hot water. Tristan took that as his cue to leave.

"I hope we will see you and Cassie at the assembly next week?" asked Ella as he took his leave. Her raised eyebrow and steady gaze suggested the question did not have a choice of answers.

"Of course," he replied, as if it was a given, though he hadn't thought to attend until just now. "I trust you ladies will each save me a dance?"

They said they would. Then Ella asked, "are you investigating the storming of the jail at Rotherfield?"

He stared at her in astonishment. *How the devil did she know about that?*

"Pish!" she said, dismissively. "You cannot keep anything quiet around here. You should know that by now. And, with David away, I was sure it would be you they'd come to."

"And do you also know where I should look for the perpetrators?" He didn't hold out much hope, but one never knew.

"One of Hadlow's tenants is in Haywards Heath, awaiting trial. John Carter. His mother is terrified for him, and I said I'd try to help."

"I can't interfere with justice."

"If he hangs, it will not be justice." Her eyes hardened. "He was coerced into his crime."

"Pressganged," mused Tristan, remembering Fremont's description of what was happening.

"That's a good way of putting it," agreed Ella. "I'm not saying he can help you. Even if he knows something, he may not be prepared to say. But it's worth the try. And if it spares him the noose, or transportation…one never knows."

Tristan didn't think he had any sway over the judges, but it couldn't hurt to try. He promised he'd go and see Carter, then collected Apollo from the stables and went home.

****

Diana lay in her bathtub and let the warm water soak

away the aftereffects of her run through the woods. Her legs and back ached from the unaccustomed exercise, and there were a couple of long, shallow scratches on her arms from the brambles. Those had stung at first contact with the water, though that had quickly subsided. She had no idea how she'd collected the bruise on her thigh and the scrape on her knee. She was simply glad her injuries were not worse.

That made her think of Ned, who had been beaten by her attacker. She hoped his injuries were not too great, and that they would heal quickly. Cook seemed to think they would, and Diana had the impression she'd treated many "wounded warriors," as she had called him. Ella had assured her that Cook knew what she was talking about.

"She's been with my family since before I was born," she said. She had come up to Diana's room and sat with her while the bath was prepared. "My governess found the sight of blood, even a small amount of it, unbearable. Since I was less of an embroidery-and-watercolor miss, and more a tree-climbing, neck-or-nothing-riding, dragon-slaying hoyden, there was frequently a cut or a graze, a bruise, and even, once, a broken arm to deal with. Add in that Bertie and David were constantly here, slaying the dragons alongside me, and Cook's ability to heal wounds and patch up injuries was very much in demand. If she says Ned will be fine, he will be fine." She laughed again. "Although, I'll warrant she'd dearly love to get him into a bath."

"He'd feel better for it," agreed Diana.

"You know that, and I know that, but Ned's aversion to cleanliness is strong. He'd have to be unconscious before it could happen. Either that, or held down by every footman, gardener and stable hand I employ. And even then I doubt we'd succeed."

The moment lightened her mood and Diana's guilt over Ned faded. If his injuries were minor, no real harm was done. The attack had failed. In more ways than one, since they would now be more vigilant, and Ella planned to increase the security of her estate. It was doubtful the man would be able to try again.

Once the bath was filled, Ella left Diana to her privacy. At first, the silence had allowed her to relive the attack, and to think through what she could have done, *should* have done. If-onlys crowded her mind until she slapped frustratedly at the bathwater, sending lavender-scented bubbles flying into the air to land on the bath edge, the floor, and her nose.

"If-onlys are no better than fairy tales," she reminded herself.

It had been one of Papa's favorite sayings, usually uttered with a philosophical shrug as a business deal eluded him, and his managers and agents lamented a missed opportunity, or a misstep they felt had cost them the success.

"It's a good saying, Papa," she whispered now. "Very apposite to today." She sank back down into the bubbles, hearing them fizz and whisper around her comfortably warm body. "Truth is, Papa, I could not defend myself. Ned bought me time. But if Lord Leonard hadn't come…" She shuddered. "I dread to think what could have happened."

And, yes. 'Could have' was another phrase that belonged with fairy tales. She smiled at the idea of Papa admonishing her for using it, especially so soon after "if only."

The fact was, Lord Leonard *had* come. He frightened away her pursuer and rescued her. Calmed her down, held her while she cried, and then…

He kissed her.

It had been Diana's first kiss. Travelling with Papa, there'd been no opportunity to meet a gentleman who might have kissed her. The eligible men she did meet were either in business with Papa and eager not to offend him, or they were easily exposed as fortune hunters, whom Papa quickly saw off.

Tristan, though, was neither of those things. He was, well, Tristan.

Diana had found comfort in his embrace. More than comfort. She'd stood there, wrapped in his arms, the warmth of him chasing away the chills within her, and she'd felt…peace. As if this was where she should be. Where she belonged.

His body was hard and firm, his arms warm and strong around her. She'd pressed closer. Closer than was strictly necessary, perhaps. Certainly closer than was proper. But she hadn't cared. All she wanted was to be with this man, held by him. Proper could go to the devil.

Without conscious thought from her, her arms had wound themselves around his waist. She'd felt the powerful muscles in his back, the way they flexed as he moved.

He'd smelled of bergamot, the spicy, citrusy scent mixing with the fresh cleanliness of sandalwood and the underlying musk of male. A hint of fresh air clung to him. It mixed with the starch lingering on his cravat, and the last of the laundry soap in his shirt, a combination of smells that enticed her, left her wanting more. This close, she could see the dark shadow on his jawline, though she

Caitlyn Callery

was certain he would have shaved this morning. The lashes around his eyes were thick and long, darker than his hair, which was mid-brown, although blond highlights weaved through it, courtesy of the sun.

He came nearer and she stretched up, trying to close the gap between them. His eyes softened, his gaze narrowing until it was focused solely on her. The bird song faded. The trees no longer shushed in the breeze. The only sound was his breathing, and hers.

Then he kissed her. His lips were cool, touched by the fresh air. And yet, his kiss was warm, inviting, full of the promise of more. The gentlest pressing of him against her, yet it felt like…everything.

He kissed her again. Firmer, this time. Deeper.

Her heart sped up, and there was a strange fluttering feeling in her stomach, as if a thousand butterflies had taken flight. Her breasts pushed against his chest, soft against his hardness. There was a tingling, aching feeling in her nipples. Something pressed against her belly, hard and insistent. It took her a moment to realize what it was, but when she did…

Triumph surged through her. She'd done that to him!

She moaned in pleasure, and her lips parted beneath his. He pressed against her mouth, and she opened wider, letting him inside. His tongue slid alongside hers, swirling, dancing, tasting. Her tongue danced back, savoring every move, wanting…she didn't know what.

A strange heavy feeling settled between her thighs, a longing for…something. She pressed her body closer to his, felt him harden even more against her belly, the tightening of his arms around her, the caress of his fingers across her back, her shoulders, her arms. The

116

ache at her center grew. She wanted more. She wanted him to teach her more. To fulfil the promise the kiss offered.

And then, without warning, he stopped. He stepped back, leaving her confused and bewildered, wondering what she'd done wrong. He couldn't look at her. Couldn't meet her eyes.

He had apologized.

The single, most profound experience of her life, and he had apologized! Called it wrong. Asked for forgiveness!

Diana had wanted to slap him. She'd wanted to rail at him, tell him what she thought of his apology. For the briefest instant, she was tempted to call on every curse word she'd ever heard—and after a lifetime of ships and sailors, there were many—and hurl them at his head.

He had apologized!

How dare he?

Pride had kicked in and refused to let him see how he'd upset her. Bad enough the heat in her cheeks gave her away. Her behavior, her words, would not. So she'd been coolly elegant—at least, she hoped she had. She hoped she'd been sensible about it. Mature.

The fact that she'd only then remembered poor Ned shamed her. How could she have been so selfish as to leave him to suffer? Thank the Lord he'd not been hurt worse. She would never have forgiven herself.

Tristan had recovered his equilibrium quickly. Their kiss had, it seemed, had no effect upon him at all. He'd cleared his throat and become Lord Leonard again, cool and aloof, friendly, but entirely proper. Nothing about him gave the slightest inkling of what they'd just done.

Diana wished she could say the same. In truth, she'd

needed to occupy her thoughts with Ned and his welfare, needed the time it took to find and help the lad, and bring him home. Even then, she wasn't convinced that Ella hadn't guessed. Thankfully, she'd said nothing.

Diana hoped her embarrassment, her shame, and her wanton wish for more of his kisses would be gone by the next time she met him. That would be at the assembly, when the whole neighborhood would be there. They would come eager to find gossip. Gossip Diana was determined would not involve her.

But Tristan—*Lord Leonard!*—had asked her to dance.

"I can do this," she murmured. "Nobody will know."

She prayed she was right.

Chapter Ten

The Assembly Rooms in Rotherton were filled to capacity by the time Diana and Ella arrived. An abundance of torches lit the building, making it shine against the night sky in contrast to the rest of the High Street, where only the Golden Goose was illuminated.

The building was much grander than its neighbors, wider than four of the other buildings on the High Street put together, and just as long. It had three stories, but each of those was as tall as two in any other building. With its white walls and steps, and the ionic columns standing sentinel across the front, it seemed out of place in the village, and would have suited somewhere more fashionable, such as Tunbridge Wells or Brighton.

Several carriages stood on the road, the coachmen talking and laughing with each other. Some drank from tankards. Others played cards.

Ella's coachman pulled up at the steps. A footman helped the ladies out, and they went inside.

The ground floor was taken up with a place to leave coats and hats, and a ladies room where they changed into their dancing shoes, straightened their dresses, and repaired minor damage to their hairstyles before making their way to the first floor, where the ballroom and the refreshment rooms were situated. The master of ceremonies greeted them at the ballroom door, but he didn't announce them. He wouldn't have been heard if he did, since the noise from the crowd already forced people to shout at near neighbors simply to be heard.

Chandeliers sparkled, the crystals in them enhanced by dozens of candles, which combined to give off the sweet scent of beeswax, strong enough to almost cover the smells of pomade and mixed colognes, powdered wigs on dowagers, and more than a hundred heated bodies. The two end walls were made up of floor-to-ceiling mirrors, which gave the illusion of more space but also made it seem that there were more people here. Several alcoves were dotted across the back of the room, open and available to the main ballroom but in a way that the occupants were sheltered from the bustling chaos and noise.

Ladies moved around the floor, or gathered at the walls, or in the alcoves, their gowns a rainbow of colors, some silk, designed to impress, others in plainer fabrics better suited to the heat of the night. Gentlemen attended them. Most wore evening dress, although Diana spotted the Reverend Mr. Fielding, garbed all in black, save for his white Geneva bands. Here and there were the red coats of militia officers. Some of the other gentlemen seemed to give the officers a wide berth, along with resentful looks. She wondered if those gentlemen had had to pay more for legal brandy, thanks to the officers' presence. She didn't want to think they were actually in league with the smugglers—not after the news of killings and attacks.

"I see Mrs. Bell," said Ella, and she pointed to an alcove in which a number of ladies sat, small tables placed near them to hold their drinks.

Diana knew most of them. As well as Mrs. Bell and her daughter, Julia, there was Mrs. Potter and her daughter, Caroline, plus a lady in a less colorful gown.

"That's Miss Thompson," said Ella. "She was Caroline's governess until last month. They've kept her on as a companion until they go to Town for Caroline's debut after Christmas."

Sitting between Caroline and Julia, talking animatedly, was Cassie Leonard. Tristan's sister. Diana looked around for Tristan, but didn't see him.

"My dear Miss Forbes-Smythe," gushed Mrs. Potter as they came into the alcove. "Do come and sit with me. We have so much to talk of."

"Oh, dear," whispered Ella, managing not to move her lips or break her smile. "Here comes gossip." She approached Mrs. Potter. "Is there room for two? I have my friend with me. Have you met Miss Wilde?"

Mrs. Potter looked Diana up and down, and her mouth pursed slightly, as if she'd tasted raw lemon juice. A solidly built middle aged woman, her hair was too dark to be natural, and had been teased and tortured into stiff curls around her plump cheeks. She wore a dress in bright pink silk. It was tight across her ample bosom, and needed a younger figure to show it at its best.

"I can sit over here," said Diana, and she joined Miss Thompson at the edge of the group. Ella didn't look happy with this, but Diana was content. She'd rather not join someone who didn't want her.

"Can you guess at the news Mr. Potter gave me today?" said Mrs. Potter, before Ella had fully sat down. "You never will, so I will tell you. Your days as a proxy landlord…" She frowned, unsure. "…landlady?" She waved a hand heavy with jeweled rings. "No matter. The point is, your duties in that regard are at an end. What do you say to that?"

Ella looked confused. "Huzzah?" she ventured. Miss Thompson gave a tiny chuckle.

It wasn't tiny enough. Mrs. Potter glared at Miss Thompson. "Did something strike you as humorous, Thompson?"

The woman's accusing and condescending tone annoyed Diana. In the last few weeks, she'd come to learn what it was like to be one of the genteel poor. Most people, once they'd decided a woman was not well off, treated her with disdain, if they bothered to notice her at all. For Diana, the situation was temporary, but she was well aware that Miss Thompson, and others like her, must endure it *ad infinitum*.

Not tonight. Diana smiled sweetly. "Forgive us, madam," she said. "I made a remark to my new friend that amused her. We didn't mean to interrupt your conversation."

Mrs. Potter glared for a moment longer, then turned back to Ella. Miss Thompson smiled at Diana and mouthed, "Thank you."

"As I was saying," Mrs. Potter said, "you, Miss Forbes-Smythe, no longer need look after the Hadlow estate. Don't say you haven't been doing so, for we all know you have. You are a saint, my dear. A neighbor in a thousand."

Ella's grimaced smile said she was uncomfortable with the compliment.

"But Mr. Potter has it on very good authority the new Lord Hadlow will be among us soon."

"It's about time," said Mrs. Bell, drily. Her expression of overdone innocence caused Diana to bite her lip. She didn't think Mrs. Potter would believe the same excuse for giggling again.

"When?" asked Ella.

"At the beginning of August. Something to look forward to, don't you think?" Mrs. Potter glanced at her daughter. "I hear he was a soldier. An officer, of course. He had to get back to England and then sell his Commission, which is what caused the delay. The workings of the army can be tediously slow." She tittered. "I expect he looked very dashing in his regimentals. And now, he's a viscount, to boot. It will be good to have some proper gentlemen in the neighborhood. As it stands, Lord Rotherton's the only one within twenty miles who is both titled and unmarried, and he doesn't seem to be, in the slightest, inclined to find a wife."

"There's my brother," said Cassie. Her lips smiled, but Diana saw the cold challenge in her eyes.

"Yes," agreed Mrs. Potter. "But I was speaking with my daughter in mind, and I'm certain you would agree, Miss Leonard, my Caroline can hope to look higher than a mere baron."

Cassie bristled, but said nothing more. Diana stiffened, fighting the urge to defend Tristan. She clenched her hands in her lap and bit the tip of her tongue to stop herself doing it. Caroline Potter's face glowed red, and she seemed to shrink into her chair, as if she hoped to disappear. The young woman had all Diana's sympathy.

"I wonder that you will settle for a viscount," said Mrs. Bell. She patted down the lap of her gown, a picture of disingenuity. "Especially one whose estate is in parlous condition."

"Caroline's dowry would go a long way toward remedying that," answered Mrs. Potter with a dismissive wave of her hand. "And, as I told Mr. Potter, it would mean she could stay nearby after her marriage. She might marry higher, of course, we are aware of that, but if she moved to the other end of the country, I would miss her."

Caroline's blush faded into a horrified pallor. The other ladies wore looks of sympathy.

The light dimmed slightly as another person entered the alcove. Ella glanced up, smiled, then looked slyly at Diana. Diana didn't need to look for herself. Even if Ella's reaction had not told her who it was, she would have known. A strange beat resonated on the air, and a breathless hush swept over the gathering. Bergamot and sandalwood filled the room, tempting and enticing.

"Ladies," Tristan said, his deep voice resonating through the space.

"Good evening, my lord," smiled Mrs. Bell.

Mrs. Potter's smile was uncertain. Diana thought she must wonder how much of the conversation Tristan had heard. He may be a "mere" baron, but he was still a peer. It wouldn't do for Mrs. Potter to insult him to his head.

Beside Tristan stood the Reverend Mr. Fielding. "Are you all acquainted with my friend, Mr. Fielding?"

The ladies said they were. Mrs. Potter complimented him on last Sunday's sermon and Mr. Fielding smiled and thanked her.

"I came," continued Tristan, "to claim dances I have been promised with Miss Wilde and Miss Forbes-Smythe. They're setting up for a quadrille now, after which there is a Scotch reel. Would you care to join me for one, Miss Wilde, and you for the other, Miss Forbes-Smythe?"

"If it is acceptable to you ladies," said Mr. Fielding,

"while Miss Wilde dances with Lord Leonard, I would very much enjoy the chance to dance with Miss Forbes-Smythe. And then, perhaps, Miss Wilde would accompany me for the reel?"

Tristan glanced around the alcove. "I also hope I'm not too late to claim dances with Miss Potter, Miss Bell, and Miss Thompson."

Mrs. Potter's eyebrows rose, and she looked at Miss Thompson as if the idea of her dancing was outrageous. Before she could say anything against it, though, her daughter answered Tristan.

"I'm sure I speak for all three of us when I say we'd be delighted, my lord."

"It is my fervent hope that I may dance this evening with *six* lovely young ladies," said Mr. Fielding. "If I may be so bold as to ask you, Miss Leonard, to add my name to your card? As well as all the other ladies here?"

Tristan came to Diana and held out his arm. With a smile and a curtsy, she put her fingers on the sleeve of his coat and let him lead her to the dance floor. Ella followed with Mr. Fielding.

****

Tristan spent much of the evening dancing, partnering the ladies who'd been present in the alcove. He had hoped to secure Diana as his partner for the supper dance, but was beaten to it by Ensign Roberts. Instead, Tristan partnered Miss Thompson and led her into the refreshment room, where she was immediately summoned by Mrs. Potter and required to sit with Caroline and a fashionably dressed young man.

He ignored the way in which Mrs. Potter made Miss Thompson's situation obvious. An employee she may be, but tonight, she was a lady at a ball, and he would treat her accordingly.

He collected a plate of sweetmeats from the buffet and brought them to her, ensured her glass was filled, then did his best to engage her in conversation, not an easy feat when her employer was nearby, listening to every word and glowering at the lady whenever she thought she'd overstepped. Tristan was almost glad when Lieutenant Paisley came to him and asked if he might have a word.

Tristan followed Paisley down the stairs to the entrance, where a soldier waited alongside Ensign Roberts, and several other officers, including a captain, a corporal and a sergeant.

"They've landed contraband at Rye," said the soldier, whose coat was dirty, and torn on one side. "We got a small force there before they finished unloading, but the bulk of our company was too far away. We were outnumbered, ten to one. We never stood a chance."

Paisley swore.

"Were any of your men hurt?" asked Tristan, and the soldier nodded.

"Three seriously wounded. One might die. The smugglers escaped." The soldier hesitated before he added, "they weren't all local men, sir. One of our lads, he grew up in the stews of London. He recognized at least two of them what was attacking us. Said they was well known in St. Giles."

Tristan and Paisley shared a look.

"That's not all," said the corporal. He reached out to a woman who stood to the side of them. She seemed reluctant to move forward, despite the corporal's coaxing. Tristan recognized her as Susie Turner, one of the barmaids at the Golden Goose. Her dress was indecently low, and her hair disheveled, but that may have been normal for her. The black eye and split lip, however, were not normal. At least, he hoped they weren't.

Tristan smiled at her and spoke in the soft, reassuring tone he would have used to calm a skittish horse. "Don't be afraid. Nobody here will harm you."

The captain, a man called Allenby, sniffed. He clearly did not approve of Tristan's promise.

Susie looked about, nervously. "I got to get back, afore I'm missed," she said, and took a step away from them.

"We can keep you safe."

She huffed out a disbelieving laugh. "Seth won't want me telling you anything."

"Did Seth hit you?" Tristan frowned. The landlord of the Golden Goose was a big man, loud, and at times obnoxious. It would not be a surprise to learn he was involved in things that were not quite legal, but though he might cuff the ear of his pot boys and stable lads, Tristan didn't think he'd hit a woman. He certainly wouldn't leave marks on one of his wenches. Tristan was fairly sure Seth encouraged them to offer services other than food and drink to their customers. A black eye would cut into what might be a profitable sideline.

"Seth never laid a finger on me," confirmed Susie, bristling with indignation at the suggestion. "And it don't matter. It'll be safe to go back now." She turned and ran back, past the line of waiting carriages, to the inn.

"Corporal?" asked Paisley. "A report, if you please."

The corporal stepped forward. "I wasn't in the taproom at the Goose when it happened, sir. But, according to people that was, there was a ruckus in there. They said as how some wrong'uns came in, looking for...recruits."

"Recruits? They were army?" demanded Allenby.

The corporal barely refrained from rolling his eyes at the question. Paisley sniffed, his own derision of his superior hardly any better hidden. Tristan guessed the captain had not been in the area long. He hoped he would soon learn.

"No, sir," said the corporal. "They weren't army. Weren't Navy, neither. Though they was using Navy tactics."

Tristan understood immediately. "Pressganging," he murmured.

"I think the Navy prefer to call it conscription, sir," sneered Allenby. "An easy mistake for a civilian to make." He looked Tristan up and down, as if calculating his worth. "May I ask your role in all of this?"

Paisley stiffened. "Lord Leonard is the senior ranking gentleman in the area, at present," he said. Upon hearing Tristan's title, Allenby lost some of his superciliousness. "Until his accession," continued Paisley, his voice carefully deadpan, "he was a major in His Majesty's Army, and fought at Waterloo."

Captain Allenby cleared his throat and looked as if his stock had suddenly become too tight. "My apologies, my lord."

Tristan nodded, then turned to the corporal, who looked as if he struggled not to smirk. The captain may be new to the area, but Tristan suspected he'd already made himself unpopular.

"The—er—wrong'uns—were   in   the   bar conscripting men?" Tristan asked.

"Yes, sir," said the corporal. "They've been doing it all over. Grabbing men and forcing them to work for them. They usually pick 'em off in ones and twos, but tonight, it seems, they were in a hurry for men, because they tried to get a whole bunch of them at once. Big mistake. There was enough locals to fight back. A few heads got broken. Made a mess of the Goose, too. But, as luck would have it, me and a couple of the other lads were—er—nearby. Some of those coachmen joined us, too. Seeing our red coats and realizing they was outnumbered, the gang scarpered. Although I've got a feeling they'll be back."

"I have a feeling you're right," agreed Tristan.

"We should get down there and find them," said Allenby.

"They'll be long gone," answered Paisley.

"Yes, but the men they fought will tell us—"

"They'll tell us nothing, sir." The lieutenant sounded exasperated. "Nobody in the place will have seen or heard anything. In fact, I'm surprised the young lady came to you, Corporal."

The corporal colored and looked sheepish. "I…might have been with her, sir," he mumbled.

"So we do nothing?" blustered Allenby. "We allow innocent citizens to be attacked in a respectable establishment, and do nothing?"

While Paisley patiently explained there was nothing they could do, that nobody would even admit there'd been an attack, let alone by whom, Tristan pondered the problem.

In some ways, Allenby was right. Something should be done. This gang was getting bolder and more brazen by the day. Tristan suspected the increase in both attacks and bravado could be traced back to the involvement of the London criminals. There was no doubt in Tristan's mind that the Hicks brothers now controlled the gang. Which meant they could expect the attacks to grow in number, and viciousness, unless and until they were stopped.

The emboldened gang were a threat to everybody. Not just to the laborers they forced into their ranks, and their loved ones, threats against whom kept their men cooperative and silent. The threat had grown now, to include members of the local gentry. Tristan was convinced the men who'd sat outside the Golden Goose the other day had been gang members, for who else could sit idly drinking in the middle of a working day? Those men had thought nothing of jeering at passersby, including Ella and Diana, though they must have seen they were ladies of quality.

That brought to mind the long-haired man, who had stared so intently at Diana. Although he'd made no move to follow her then, he had turned up the next day on Ella's land. He must have followed the ladies, then hidden, watching and waiting for his chance.

Tristan wanted to race back to the ballroom and ensure that Diana was all right. If anything happened to her…

He was being absurd. She was in a crowded ballroom, surrounded by her friends, and dozens of gentlemen, all capable of coming to her defense. The long-haired man would be stupid to try to attack her there, and on her way home she would have the protection of Ella's footman and coachman. There was nothing to worry about.

Nevertheless, he decided, he would accompany the

ladies back to Amberley. And then he'd encourage Ella to increase the number of men guarding the place. He could do no more than that.

****

Diana watched the red-coated officers leave the ballroom, including Ensign Roberts, who apologized profusely for abandoning her. She assured him she was not offended, that of course he must attend his duty, and she hoped he would return soon. That was not something she truly expected would happen: if the situation was serious enough to drag away every officer in the place, it would likely occupy them for the rest of the evening.

Lieutenant Paisley spoke to Tristan, who followed the officers. That told Diana the problem involved the smugglers. As the highest-ranked gentleman currently in the neighborhood, Tristan had to work with the militia for the safety and well-being of the people. Diana prayed that safety extended to himself.

The supper finished. The officers did not return. The music started for the second half of the evening, but there were noticeably fewer dancers, and the mood was subdued. Mr. Bell and Mr. Potter emerged from the card room and collected their families, as did several other gentlemen.

"Time to go home, by the look of it," said Ella. "No point staying when everyone else is leaving."

Diana agreed. "What about Cassie?" she whispered. "Her brother left at the same time as the officers."

Ella moved to where Cassie sat and offered to take her home.

"I'm sure my brother will be back soon," said Cassie, as she declined the offer.

"You're probably right," replied Ella. "But I would

feel better knowing you were safely inside the vicarage. His lordship would want it, too, I make no doubt. And, considering that all the officers have left as well, he may be some time."

Cassie thought for a moment, then agreed to come with them. The three ladies collected their coats and changed their shoes, then made their way to Ella's coach.

They were almost at the vehicle when Ella stopped, her spine rigid, shoulders stiff. She looked around, urgently. "Where's Terrence?" she whispered.

"Terrence?" asked Cassie.

"My footman."

Diana peered into the darkness. Terrence should be standing at the coach, ready to help them in. He was not there. For that matter, the driver was not in his box, either.

"Perhaps they are with…" Cassie turned to look and see if the men were with other coachmen. Most had gone, and the few who were left were with their vehicles, waiting for their employers. Her voice trailed off, sparking a new anxiety in Diana.

She followed Cassie's stare and gasped, horrified. There, beside the coach, lying in an awkward heap, was Terrence, his blond hair dark and matted with what looked suspiciously like blood.

Chapter Eleven

Diana looked around, shock and horror sinking in. Someone had attacked Terrence! She prayed he wasn't badly hurt. Although why anyone would attack him in the first place was beyond her. He would have little, if any, money; he wasn't worth robbing.

And where was the coachman?

"Tom?" called Ella, clearly searching for him.

On the edge of Diana's vision, a shadow moved. She turned to see three men run from the trees toward them. They were burly men, roughly dressed, wearing fishermen's knit caps, jerkins, and the loose-legged breeches that made a man less likely to drown if he went overboard. Their calves were bare, their shoes well worn. One carried a cudgel, another held a burlap sack.

All those details registered in her mind in an instant.

The man in front stopped just short of the ladies and looked from one to the other of them in confusion. "Which one?" he asked.

"The youngest," growled the man with the cudgel, standing to their left, blocking that avenue of escape. The first man glanced at Cassie, who stiffened her shoulders and fisted her hands, clearly expecting to fight.

"She's not blonde," said the man with the sack. "He said she was blonde." He moved to the right, boxing them in.

Diana knew then who they wanted. Her heart

jumped to her throat. It was difficult to breathe. Impossible to swallow.

"Let's take all three," said Cudgel Man. "To be sure."

"I've only got one sack," said Sack Man.

"It's this one," said the third man, pointing at Diana. He moved forward.

"No, you don't," murmured Ella. She grabbed the coachman's whip from its holder on the coach. Thankfully, the vehicle was low-slung—if the seat had been higher, she would have had to climb to it and likely would not have succeeded.

The whip was short, designed to make a noise over the horses' heads rather than to touch their backs. That made it easier for Ella to wield it in the confined space, and she cracked it at the man nearest to her. He was half as big again as she was, and carrying that cudgel, but he flinched away from the whip's tip.

Both the other men went for Diana. She swung her reticule at them. All it contained were her dancing slippers, a comb, and a fan. Those things were not heavy enough to do much damage, but it bought her precious seconds as the men swayed back, out of reach.

Cassie grabbed at her bonnet and pulled out a long, sharp hatpin. She skewered the man nearest to her, and was rewarded by his yelp of pain and a string of obscenities, even as he swung around and backhanded her across her cheek. The blow seemed to enrage her rather than cow her, and she pounced on him, somehow managing to get onto his back, one arm clinging tightly around his neck while she repeatedly stabbed at him with the hatpin in her other hand. He yelled as the pin penetrated the skin on his neck, cheek, and chest. He shook her like a dog with a rabbit, but she clung on, her legs around him as if she sat astride a horse. Frantically, he batted at her, but he couldn't reach to make effective strikes.

Diana swung her reticule at the third man and yelled for help at the top of her voice.

There was a shout, and the sound of boots against the hard ground as rescue rushed in. Both her attacker and the man menacing Ella turned and ran, disappearing into the shadows. The third man slammed his back against the carriage wheel. Cassie grunted and let go of his neck, slithered to the ground, and sat in a crumpled heap. He ran after his mates.

Men in red coats raced past and chased the attackers. Tristan stopped beside the coach, as did Lieutenant Paisley and Mr. Fielding. The lieutenant knelt beside Terrence.

"Woo!" Cassie sounded exhilarated. "That'll teach them!"

"Are you all right, Miss Leonard?" asked Mr. Fielding. He looked both horrified and concerned. Tristan grabbed his sister's chin and turned her head so he could see her cheek more clearly. In the dim light of the few remaining torches, Diana could see it was already swollen and beginning to bruise.

"I'll kill him," he growled.

"I think I beat you to it," Cassie said. Her voice was full of unnatural elation. "I've scarred him, at the very least." Then she seemed to remember herself, and the bright grin fell as she looked from Ella to Diana. "Are you two all right? They didn't hurt you?"

Ella and Diana reassured her they were unhurt. "But my footman…" Ella turned to where Paisley tended to

Terrence.

"He'll live," said Paisley. "Though he'll have a blinder of a headache, and he may not be fit for duty for a day or two."

"He will have the best of care," vowed Ella.

A soldier opened the coach door, and caught the driver as his limp form tumbled out. He, too, had a gash on his head, and a bloodied face. He was groggy, but coming round, groaning softly.

"Can someone send for the doctor? Both men should be seen to at once," said Ella. She was calm and controlled, whereas Diana was shaken, her insides fizzing and bubbling, hands trembling, breath short and shallow. She felt inadequate and helpless. Ella had threatened her man with a whip. Cassie had scarred hers. Diana had…swung her reticule.

"Tell the doctor to come to the vicarage," Tristan added to Ella's request. "Best not to move them too far until we know the damage they've sustained," he explained. Ella nodded and thanked him.

At last, Diana found wits enough to whisper, "I'm so sorry. This is my fault."

"Nonsense!" said Ella.

"This is the fault of those ruffians," agreed Cassie. "Who, hopefully, will think twice before attacking helpless females again." She grinned at her brother. "Did you see us, Tris? We routed 'em!"

Tristan closed his eyes and muttered something that sounded like, "God help me!"

As gently as they could, the soldiers loaded Tom and Terrence into the coach, then walked it to the vicarage, where they took both men in and made them comfortable in the parlor at the front of the house, watched over by

Lieutenant Paisley and two of his men, while the rest of them settled in Cassie's sitting room at the rear. Tristan's manservant made tea for the ladies, though the men helped themselves to brandy.

"Would somebody tell me what happened?" asked Tristan. Then he pointed at Cassie, and added, "Not you. You can give me your story when you've calmed down."

"I am calm," she argued.

He shot her a sidelong look, then turned to Ella and Diana. "Was it a robbery? Did they take anything?"

"It wasn't a robbery," said Ella.

"They were after Diana," added Cassie.

"They were after me," Diana confirmed.

****

Tristan felt sick. Those blackguards had attacked Diana and her friends outside a crowded building, on a fairly well-lit road. How brazen could they be?

He hadn't seen the long-haired man amongst them, but he had no doubt he was involved, because all three ladies said the attackers were clearly under orders. The men had spoken of a "he" who had told them to bring "the youngest blonde."

Was this an obsession with a woman who had caught his eye? If it was, the man must be powerful, to be able to direct three other men to try to abduct her. Kidnapping was a capital crime; very few men would be willing to hang solely for a friend's lust. Which meant there had to be more to it. He frowned and tried to fit the pieces into a sensible whole.

Firstly, the long-haired man had stared at Diana on the High Street for far longer than was warranted, even for a man captivated by her beauty. His friends had jeered and mocked others as they passed by that day, but their interest in their victims soon waned. Most of them had quickly lost interest in Ella and Diana too, but that man had continued to stare after her, frightening and unnerving the ladies enough that they'd grabbed makeshift weapons, prepared to fight him off.

Then there'd been the incident in the wood. The same man had chased Diana, and hurt Ned Fellowes. There'd been no question of simply staring at her then.

"They will be found," said Mr. Fielding, reassuring the ladies and bringing Tristan out of his musings. "Fear not, for as we learn in the Book of Job, 'there is no darkness, nor shadow of death, where the workers of iniquity may hide themselves.' "

"I certainly hope not," answered Ella, grimly.

****

Diana didn't want to answer any more questions. In truth, she didn't know how to answer them. She desperately wanted to be truthful with Tristan. He was trying to help her, to ensure the villains were brought to book. He needed the information. But confiding in him meant going against everything Fremont had insisted she do.

Fremont had said she must tell nobody. She'd promised him she wouldn't say a word. He was the person most responsible for keeping her safe, and she'd vowed to listen to him and do only what he said.

Besides, if she confided in Tristan now, in this room, she would also have to tell Mr. Fielding, widening still further the circle of people who knew. Mr. Fielding was a man of the cloth, of course, and should be trusted with secrets. Yet Fremont had chosen not to take him into his confidence. Fremont hadn't confided in Ella, either, although they'd seemed close friends. If he thought that even his close friends should not be told the truth…Diana was in no position to argue.

Fremont and Tristan were not friends. Diana knew that. When they arrived in Rotherton, Fremont had been decidedly cool toward Tristan. He didn't seem to like or trust him at all.

It was a conundrum. Ella was her friend, and Tristan the closest thing to a magistrate in Rotherton at the moment. But Diana had promised Fremont that she would follow his advice, to the letter. She'd agreed to obey his edicts. She had no other choice, not if she wanted to stay safe, out of the hands of her pursuers.

Obedience was a lesson she'd learned the hard way, and one she would not soon forget. If she'd obeyed Papa's edict when he told her to stay in Norfolk, perhaps Papa would still be alive.

She stared into the cold hearth of the fireplace and thought back to the fateful day when her disobedience had cost so much.

Chapter Twelve

Papa had been angry at her return to London. Rightly so, as she'd discovered when those dreadful men had kicked in the door to his study moments after she'd hidden, their grins cold and wicked, the glint of murder in their eyes.

"Where is she?" asked the smaller man, looking around the room. From her vantage point on top of the bookcase, Diana recognized him as the man she'd seen across the road. His accent was broad, with the rounded vowels of the stews. As well as a patched coat, he wore boots that were cracked, the heels worn unevenly. His hat was stuffed carelessly into his coat pocket, allowing her to see his unkempt hair, grimy skin, and the vicious ice in his eyes. The end of his nose was swollen, its strange puce color indicating a love of strong drink. In fact, the stench of alcohol was strong enough on his breath that she could smell it even from ten feet above him.

"Get out of my house!" blustered Papa, but Diana heard the tremble in his voice and knew he was scared. It shocked her to the core. She had always thought her father fearless. He'd faced recalcitrant seamen and arrogant rulers, storms at sea and robbers on the roads and never once shown that he was afraid. But these two men…

"I'm sorry, sir," said Addams, from behind the

intruders. The servant's nose was bent out of shape, and his eyes were starting to blacken.

Papa swallowed. "Not your fault, Addams. That will be all."

"Yes, sir," said Addams. He made to leave the room, but the second man barred his way.

"You stay here," he commanded. He dropped the aitch.

"Let him go!" demanded Papa. In response, the second man grabbed Addams, then shoved him, full force. Addams stumbled and Papa caught him, stopping his fall.

"That's better, innit?" The second man grinned. "Now we're all cozy-like. And we can be certain nobody's going to run to fetch help, can't we?"

This man was taller than his colleague by a good six inches, making him close to six feet in height. Whereas the first man was rotund and unkempt, the second was lean and trim. His clothes were not in the first stare of fashion, but they were cared for and respectable. At first glance, Diana thought, the pair might be mistaken for master and servant, but there was a similarity about the mouth and the shape of the nose that suggested they might be related.

"This is an outrage!" said Papa.

"I'm sure it is," agreed the taller man. "But where are your manners? My brother asked you a question, and you, Mr. Villiers, have not had the decency to answer him. So I will ask you again. Where's your daughter?" The "*t*" in the word "daughter" was replaced with a glottal stop.

Papa drew himself up to his fullest height and his chin lifted defiantly. Diana bit her bottom lip, trying to stop it trembling. Fear ratcheted her heartbeat and made her breath shallow, and she had to work to stop herself being heard.

These men wanted *her*. They'd been looking for *her*. Why, oh, why had she not done as she was told and stayed in Norfolk? Now she'd put Papa in danger of a beating. Addams, too, by the look of it.

She tensed to stop her trembling, and stayed as still and quiet as she could. Papa had commanded her to remain hidden. She may not have obeyed him before, but from now on, she vowed, she would.

"You stay there," he'd said, as he made her climb the bookcase ladder. *"Whatever you hear. Whatever happens. You do not show yourself. You do not make a sound. Promise me!"*

Diana had promised, and she would keep her word. There was no choice. These men were dangerous. They menaced Papa now, implying that he could avoid pain and injury by giving them what they wanted. If she'd thought that was true, she might be tempted to try and save him. But whatever they said, whatever they implied, Diana didn't think he'd be any safer if they found her. So she lay, absolutely still and silent.

The tall man sighed. "Mr. Villiers," he said, in the tone a weary tutor might use with an obtuse student, "I appreciate that, in your world, you're not used to doing another's bidding. You're an important man. I understand that. But what you've got to understand is, this is not your world now. For the duration of this conversation, this room—heck, your whole house, for that matter—is not part of the upper-crust world. This place is now in the domain of my boss. And, Mr. Villiers, you should be warned, my boss is not a man to be crossed. What he wants, he gets."

"He shall not have my daughter." Papa's words came out in a determined hiss. Nausea churned in Diana's stomach and tasted bitter in her throat.

"Mickey," said the tall man.

The shorter man grinned, viciously. His fist shot forward at lightning speed and connected with Papa's face. Papa staggered back. Diana bit her bottom lip so hard that she tasted blood.

"Where. Is. She?" insisted the tall man.

"She isn't here," said Papa.

The smaller man—Mickey—hit him again. Papa slammed into the bookcase next to the one Diana hid upon. The shelves rumbled and shook.

Addams moved to try to help Papa, but the tall man grabbed him, spun him round and threw him into the opposite corner, where Addams crumpled into a dazed heap.

"I saw her come in," said Mickey. "So where is she?"

"She's gone," said Papa. "You'll never find her."

Mickey hit Papa again. Diana flinched at the sound of his knuckles against Papa's face. The second man stood over Addams, silently warning him not to get up. Addams looked up at his tormentor and Diana saw the fear in his eyes. It was at odds with the sheer determination on his face. In that instant, she knew that neither he nor Papa would give an inch. They would keep her safe. No matter what the villains threw at them.

This was her fault. Her selfishness had brought this torment upon them. She'd thought only of the Season she was missing, believed herself hard done to because she wasn't part of it. She'd given no thought as to why that might be. If only she'd pondered the question a little more, she would have realized Papa wouldn't deny her for the sake of it. If he said no, he had a good reason.

And if she'd trusted him, obeyed him, stayed away, none of this would be happening.

I will do as I am bid in future, Papa. I promise. Which was neither help nor comfort now.

Mickey hit Papa several more times. Papa tried to defend himself, but stood no chance against the Rookery-hardened man. In the far corner, Addams began to rise, but stopped when the tall man pulled out a knife. He didn't brandish it, just seemed to examine it, feeling its sharp edge softly with the pad of his thumb. It was all he needed to do. Addams stayed where he was.

Papa said, over and over, that Diana was gone. She was not here. They would never find her. Each defiant utterance earned him another thump. His face was a bloody mess, his nose broken, eyes swelling shut, lips thick and bleeding. There was a cut on his cheek, and his cravat was stained with blood, and the gore from his nose. His breathing rasped, heavy and labored, and his voice grew more nasal with every hit.

Diana prayed it would stop. She prayed these men would leave, search for her elsewhere, so that she and Addams could tend Papa's injuries and work out what to do next.

But they didn't leave. They did not let up in their interrogation at all. Mickey continued, punch after punch, slap after slap, the question repeated incessantly, Papa refusing to answer.

Then Mickey hit out once more. Whether his frustration lent power to this last punch, or whether Papa was just too beaten to stand his ground any longer, Diana could not say. All she knew was, Mickey hit Papa, Papa lost his balance and fell, and there was a loud crack as his head hit the stone surround of the fireplace.

He groaned once. His eyes flickered. He seemed to look up at her, though he could not possibly see her.

"No!" cried Addams. He tried to move forward, but the tall man pushed him back.

"What the bleedin' 'ell have you done?" said the tall man, glaring at Mickey.

"I didn't mean…" Mickey knelt beside Papa, and looked him over, as if searching for a clue about what he should do next.

Diana saw the light dim in Papa's eyes. His jaw slackened, and his chest stilled. It took everything she had to keep the scream of agony silent within her.

"You bloody killed him," whispered the tall man.

"Mr. Villiers?" sobbed Addams. He pushed past the tall man and knelt at Papa's side, his hand shaking as he reached out to his master.

"You idiot!" the tall man shouted at Mickey. "How're we going to find her now?"

"Murderers!" said Addams. "You murdered him!"

"It was an accident," said Mickey.

But what he did next was no accident. He got to his feet, grabbed the knife from his accomplice, and plunged it into Addams' back. The servant fell, covering his master's body with his own.

"No witnesses," said Mickey.

"And no bleedin' heiress, neither." The tall man glared at Mickey. Diana wasn't sure which horrified her more: that Mickey had just killed two men, or that neither of them seemed fazed by that. Their only concern was the lack of information that could be gleaned from a dead man.

"Stop fussin', Simon," said Mickey, when the tall man called him an imbecile for the third time.

"You do know what the boss'll do to us for this?"

"Only if we don't find her." Mickey sounded petulant.

"And how will we find her? You've killed the only man who knew where she was!"

The numbness of shock began to wear off, leaving a yawning hole in Diana's heart. She felt it crack, the sharp pain fueling the hot tears chafing her cheeks and wetting the dusty wood shelf beneath her.

"There's got to be a clue round here somewhere." Mickey pulled out the drawers of Papa's desk and lifted out papers, rifling through them before throwing them to the ground.

Simon nodded. "I'll look round the rest of the house," he said, and he left the room.

Diana had no idea how much time passed. Mickey emptied the desk, and the cupboard where Papa kept his ledgers. He looked on the bookshelves, taking down the books he could reach, shaking them before throwing them into a heap on the floor. Diana cried silent tears until her eyes were hot and her nose too blocked to breathe through it. She committed every detail of this man to memory. If—when!—she got free of here, she would make sure every constable and watchman in London knew who had done this.

Finally, Simon returned. He held a letter in his hand. "I think I know where to look," he said. "This is a letter from some woman in..." he checked the paper, "Downham Market in Norfolk. She says Miss Villiers is with her, and is comfortable and happy."

Oh, Lord, no! They had Aunt Mathilda's address. Was Diana's aunt in danger now, too?

Thoughtful, Mickey scratched at his neck. "She's not there now, though, is she? Can't be. I saw her here. Today. That letter had to come before today."

Diana closed her eyes, relieved.

"What if she went back there?" argued Simon. "Foxes run for their holes when the hounds are about. And seein' as how she's not here…"

Oh, God! No!

"Besides, there wasn't nothin' else I could find," continued Simon. "It's as good a place to start as any. Maybe this woman'll know where else she may have gone."

Diana pressed her lips together as more tears fell. Any and all friends she had would now be in danger. Worse, none would know until it was too late. She had to get away, to warn them all. The thought renewed her determination not to be caught.

Below her, Mickey frowned at Simon, skeptical.

"It strikes me," said Simon, "we ain't got much choice. We either go to Downham Market and see what we can find there, or we tell the boss we lost his heiress and you killed the one person who could lead us to her. Do you fancy doing that? Because I certainly don't."

Mickey chewed his bottom lip, thinking. "He might not be too unhappy," he said. Simon's eyebrows raised in disbelief, and Mickey went on, quickly. "Look at it sideways, Si. Yes, it'll cause a delay. But with Villiers dead, it's better for him in the long run. I mean, everything's hers now, innit? If he marries her, he won't just get the dowry. He'll get the whole kit and caboodle."

Diana's eyes widened to the point of pain. She only

just stopped the horrified gasp before it gave her away. Their boss planned to marry her? That was why Papa had sent her away. He'd done all he could to protect her, and she…fresh tears pricked at her eyes.

"This address is better than nothing," said Simon. "We can leave now. Tonight. Best get out of London before he finds out about…" He gestured at the bodies.

Mickey scratched his stomach. "What if he didn't find out?"

Simon's eyebrows raised. "He was a wealthy merchant, Mick. I think his death will be remarked upon. And before you say it, his disappearance'd be noted, too. No. We've got to get out. Before we end up feeding the fish in the Thames."

"What if they died in a tragic accident? If they died in a…fire, say?"

They were going to burn Papa's body? Revulsion shivered through Diana. Somehow this—this desecration was as bad, if not worse, than the actual act of murdering him! They were going to set him on fire! Destroy everything that was left of him. And at the same time, they would destroy this house, her home. A new wave of terror rolled over her as she realized what that meant. They would set this house alight! With her inside it!

Had she survived the assault on her home and evaded capture by these men only to burn to death? Her heart beat so fast now it seemed to bounce off her ribs, painful and loud. She was shocked they could not hear it. Panic threatened to engulf her. She had to fight to even her breathing. Bile burned her throat.

"S'pose it might work," said Simon. "Though we can't start the fire in this room. They can tell these things, you know. They can tell where a fire started, and what-have-you."

Mickey gave him a look of disbelief. "How?"

"I don't know how, do I? But I heard they can. We'll start it in the kitchen. Then if we throw lamp oil, and perhaps some brandy, over them, they'll catch quick enough. The house being empty, by the time anybody notices the fire, it will have spread to here. With a little luck, when anyone gets in to put it out, these two'll be burned beyond recognition. Mr. Percival will think they had an unfortunate accident, and thee and me, we'll be far enough away that nobody will ever connect us to it. If he asks, we'll say we were following a tip. How were we supposed to know the cook'd start a fire while we weren't here?"

The two men argued back and forth a little more but, in the end, Simon got his way. They broke Papa's desk lamp and spilled the oil over the bodies, then added the contents of his decanter before they headed to the kitchen to set their fire.

Diana didn't immediately come out of hiding. She didn't dare until she was certain the murderous pair were gone. The last thing she needed was to be discovered by them just when escape was in sight. If she was caught, Papa and Addams would have died for nothing, and justice would never be done.

So it was only when thick, acrid smoke billowed into the room, stinging her eyes and stealing her breath, that she climbed down on shaky legs.

"Goodbye, Papa," she whispered. She coughed on the smoke, and brushed the tears from her sore cheeks. Then she climbed out of the study window and made her escape through the overgrown gardens before heading to the only place she could think of where she might now be safe.

The home of Papa's friend, Philip Unsworth, Lord Fremont.

****

In the sitting room of Rotherton's vicarage, Ella said something to Tristan. Diana didn't know what it was, but it brought her out of her memories and back to the here and now, where Tristan investigated the attack on them this evening.

As much as Diana wanted to help him get to the bottom of it, as much as she wanted those men arrested and the threat lifted, she could not tell him the truth. She'd promised Fremont she would tell nobody.

Although, what if the information she held back was exactly what Tristan needed to stop not only the attackers, but everything? What if he could flush out the Hicks brothers and their minions, and even Milton Percival, and bring this awful nightmare to an end?

Diana massaged her forehead with the fingers and thumb of one hand, trying to stop the headache that was building. She was torn and confused, uncertain which way to turn.

In the morning, she would write to Fremont. He'd know what to do, and who to trust. Until then, she would keep her own counsel and hope it didn't make matters worse.

Chapter Thirteen

The ladies knew more than they said. Tristan was convinced of that. It angered him that they would willfully withhold information, for how could he find the villains and keep them safe if he was missing vital evidence?

"You're absolutely certain," he asked for the fifth time, "you don't know who these men were?"

"Never saw them before in my life," said Ella. Her frustration was also showing. She was as sick of answering him as he was of asking. "They aren't Rotherton locals. I would have recognized them if they were."

"I don't know them, either," said Diana, softly. He eyed her, skeptically. She lowered her gaze, so he could not gauge her thoughts and emotions. Why wouldn't she help him?

"Who might have sent them, then?" he persisted. She glanced up. For the briefest of moments, he saw something in her expression, a fear behind her eyes, a slight paling of her skin. He wanted to reach out, take her in his arms, and promise he would find the blackguard that would send such men after her. Find him and pummel him to within an inch of his life, before dragging him to jail and throwing away the key.

The violence within him shocked him. He pressed his lips tightly together and tensed his jaw, willing himself to calm down. He was acting as magistrate, for God's sake. It was his job to see that justice was done, not act the vigilante and commit a crime himself.

But they attacked Diana! The thought raced through his brain, pushing aside all others, overcoming rationality, stripping him of civilized trappings.

They had attacked Diana! Tried to take her. Anger swelled within him again, painting the room a vivid red. It took several moments to push back the rage and maintain a veneer of cool respectability.

Diana took a deep breath in, blew it out, and shook her head, all traces of vulnerability once again hidden. "I cannot say," she answered his question.

Tristan frowned. *I cannot say?* That might mean she didn't know, but he wasn't convinced.

"I have no idea," said Ella. From the way she spoke and the look on her face, he believed she told the truth. If Diana was keeping secrets, she hadn't shared them with Ella. Which begged the question, what could be so secret she couldn't even tell her friend?

He wanted to shake her. To remind her that he was trying to make her safe. He needed her to trust him. That she did not, rankled. More than rankled. It actually hurt, a physical pain, somewhere between an ache and a sharp stab behind his breastbone.

"I can't think of anyone," said Cassie. He glanced at his sister. She was still bright-eyed and tense, her knee bouncing up and down as if she needed to run, or dance around the room.

At least her speech was calm now, and her color had faded, so perhaps the worst was over. Tristan had seen behavior like hers before, in men after a battle. Their blood was up, nerves tuned to the fight, and it took time for them to relax again. That was, he knew, when they were at their most dangerous. Volatile and uncontrolled, spoiling for action, they would pick fights, defy officers, attack civilians.

Not that he thought Cassie would attack anyone. Although, considering the exasperated way she looked at the curate every time he fussed over her, Tristan wouldn't wager on that.

"Of course you cannot think of anyone," Mr. Fielding answered Cassie. "None of you would know anybody like that. I am sure ladies such as yourselves would never know people with evil on their minds, and in their hearts."

If he quotes the Bible at her now, I will not be held responsible for my sister's actions.

"I'm sorry we're of no help to you," said Ella. She glanced at Diana before she added, "I wish we could be. The sooner those men are caught, the better for everybody."

"Hear, hear," agreed Cassie. Mr. Fielding nodded sagely. Diana chewed her lip, nervously.

You are the key, Diana. He knew it. So must she. It was, after all, Diana that the long-haired man had watched in the High Street. It was she he'd chased in the wood. And it was she the three men had tried to take tonight. Clearly, she was the one in most danger. But until she confided in him, there was little he could do to help her.

Well, no. That was not quite true. He couldn't fully investigate, and he couldn't pinpoint his search for the men. But he could do something. He could make sure she was protected, so that another attack was unlikely to succeed.

153

Almost as if she read his thoughts, Ella spoke again. "I'll have my gardeners, and most of my footmen, stand guard," she said. "There are enough of them to deter quite a force."

Which was good, as far as it went. "That gives you protection in the short term, but it doesn't solve the problem." Tristan batted away the feeling that gardeners and footmen could never protect Diana as he would. It was absurd, to say the least, but even so, it forced its way into his consciousness, insistent and forthright. The men might be big and burly, and there would be several of them, but they didn't care for her as he did, weren't as…

Weren't as what? What did he think? That because he'd kissed her, he somehow had the power to fight off all comers, protect her from all life's woes and hold her, steady and safe, in his arms? He was a fool!

"The real trouble is," Mr. Fielding said, "there aren't enough soldiers in the area." He shook his head, sadly. "How many officers and men languish on half pay, when they could be employed to make the fight against evil so much more effective?" He sighed. "As we learned tonight, the militia barely have enough men to take on the landing of run goods on one small beach. They cannot be everywhere, and we cannot call upon them, thereby reducing the numbers at the ready even further."

"I heard there was a raid on the Golden Goose tonight, as well," added Cassie.

"By the militia?" Ella was incredulous. "That's a waste of time. Seth Fayers isn't daft enough to store illicit brandy on his premises."

"Not by the militia. By the smugglers." Cassie's eyes were round. She clearly enjoyed telling her tale.

Tristan stopped listening. Instead, he watched

Diana. She sat on her chair, perched on the edge of its seat as if ready to spring to her feet at a moment's notice. Her hands were clutched together in her lap, the fingers entwined so tightly her knuckles shone white. Her head was bowed, eyes cast down.

What are you hiding? Tristan couldn't think it was anything too bad. She didn't strike him as the sort of person who would be in league with smugglers, especially not with the caliber of men who were engaged in smuggling in this area of late. Whether Milton Percival was involved or not was still open to debate, but the Hicks brothers had definitely been sighted. No lady of breeding would associate with those two. After Tristan had heard them discussed by Fremont and Rotherton, he'd made a point of learning more about them. Percival's reputation was already known to him, but the Hicks brothers had been an unknown quantity. What he'd learned about them appalled him.

The brothers worked as a team, so his informant had said. Both committed violence without mercy, and showed no remorse afterward, although Simon, the elder brother, apparently used that violence more as a means to an end, unleashing it only when he had to, only as far as he must. The mere threat of it kept his victims subdued.

Mickey, on the other hand, relished it, and actively sought it. There were tales of beatings and maimings, of broken bones and disfiguring scars. There were also rumors of murders, although those were, so far, uncorroborated.

For all that was said about them, neither had spent so much as one day in prison in their adult lives. Which didn't surprise Tristan. Witnesses were reluctant to come forward if doing so put them in danger.

Was that Diana's fear? That they would come after her if she spoke of what was happening?

Tristan couldn't think so. Not unless she'd seen or heard something truly awful. But certainly, there must be some compelling reason for her fear, because those men had not simply seen her and chased her, out of the blue. They had actively sought her, deliberately targeted her. And, unless he missed his guess, she had known—or at least suspected—that they would do so.

She had arrived in Rotherton with Fremont. That might or might not be significant, since the viscount had also taken up the curate and brought him here, and Tristan did not see anything about Fielding that hinted at subterfuge, secrets, and lies.

Whereas Diana...Fremont could have brought her here to protect her from the retribution of the violent and malicious men.

That would explain the secrecy. Although when, where, and how a gently bred lady like Diana Wilde might have witnessed the Hicks brothers committing a crime, Tristan couldn't begin to fathom. Their stomping ground was the Rookery of St. Giles, and the filth of Devil's Acre. Someone like Diana should never have been anywhere near either place. Even though she was clearly not out of the top drawer, she was obviously well above the touch of the Hicks brothers. Poor she might be, but not as poor as some. She was certainly not poor enough to have lived in the slum tenements of London. She would have stood out there like the proverbial sore thumb, no matter how empty she thought her purse was.

Could she have seen the brothers commit a crime in the more upmarket areas of the city? That didn't ring true either, for if they'd attacked someone in a respectable place, the crime would have been taken seriously, arrests made, and she would be safe.

Unless, of course, Diana was the only witness. Not all judges accepted the uncorroborated testimony of a woman, even today. She might need to hide until a judge was found who would hear her. Which would explain why Fremont had brought her here, where she could be safe.

Except she wasn't safe. Those men had made a concerted effort to take her tonight, on top of the attempts of the last week or so. Nor did it seem the problem might go away, for the villains had proved persistent.

All Tristan could do was watch and hope he wasn't too late when she needed him.

She wasn't the only person in Rotherton who wasn't safe, though. All the people here were threatened now, because of the smuggling gang. Especially if it was true the gang was run by London thugs.

Earlier, Tristan had ridden to Haywards Heath, taking Ella's suggestion that he talk to John Carter. It had been a waste of time. That Carter was an unwilling accomplice to the smugglers, Tristan didn't doubt. The man struck him as decent and hardworking, the sort of man who would abide by the law if he could. But he'd also made it clear he had no intention of testifying for the prosecution, no matter what he was offered to do so.

"I can swing as a smuggler," he'd said. "Or I can avoid that fate by testifying, and then end up lying in an alley with a knife between my ribs. Either way, I'm dead. Difference is, if I testify, my mum and my sweetheart will be in that alley with me. Unless you can guarantee their safety, I'm not your man."

Every other man in the cell had said something similar.

Tonight's raid on the Golden Goose had brought the truth home, too. The smugglers were growing bolder, their actions more brazen. In the past they'd "recruited" people in ones and twos. Tonight, they'd attacked an entire taproom full of men. Their overconfidence had been punished; there'd been enough people to fight back and see them off. But that wouldn't be the end of it. The men who'd successfully defended themselves in a crowd would now be picked off in smaller numbers, and the smugglers would win in the end. The only thing that would stop them would be protection from the militia. But the militia had neither the manpower nor the will to defend Rotherton when there were so many other demands on their resources.

And Tristan's thoughts had come full circle.

Except…he now had an idea.

The militia based in Winchelsea did *not* have the wherewithal to protect the inhabitants of Rotherton. They were, as Fielding said, stretched to capacity. Even if they could spare a few men, they couldn't be everywhere. And they couldn't be here forever. All the smugglers needed to do was wait them out, then act.

For the level of protection necessary to end the threat altogether, Rotherton would need a militia of its own, dedicated to protecting this place and its people, permanently.

Lord, but he was a slow-top! The solution was staring him in the face. Rotherton could form its own militia.

There were enough able-bodied men in the area to

make up a decent force, and tonight had shown him, and more importantly, the smugglers, that those men were willing to fight. It was a given that some of them would have military experience, although even those that hadn't been in the army or navy would soon learn the rudiments, if they put their minds to it.

As for training them... Tristan had been an officer. He was capable of forming volunteers into a force to be reckoned with. Volunteers who would see off the threat and make themselves and their loved ones safe.

He wasn't naive enough to believe it would be that simple, of course. The gang would not give up without a fight. But, if the men Tristan recruited showed willing, he made no doubt that, sooner or later, they could make the gang cut its losses and move on.

In the morning, he would talk to Lieutenant Paisley and to Seth Fayers. The landlord would likely be key in persuading the men of Rotherton to rally together. Tristan would also need to write to David and tell him what he planned. He didn't think David would object, but this was his village and these were his people, so he had a right to know.

As he pondered the logistics of his idea, and tried to work out how quickly he could have an effective fighting force in place, there was a knock on the door and Paisley came in.

"Beg pardon, my lord, ladies," he said with a curt bow. "The doctor has gone, and I thought you would appreciate knowing what he said."

Briefly, he said that both the injured men had been treated, and pain-relieving medication administered. Tristan's manservant had readied beds for them behind the kitchen in what would have been the housekeeper's room, had Tristan employed a housekeeper. The doctor advised that the men should stay there for at least two days, resting and recovering, before they attempted the journey home. If they were attended properly, they should both make full recoveries.

"Thank goodness," said Diana. Her words were heartfelt, her sincerity reinforced by relieved tears. Tristan watched her. Briefly, she met his gaze, then looked away, flustered.

"Amen," agreed Mr. Fielding. "A prayer answered."

Ella sighed with relief. "In which case, there's no reason for us to be here. Diana and I can go home to Amberley and leave you good people to your own peaceful beds…"

"Not without an escort, you can't," interrupted Tristan.

Ella stared at him for a moment before she answered, "you're right, my lord. We have had more than enough excitement for one evening. Best not to tempt fate into bringing us more."

"I will escort you," Tristan said.

"As will I," said both Paisley and Fielding together.

"Do you ride, sir?" Paisley asked Fielding.

Fielding grimaced. "Never had occasion to. As the second son of a clergyman, who entered the church myself straight after my education, I've never had the luxury of owning or riding a horse." He winced. "It would be difficult to be in the escort party if I cannot ride, would it not?"

"Should I not be protected, too?" asked Cassie. "I will be quite alone here, until my brother returns." Her smile was wide-eyed and disingenuous as she saved the cleric's pride. Tristan smiled at her, and put his hand to his chest in a silent thank you.

Half an hour later, with the servants settled in their makeshift hospital and Cassie sipping tea and showing Fielding just how charming she could be, Tristan, Paisley, and the two soldiers took Ella and Diana home to Amberley.

It may have been their escort, or it may have been the hour, for the dawn was beginning to smudge the inky blackness of the night, bringing in shades of grey, indigo and violet. Perhaps it was simply that the failures they'd accrued tonight had sent the smugglers home to lick their wounds. For whatever reason, the ride to Amberley was without incident, and they were able to see the ladies safely inside the house. Once they knew the doors were locked and the windows secured, they rode back toward Rotherton.

"I'll be glad when this night is done with," said Paisley, wearily.

"Agreed." Tristan grinned. "So much for the sleepy idyll of the countryside, where nothing much happens, eh?"

Paisley chuckled, and they rode on.

Chapter Fourteen

A week after the ball, Cassie came to visit Ella and Diana at Amberley. She brought with her Mrs. Bell and her daughter, Julia. Mrs. Bell was unnerved, to say the least, to find the house so well guarded, a fact which disgusted Ella.

"Fiddlesticks!" she muttered. "Are the guards that obvious to you?"

"As obvious as the tower on St. Bartholomew's Church," confirmed Mrs. Bell.

"I wanted them to look as if they were going about their business, but close to the house," said Ella. "They're supposed to guard *discreetly*."

She had told Diana the same thing when she'd set the men to guard duty. "The gardeners will work on the land closest to the house," she'd said. "They will look as if they are renovating the area. That way, nobody will realize they are armed and ready for action. And, on the bright side…" She'd grinned and added, "By the time the villains are rounded up, I will have the best formal, kitchen, and herb gardens in all of Sussex."

Diana hadn't been convinced, but she'd said nothing. She was still smarting from the confirmation that the men who had attacked the coach, and who were now a possible threat to Ella's home, had come for her. If she wasn't here, there'd be no danger to Amberley. The morning after the attack, she'd written to Fremont, explaining what had happened and asking him to remove her for the safety of everybody else.

The letter was never posted. Ella had realized what Diana had done and had forbidden it.

"I can keep you safe here," she insisted.

"But the men who attacked you…"

"Pish!" Ella straightened, bringing herself up to her full height, which was still several inches shorter than Diana. Her eyes glowed with annoyed determination. "If you think this is entirely about you, you are mistaken. Do you think you're the only person in this area to fall foul of those fiends? That they only arrived to cause trouble after you came? I do grant you, on this occasion, they were looking for you. But they've been attacking people here for months. They started long before you came. And their attacks upon us won't stop just because you've taken yourself to…wherever you think you're going to go. The wilds of Yorkshire, perhaps? Wales? It doesn't matter what destination you have in mind, because I'm telling you, Diana, there is nowhere for you to go. You are as safe here as you are anywhere." She patted Diana's arm, reassuring her. "Besides," she continued, "I would miss you if you went now." She gave Diana her attempt at a winsome smile. Winsome, it wasn't, not really. But it did make Diana laugh, and before much longer she'd agreed to stay—and had burned the letter to Fremont.

Now, here she was, a week later, drinking tea and entertaining Mrs. Bell.

"Then again," said that lady, "it isn't just your home that is surrounded by would-be protectors. Lord Leonard has turned the whole of Rotherton into a parade ground for men playing at being soldiers." She shook her head. "They spend their time marching to and fro, and learning to keep formation. And goodness knows what else he's teaching them. Mr. Bell said they were wrestling in the vicarage gardens the other day. Can you imagine?"

"He's teaching them to defend themselves in hand-to-hand combat," explained Cassie. She reached for one of the shortbread biscuits Ella's cook had made, then nibbled on it, ignoring the look of disdain Mrs. Bell threw at her.

"Your brother is a military man," the woman said with a sniff. "I understand he feels the need for action. It's what he's used to. And, I think we can all agree, most men are little boys at heart, so joining a militia or wrestling in the mud are things they want to do. But they should not be doing that in full view of an innocent maiden such as yourself, Miss Leonard. Your brother is very much at fault for permitting that to happen. Somebody should tell him that his actions are inappropriate. Before you are ruined by them."

Whether it was the woman's narrow-minded focus on the propriety of the situation, or whether it was a need to defend Tristan from her disapprobation, Diana wasn't certain. Before she had time to second-guess her decision, though, she had leapt to his defense.

"Lord Leonard is trying to ensure the safety of everybody in Rotherton. We should support him in that ambition."

"Pah!" said Mrs. Bell. "What's the army for? It is not in the remit of Lord Leonard and his band of eager followers to do the soldiers' job for them. He isn't even a magistrate. Not in this area, anyway. He is simply a guest of Lord Rotherton, and he overreaches his authority."

"He is Rotherton's proxy while the earl's away,"

Ella reminded her. "He has Rotherton's blessing to do whatever he deems necessary." She took a bite of biscuit.

"Therein lies the problem. Authority was given to a man who ought never to have had it."

Cassie rolled her eyes. She had clearly heard this before and didn't deem it worth the answer. Julia looked away, her cheeks flushed, betraying her embarrassment at her mother's forthrightness. Ella chewed on her shortbread.

Diana lifted her chin and fixed Mrs. Bell with a steely stare, the one she'd learned from Papa. Growing up, she'd seen him employ it in many a terse situation. It had always worked for him. She prayed it would work now.

"Lord Leonard is a baron," she said. "A peer of the realm." Her voice was cold and brooked no opposition, another thing she had learned from Papa. "Before he was a baron, he was a major in His Majesty's army. He is well used to wielding authority and, I suspect, is capable of assessing a threat and the best way of dealing with it. I, for one, am grateful for his willingness to use his experience to protect us all."

The moment she'd spoken, she wondered if she'd gone too far. She'd spent the last month in Rotherton hardly saying a word, avoiding confrontation and any situation that might make her noticeable. All in an effort to keep herself safe. It was what Fremont wanted her to do, and she'd done it, although it ran contrary to her character. Before Papa's death, she'd been much more confident, more willing to speak out when she knew something was wrong. She'd hidden that aspect of herself here.

For what? The Hicks brothers had found her

165

anyway. Hiding had not worked. All it had done was put other people in danger. And now, Mrs. Bell denigrated the efforts of a man who had done what he could to make sure she—and everyone else—was as safe as they could be?

Diana would not allow that.

Tristan Leonard worked tirelessly for the good of this community. He'd formed the Rotherton militia and begun training them. From what Diana had heard, most men in the area had been enthusiastic to join, though they'd had little in the way of equipment or weapons to use in their fight. Some had pistols of their own, of course. Many had knives. One man had an ancient musket. But regardless, each man was prepared to stand with what he had, and take on a formidable, battle-hardened enemy. As far as she was concerned, the men of Rotherton had hearts as sturdy as English oak, and Mrs. Bell had no business criticizing them.

Not only had Tristan worked to secure the safety of the village, he'd made time each day to come to Amberley and check that Diana and Ella were safe, and that their perimeter remained secure. He hadn't trained Ella's men as such, though he had advised them and helped them improve their vigil, increasing their chances of success, should an attack come.

Both she and Ella had greeted him warmly for the first four days, inviting him in, drinking tea and indulging in polite conversation. They'd answered his questions, and taken his advice. Diana had assumed that would continue for as long as the threat remained. She was, therefore, shocked, two days ago, when Ella announced she would be visiting her tenants and would be gone for most of the day.

"I don't think you should come with me this time," she'd said, pulling on her gloves. "It doesn't do to take you into the open. You must stay in the house, although I daresay you may walk on the terrace, or perhaps in the gardens near to the building. Areas from which you can quickly run to safety, should you need to."

"What about you?" Diana asked, eyebrows raised. "You won't be safe, either."

"I believe I shall be," said Ella, with a dismissive wave of her hand. "I'm not the one they want. Plus, I'm taking two footmen with me, as well as a driver who spent a dozen years fighting the French on the peninsula. To quote him," Here she adopted a deep voice and a Sussex burr to continue, "What I picked up about fighting dirty from those Frenchies, the villains here in Rotherton haven't had time to learn." She smiled, slyly. "You may tell Lord Leonard that, when he comes to call."

Diana pointed out that Tristan would likely be upset to discover Ella gone.

"Nonsense!" Ella pulled the veil attached to her hat down so it shielded her eyes. "It's not me he's coming to see, is it?"

Diana wasn't having that. "He comes to see us both, to check on our safety."

Ella rested her gloved hand gently on Diana's cheek. "So naive."

Then she'd left and hadn't returned for hours.

In one respect, she'd been right. Although Tristan expressed concern for Ella's welfare, he hadn't seemed too put out by her absence. "I'm sure she'll be all right," he said. "She isn't silly enough to travel without adequate protection. But tell me, how have you been today?"

They had shared tea and polite conversation before he asked if she would like to walk in the garden. He opened the French door for her, and they stepped out onto the terrace.

It was a pretty day, the sort of day one remembers when one thinks of Julys gone by. The sky was a vivid blue, with just the occasional fluff of white cloud. The sun warmed the day comfortably, and bees droned in the flowers, giving the air a lazy timbre. Gardeners worked on the already perfect borders and tidied the sharp edges of the shorn lawns, wheelbarrows beside them half filled with leaves, twigs, and small branches.

The terrace stretched past three of the ground floor rooms, each with French doors that led out onto the flagstone area. At either end, the terrace was bordered by fatsia japonica, the height of the bushes and the lushness of their waxy green leaves proving they'd been given exactly the right spot to grow. They created an aura of privacy the terrace would otherwise have lacked. The front of the terrace was bordered by a stone balustrade, with a break in its line where steps led to the gardens below. A fountain took up the middle of one lawn, the gravel around it soaking up stray spray from its joyful flow.

On the other side of the lawns was a blood-beech hedge, its leaves now the dark red the plant adopted in high summer. Behind the hedge were woods. From here she could see a mixture of white-barked silver birch trees and tall, green Scots pine. Birds chirped incessantly, some of their songs melodic, others tuneless and harsh. A faint trace of roses mixed with scented stocks to sweeten the air.

They strolled along the terrace. Tristan clasped his hands behind his back. His coat was open, displaying a light blue waistcoat and a white cravat, held in place with a plain silver pin. He carried the scent Diana had come to associate with him: sharp bergamot tempered by softer sandalwood. Streaks of sun-kissed blond were woven into his nut-brown hair, and the skin on his jaw was slightly darkened by an undergrowth of new beard. There was a slight bulge under his coat, an interruption in the otherwise perfect line of the garment, which told her he was armed.

The thought unsettled her. Not for herself, so much—she had spent years walking beside Papa and his men through less than safe places, and oftentimes, they'd been armed, ready for any threat. She had trusted them to keep her safe then, and she trusted Tristan to keep her safe now.

No. What unsettled her now was *his* safety. She knew, without a doubt, should it come to it, this man would put himself into danger to save her, and the gun behind his coat was a reminder that such a scenario was possible. Diana hated that.

They made their way around the perimeter of the formal garden, slowing here and there to admire plants and to breathe in the delicate perfumes of the flowers. Their talk was light and inconsequential, until they came back to the steps that led to the terrace.

"I still have men on the lookout for the blackguards who accosted you," he said as they climbed.

Diana nodded. "Thank you."

He cleared his throat. "It would help if we had any idea who they were."

"I can see that."

Tristan studied her for a second before he asked, "You don't have any suspicion?"

She shook her head and hoped she looked truthful and innocent. "I had never seen any of those men before in my life."

It was the truth. Although it had been late at night and the area around the carriage had been dimly lit, she'd seen enough to be certain of that. In the days since, she had pictured them in her mind's eye, examining every detail she remembered, hoping for a spark of recognition. There was nothing. The three were complete strangers to her.

"What about the man who chased you in the wood?"

Diana shuddered. That man had frightened her, perhaps more than the other three combined. She'd recognized the three for what they were: ruffians out to make what they thought was an easy profit. The long-haired man…there'd been something about him. More menace.

Even so, "He was a stranger, too," she answered Tristan's question. Again, it was the truth. Although she suspected she'd learn he was closer than the others to the Hicks brothers, she had honestly never seen him until she came to Rotherton.

"Yet you recognized him as a threat."

She shook her head. "His actions alerted me to the threat he posed. He stared at me so intently, both on the day you saw him, and on the day I arrived, and I suppose it was that, the fact that it happened twice, which made me uneasy."

Now at the top of the steps, Tristan fixed her with a horrified stare. "You saw him the day you arrived?" He clenched his jaw, exasperated. "Why am I only hearing of this now?"

Diana opened her mouth to answer, then shut it again. She could think of nothing to say.

"Damn it, Diana!" He sighed and closed his eyes. "I apologize for my language. But I needed to know this. How can I keep you safe when I have only half the facts?"

"I'm sorry. It—it slipped my mind."

They stepped through the French doors, into the sitting room. After the bright heat of the garden, the room was dark, with the green tinge of unadjusted eyes. It was also blessedly cool.

Tristan turned to face her, his hand on her arm, preventing her from moving away from him. Not that she wished to move away from him, she realized. His eyes held hers, his gaze compelling, mesmerizing.

"Diana." He cleared his throat. "Miss Wilde. Nothing is more important than your wellbeing. You should know you…you are…you have become dear to me. If anything were to happen to you, I…please, Diana. Please, you must tell me these things. You must allow me to protect you to my utmost best."

She swallowed, hard. He was right. She should tell him. She would tell him. She would say…she didn't know what she would say. The words disappeared from her head. Within her there was suddenly no thought. No reason. Nothing but him.

His hair flopped over his forehead, softening the shape of his face. His eyes, almost black in the half light of the room, roved over her face, as if he wished to commit every inch of her to memory. He licked his lips with the tip of his tongue.

Of its own volition, her hand moved up and caressed

his cheek. His skin was raspy, the new beard pushing through. He took her hand in his own, guided it gently to his lips, and kissed her fingers. Her heart missed a beat. A soft moan escaped her. His eyes held hers, and she saw the triumph in his gaze at the sound. This close, she could smell the wind on his coat, the sunshine in his hair, the musk of him underlying the citrus and sandalwood of his cologne.

His lips touched hers. He tasted of tea and shortbread, and outdoors. He deepened the kiss, his tongue pressing against the seam of her lips. She opened and he slipped inside, his tongue moving with hers in that delicious dance he'd shown her before. It was as wonderful as she remembered. Better, for this time there was no hesitation, no shock. This time, she expected it, welcomed it.

He growled into the kiss as she wrapped her arms around his neck. Her fingers played with the ends of his hair, as soft and cool as silk. Her own hair loosened as the pins holding it in place fell to the carpet. Her curls came down, over her back and shoulders, scandalously heavy, and free. He pushed his hands into them and smiled against her lips.

"So beautiful," he whispered. He pulled her closer. She could feel his heart, beating a rapid tattoo in his chest. The soft whisper of her hair tumbled between his fingers. Then he cradled her head, holding her to him.

Without once breaking the kiss, his hand moved from her back to her shoulder, to her neck, his fingers warm on the bare skin of her throat. His fingertips wore mild callouses; their roughness sent a frisson of desire through her, making her heart stutter and her breasts grow heavy. Her nipples ached. They seemed to grow, as if they stretched toward...she knew not what. They pressed against the cotton of her shift, which suddenly felt tight, restrictive. She wanted to rip it from her body, to leave herself open, accessible to him.

A strange, almost overwhelming ache filled her belly and spread down to the core of her. She wanted—needed—to press herself into him, to feel him against her, alleviating the urging within her.

Something pushed against her stomach, hard and insistent. It took Diana a moment to realize what it was, what it signified. When she did, triumph surged through her. This, this was the evidence she craved, the proof that he wanted her every bit as much as she did him.

His hand moved from her throat to her shoulder. He pushed against the edge of her gown, slipping it down, revealing more of her to his touch. His lips left hers, and he feathered kisses, soft as a butterfly's wing, along her jawline, her neck, her shoulder. Each touch of his lips left a flame in its wake, searing her. She gave a tiny mewl of pleasure. In her head, she begged, "Don't stop!"

The bodice of her dress slipped to her waist, taking with it her shift, freeing her breasts. She felt the cool air on her skin as he gazed at her, his eyes unfocused, adoring. His lips curved in a half smile, he pressed his palm over one breast, and gently began to knead it.

Then, somehow, Diana would never know how, she was lying on the chaise longue in the corner of the room, her head against the armrest at one end, her legs splayed over the seat, skirts lifted, exposing her thighs to him.

Tristan kissed her again. His lips on hers brought her to heights of delicious dizziness. Then he let his wicked mouth trail down, down, across her skin, until he took one aching, erect nipple into his mouth, and nipped at it.

173

Diana cried out, more in surprise than pain, and held his head against her breast, trying to keep him there.

He took her other nipple between the finger and thumb of one hand, and tweaked it. It was painful, yet not. She arched her back, inviting him to do more. The ache between her legs built, hot and wet and wanting. It seemed to Diana as if every moment of her life so far had been leading to this. This was all that mattered. All that had ever mattered.

She felt his other hand on her thigh, just above her knee. A nerve jumped and her leg jerked. She could not have said whether it was a good feeling, or a bad one. It just *was*.

Her skirts rustled as they slid slowly up, tickling against her stockings, pushing higher and higher, teasing her, tormenting her. She wished she could do the same things to him, wished she could make him feel what she felt, but she didn't know how. All she knew was the feel of him against her, his weight on her, the heat within him building, touching her, bringing her to…she didn't know what. She just knew it had to happen, or she would go mad.

He touched the bare skin at the top of her stocking. She moaned again, thrusting her hips toward him, urging him on. His hand moved, devastatingly slowly, making her cry for more. At last, at long last, his fingers skimmed the springy curls at her center, and found the nub where everything gathered.

Higher, higher, she soared. She smelled the musk of him, and the strange salty sweetness that she somehow knew was her. Stars swirled behind her closed eyelids, and her ears filled with the rushing river of her pulse, too fast for individual beats. Tristan murmured. She could not tell what he said. She didn't care.

He stroked one finger up and down, over the lips of her most private place. A hesitation, then he slid it into her. She sobbed and moved her hips, wanting him to go deeper, further. He withdrew. In her mind, she cursed him, begged him for more.

Once again, he pushed his finger into her. No. Not one finger. Two. She felt the stretch as they entered, the slide of them as they moved within her, faster, further.

Her hips bucked. The stars behind her eyelids turned to fireworks, bursting into color and flame. She couldn't catch her breath. Couldn't think. Couldn't speak.

All at once, a dam broke and she cried out as feelings flooded her. His mouth came over hers, swallowing her sobs.

It was seconds. It was an eternity. Her body pulsed, hot and fast. She didn't know where she was. She didn't know *who* she was. There was no her. No anything. All that existed was this.

Gradually, Diana floated back to earth. Her senses returned. Once more, she was lying on the chaise longue, dress disheveled, hair in disarray. Tristan sat, gazing down at her, his eyes crinkling with his smile.

"Diana," he whispered. Then he shook his head. "I'm doing this all wrong. I was going to tell you I—" He looked up sharply and swore, a moment before she heard what he'd heard.

"Diana?" called Ella from the hallway.

****

"Diana? Are you all right?"

The shadowed sitting room of that time with Tristan disappeared and, once more, Diana was in Amberley's brighter, more public morning room, its cream, blue and

175

gold decor bringing the sunshine into the house. Her dress was exactly where it should be, covering her demurely, and her hair was held in a tidy, somewhat austere, bun. Ella sat across from her, her head cocked to one side like an inquisitive bird, a knowing smile twitching at her lips. From an adjacent sofa, Cassie and Julia studied her. They seemed puzzled.

Mrs. Bell placed her empty cup onto the table beside her. "Woolgathering, Miss Wilde, is all well and good when you're on your own, and performing necessary but mindless tasks. It's not quite the done thing when one has company."

Heat infused Diana's cheeks. She was grateful to Mrs. Bell for scolding her. It gave Diana the perfect excuse for her deep blush. Which meant she did not have to fabricate some pathetic reason for it that would likely fool nobody. Because, of course, never in a thousand years could she ever tell these ladies the real reason for her embarrassment: the highly inappropriate memories that had been playing in her mind, almost nonstop, over the last few days. Memories that surfaced whatever else she was doing, no matter where she was, and who she was with.

Memories that would have to cease. Now.

"Forgive me, madam," she said to Mrs. Bell. "I had—er—remembered a letter I must write later. And—you know how it is with these things." She smiled, glanced up at Mrs. Bell, and looked away again. "Once you think on them, you begin to put together the details. What you will write, how you will say things…"

She shut up. Papa always said the way to tell a liar was that they protested too much. *"The truth is encapsulated in a sentence,"* he told her. *"A word or two. A lie needs embellishment."* Diana stared down at her hands in her lap, hoping the conversation would move on.

Mrs. Bell sniffed. "Not that it matters much. My question to you was not one to change lives. I merely wondered if you'd ever been near Brighton?"

Brighton? How on earth had the conversation moved to Brighton? The seaside town, less than thirty miles from here, was fashionable, partly because the Regent favored it. He'd bought and refurbished a residence there—if residence was what one could call the Pavilion with its grandiose buildings topped with domes and peaks to rival the palace of any Indian moghul. Papa had gazed at it, shaken his head, and murmured, "Good Lord, what next?" as he walked away.

Which didn't explain why they were talking of the town now.

"We're going there for the summer," said Cassie, clapping her hands together and grinning with glee. "I am invited as Julia's particular friend."

Diana's eyes widened in surprise. Ella busied herself with moving the empty teapot on the tray, making room for the other crockery. A subtle if sure sign the visit should end soon.

"Julia will make her come-out in the new year," explained Mrs. Bell. "And with her older sister marrying the heir to a viscountcy…"

Ella rolled her eyes at the familiar boast. Diana bit the inside of her bottom lip and schooled her expression to one of polite interest.

"…We didn't think it fitting for Julia to turn up in Town a complete ingenue. What better way to ease her into Society than with a visit to the most fashionable resort on the south coast? There should be enough people there to make it worthwhile, and she will have friends when we arrive in London." She smiled, once more. "But, la! You must forgive the young ladies their boasting. They are young, and they forget that not everyone is to the manner born."

Diana stiffened at the implication in the woman's words, but she said nothing. After all, she and Fremont had fostered an impression of her humble circumstances in her new neighbors. She should be glad they'd been successful.

But, oh! how she longed to put this woman in her place with the truth. To say, *"Actually, I've stayed there several times. My father owns a townhouse in Brunswick Square…"*

The thought brought the threat of fresh tears, because it wasn't Papa's townhouse anymore. It was hers. She wished it was not.

Ella put the biscuit plate onto the tray with more force than was needed. The sharp snap made Diana jump, and brought her back from her maudlin thoughts.

"It is indeed a fashionable place," said Ella, a quiet fury in her voice. "I do hope Miss Bell and Miss Leonard enjoy their summer there. We did, didn't we, Diana?"

Diana looked up, met the challenge in Ella's eyes, and nodded.

Ella then made a show of looking at the clock on her mantelshelf. "Goodness!" she said. "Is that the time? You will excuse me, I'm sure, Mrs. Bell, but I have things to attend, which must be done today. You must come and tell us about your visit to Brighton when you return. I, for one, will be agog."

She managed to usher the ladies from the room

without causing them offense, leaving Diana to breathe a huge sigh of relief.

Chapter Fifteen

Tristan sat in the study at the vicarage, David's books spread open on his desk. From outside, he heard shouts and responses as the volunteer militia trained on the lawn. He'd been lucky to find three former soldiers among those who'd volunteered, one of them a sergeant with parade ground experience. He was currently putting the men through their paces, teaching them skills they would need if—or, more likely, when—the smugglers took them on.

It was heartening to see their enthusiasm. Heartening, but not surprising. Defending his home and loved ones motivated a man. So far, the volunteers were learning well, and had come on in leaps and bounds. It gave Tristan hope that, soon, the smuggling gang would be sent on their way, and the people of Rotherton would be able to resume lives of peace and tranquility.

He would, of course, be amazed if it was as simple as that. It might well take two, three, or more blows before the gang relinquished their hold on Rotherton. They would hit back, hoping to quell a revolt and pull the people back into line. They couldn't afford not to. If Rotherton succeeded in defying them, other villages would follow suit and the gang's power would be diminished, if not destroyed. Tristan had pointed that out to his men from the start. He did not want them thinking this would be quick and easy. That would be a disservice, and less than their bravery deserved.

Even after his warning, though, not a man-jack of them had walked away or wavered in his determination. Tristan was proud to know each and every one of them.

Ella's servants had shouldered responsibility for Amberley's security equally well. The gardeners had, to a man, pledged their willingness to protect the ladies, and had prepared for any kind of attack. Some of them were not young men, but they'd still been willing. The oldest gardener, a wizened man with a bent back and arthritic hands, had accepted that he couldn't fight, but insisted he could keep a look out and sound the alarm. Meanwhile, Ella's footmen patrolled the grounds and the house, ready to inflict damage on any would-be assailants. He prayed they would be enough.

Thoughts of the security arrangements turned to thoughts of the lady whose protection made them necessary. Diana Wilde. Oh, Ella needed protection, too, but Ella wasn't the principal target, and any danger to her was purely collateral. The real threat was to Diana. The only uncertainty was, why? And what could Tristan do, that he wasn't already doing, to keep her safe?

He couldn't answer the first question, although he was sure Diana could. She must know, or at least suspect, why she'd been targeted, but she wasn't prepared to tell him. She didn't trust him.

At first, that had rankled. He'd done nothing to earn her mistrust. Then again, he'd done nothing to earn Fremont's mistrust, either, but the man had made it clear how he felt. Since Diana was a friend of Fremont's, perhaps it was his influence that made her so wary of Tristan.

Then again, Tristan had done nothing to improve her

opinion of him. In fact, after his behavior the other day, he wondered why she'd have anything more to do with him at all. She might have slapped him for his actions, and she would have been justified.

He hadn't intended to take advantage of her. He only intended to speak with her. But as they walked in Ella's gardens, he found himself more and more aware of her beside him. Being in a private garden, she'd not worn a bonnet or a coat. The sun shone on the crown of her head, making her honey-blonde hair gleam, and her cheeks seemed to glow. She carried the scent of lavender, sweet and feminine, and entirely right for her. Her eyes sparkled, bright and blue as the endless sky. She laughed at something he said, and it made him think of a tiny waterfall in a bubbling stream, though when she spoke her voice was deep, throaty. A voice of seduction trapped in an innocent miss. She was a mass of contradictions. It would take a man a lifetime to untangle them all, one from another.

His hand froze in midair, his pen poised over the inkwell as he realized he wanted that lifetime. He wanted to learn all there was about Diana Wilde, the many facets of her, facets which should be completely dissonant, yet which came together into one harmonious whole.

She was endlessly fascinating, endlessly wonderful. If he spent the next fifty years learning about her, he would never reach the end, never know all of her. But he would never tire of trying.

Tristan hadn't been in the market for a wife. Never, not once in his life, had the thought of marriage been a serious one for him. As a soldier, he'd felt no need. If he'd been asked, he supposed he would have said he didn't care to give a lady an uncertain future—soldiers had a tendency to leave widows.

Then, he'd inherited the barony. He knew most people of his class would say that increased his need to wed, to secure his line and create his heir. Tristan disagreed. He saw no point in creating heirs when there was nothing for them to inherit. Apart from his entailed estate, Tristan had nothing to pass on, and that estate was so starved of investment it was more a burden than an asset. If not for the rents paid by his tenant, there would be no money to spend on it at all, and it likely would have fallen down by now. Who would want to inherit that?

And what lady of quality would want to live like that if she didn't have to? He knew Cassie hated it, though she rarely complained, and she accepted there was nothing to be done about it. But she was his sister; she had no choice. No other woman would willingly take on the life Tristan now led, stripped of every valuable asset, unable to enhance the value of his last remaining estate, living on the generosity of an old friend...

Then again, wasn't that exactly what Diana was doing? If Ella hadn't taken Diana in, had not provided her with home and comfort, where would Diana Wilde be now? Probably looking for a position as a paid companion to a cantankerous old lady with an ear trumpet and a family who didn't want the care of her. Or as a governess for spoiled children...no. He couldn't think of her in such a post. He knew the dangers faced by beautiful governesses. The sons of prosperous houses often saw their sisters' governesses as fair game. As did many of their fathers. Tristan would not wish that fate on Diana.

His thoughts tumbled over in his head, round and round, up and down, like acrobats in a circus until, finally, they returned to the memory of that cool dark sitting room, and what had happened there.

He'd wanted to impress upon her that she could trust him, to persuade her to tell him what he needed to know to make her safe. So he'd reached out, touched her arm. It had been his biggest mistake.

A frisson of awareness had run through him. There was nothing salacious about the touch, nothing untoward at all. Yet the feelings it engendered were so heightened, so tender and intimate... His hand on her arm aroused his entire being. Every part of him responded—his breath shortened, his heart sped up, the muscles in his stomach clenched. The hairs on his arms stood to attention. His clothes grew too tight. He felt the feather-soft air on his face, heard the ticking clock, loud in the ringing stillness. He smelled the beeswax on the furniture, the lingering sweetness of logs by the fire, the lavender in her hair. And, when he kissed her, tasted the fresh summer day on her skin, he'd been lost.

He didn't regret what happened. He'd be a hypocrite to say he did, for had he not gone to bed each night dreaming of it? It was everything he wanted, and more. All he'd imagined it would be. No, he didn't regret it.

What he did regret was that it had happened *then*. He regretted his loss of control, his need to touch her, to kiss her, to feel her come apart in his arms. She'd deserved more, so much more.

She'd deserved respect.

He'd meant to talk to her, to tell her how he felt, to ask for reason to hope. Knowing he had little to offer, he'd been prepared to go to his knees and beg for the chance to deserve her.

She could do so much better than him. He knew that.

Other men could give her jewels, and gowns, and a fashionable life in the *ton*. Those things were not in Tristan's gift. But there was one thing he could give, something he hoped would make up for all else: the way he felt for her. He'd meant to tell her that.

One touch, and all his intentions had gone to the devil. He'd compromised her. All but ruined her. And as he sat, watching her in the aftermath, he wondered if he'd ruined himself as well. Robbed himself of his chance. For what gently bred lady wanted a fiend who couldn't control his actions and his emotions?

He'd begun his apology, and his explanation. Braced himself to say what he wanted to say. Only to be interrupted before he could finish the first sentence. Blast Ella and her impeccable timing! Could she not have stayed away five more minutes?

Tristan looked down at the ledger. He hadn't written a single thing. The figures in it didn't make sense to him today. He rested his elbow on the desk, put his head on his hand and rubbed at his forehead with his fingers, trying to ease the headache building behind his eyes.

The study door was flung open. Tristan tensed, ready for the fight, then relaxed when he saw it was his manservant, then tensed again when he saw the man's flustered demeanor.

"Beg pardon, my lord," he said, his voice breathless. "They're attacking the Goose. Seth sent for you, said it's time to show what your men can do."

All thoughts of Diana and his feelings for her fled. He was, once more, the officer he had been, all his concentration on the coming action, his men, and the plan to rout their enemies. Grabbing his coat from the back of his chair, he raced to the vicarage garden. The lawn had dried in the two weeks of unrelenting sunshine, making the grass wheat-yellow over the hard baked earth. Which was just as well, for a dozen men learning hand-to-hand combat had done damage enough. He could only imagine the mess if the earth had been soft and muddy, churning beneath their feet.

Sergeant Busby had the volunteers lined up. Some carried pistols, but most had knives, hammers, and cudgels. All were eager for the fight. As Tristan left the house, he heard calls of, "Time to teach 'em a lesson," and, "What are we waitin' for?" They quietened at his arrival.

He looked from face to expectant face. "Seth Fayers has called for our help," he said. "Over the last week I've watched you train, and I've seen the type of men you are. I know you will do your duty for the good of Rotherton. But remember this: we have the moral high ground. We will keep it. Use what force you need to send the villains running, and *no more*. Give no one cause to accuse you of heavy-handedness, unnecessary violence, or anything that could be construed as either a crime or conduct unbefitting the gentlemen I know you to be."

A murmur of agreement sounded.

"That said, let's get them to leave our village."

A ragged cheer went up. Sergeant Busby barked at the men to remember their training, and they followed Tristan along the road to the Golden Goose.

The stable lad stood outside the inn, together with the ancient ostler. They looked scared. The volunteers fanned out around the inn, getting into their predetermined places, ready for action.

The boy saw Tristan and ran forward. "You come to stop 'em, my lord?" he asked.

"We intend to. What's been going on?"

"Seth said as how they must pay for their drinks from now on," said the youngster. "And the same if they wanted a tup."

It saddened Tristan to hear a lad of no more than ten talking so casually about men paying for sex, but that was not his greatest concern now.

"He told them he wasn't a…" the lad hesitated and spoke the next words carefully, as if they were new to him and he was unsure of them, "…a ben-ev-ol-ent org-an-i-za-tion."

"I take it they haven't paid for those things before?"

The boy shook his head and Tristan frowned. Things were worse than he'd thought. Seth Fayers was not a man who would hand out his drinks for free, let alone the favors of his women. Not if he wasn't compelled to.

"No, my lord, they haven't," said the ostler, his Sussex burr softening his vowels and elongating his words. "Been driving Seth to distraction, it has."

Inside the inn, there was a crash, a short scream which ended in a sob, and Seth's voice shouting, "There's no need for that!"

Laughter followed. More than one man's. It wasn't good-humored or pleasant.

Seeing his men were ready, Tristan nodded at Busby, then pushed open the door to the inn.

The taproom was a mess. Bottles and glasses were broken, sharp shards across the bar and tables, crystal pellets on the floor. At least two chairs were broken, others were upended. Two men had control of an ale barrel, and were filling tankards from it, although more was spilling to the floor than was going into the cups. The bitter, yeasty smell of it filled the air. Food littered the floor, and Seth clutched a box to his chest. Tristan guessed it contained the day's takings. Two men stood before Seth, their intention clearly to relieve him of the box.

Three women in low-cut dresses huddled into a corner, armed with whatever was to hand. Susie Turner had a poker which she brandished like a sword. Another woman held the fireside shovel like a cosh, and the third had a skillet. Even so, they'd be no match for the half dozen men surrounding them.

Tristan drew himself up to his full height and called out, "Enough!"

There was a momentary lull. Men looked at him. Most swiftly decided he wasn't a threat, and turned away again.

"You've had your fun," he continued. "It's finished." His voice rang strong, authoritative, brooking no dissent. Exactly the way it had always sounded when he'd worn the King's uniform. Some things, it seemed, never left you.

"Who might you be?" sneered a man who sat on a bench near the front door, nursing a tankard of ale in his meaty fist. He didn't seem to be a tall man; even sitting, his lack of inches was obvious. He had a large stomach that flopped over the waistband of stained pantalons that sagged at the knees. His shirt was half untucked, his cravat skewwhiff, and his coat had seen better days. His hair hung loose to his shoulders, slick with grease. The color was high in his cheeks, and his nose, and his eyes swam in their sockets, signaling that he'd been drinking.

There was no humor in those watery eyes. In fact, there was nothing. The man had the deadest eyes Tristan had ever seen. A shiver travelled his spine, as he thought, absurdly, that this man had no soul.

"Show him, Mick," encouraged another man. He'd stopped filling tankards, but he hadn't shut off the barrel's tap. The ale splashed to the floor, forming a foamy puddle.

"I am Lord Leonard, and this place is under my protection," Tristan announced. "I'm asking you, politely, to leave. I will ask only once."

The room fell silent as the men processed his words. Their shock was palpable—they were not used to being challenged. He could see them weighing up the pros and cons. On the one hand, as far as they knew, he was only one man. On the other hand, he was an aristocrat. A man might be fined, or given a few nights in jail for brawling with another working-class man. He could expect a far harsher punishment for attacking a peer.

The man on the bench, Mick, studied Tristan for a long moment. Was this the Mickey Hicks Fremont had spoken of? It was said he enjoyed violence. Those eyes said that assessment of him was correct.

Mick huffed a laugh. The edges of his mouth curled upwards. "We're having a party," he said, his accent thick with his St. Giles upbringing. "It's impolite to interrupt a man when he's having a party. Teach his lordship a lesson, boys."

Everything happened at once.

The smugglers turned to Tristan. Some took a step forward.

Tristan yelled, "Now!"

His men swarmed the taproom from every doorway: front, rear, kitchen.

Taken by surprise, the gang members hesitated for a fraction of a second. It was all the militia needed to get

189

the upper hand. They barreled in, fists flying, feet kicking. Once or twice a blade flashed, though nobody went down, or seemed badly hurt.

The women joined in, hitting out with their makeshift weapons at their erstwhile tormentors. Seth held onto his money box for dear life with one hand, while belaying his attackers with a cudgel he'd grabbed from beneath the bar. One villain slipped on the puddle of beer and went down, then couldn't get up under the assault of boots kicking out at him.

There was, perhaps, a little more force in the punishment the militia meted out than was strictly necessary, and—possibly—they took a little more pleasure than they should in giving it. But these men had been at the mercy of this gang for months and, Tristan decided, as long as it didn't go too far, they deserved a little requital.

From the corner of his eye, he saw the silver flash of a blade and turned to see Mick, his eyes on the back of Busby's coat. Busby fought with one of Seth's would-be robbers, totally oblivious to the danger behind him.

Tristan pulled the knife from his boot and threw it, underarm, at Mick. It hit the edge of his forearm, not squarely, but taking the top of his sleeve with its force. Mick's arm jerked backward, and he dropped his blade as Tristan's knife bit into the back of the bench behind him. It didn't penetrate the wood deeply. It wouldn't take much to pull it out.

Mick didn't even try. Instead, he pulled his arm down, tearing his sleeve free, and leaving the blade in place. He held his injured arm with his other hand and glared at Tristan, before he stormed out of the inn.

Seconds later, the fight was finished. Gang members

scrambled away, pushing aside tables in their haste to leave. One man cupped his hand over his nose, trying to stem the flow of blood. Another had the beginnings of a black eye, which Tristan suspected was courtesy of the woman with the skillet. Seth rushed to turn off the barrel tap, saving whatever was left of the ale inside.

A deafening cheer went up as the militia realized the enemy had run away. They hugged each other, patted backs, embraced the women. One or two grabbed the half-finished tankards of ale the gang members had left behind, and swigged them down.

Busby grinned. "We did it, my lord. We sent 'em packing."

Tristan nodded. "For now."

He would let his men celebrate this triumphant moment. Tomorrow, they would be back in training.

Their struggle to reclaim their village had begun.

Chapter Sixteen

Diana sat at the escritoire in the morning room at Amberley. A piece of paper lay in front of her, and she held a quill. The trouble was, she had no idea what to write. "Dear Lord Fremont," was a given. That and the date at the top of her letter were already set down. It was what came next she was less certain about.

How did one tell the man whose rules one had promised to obey that those rules needed to change? They had kept Diana safe so far, had possibly even saved her life, but they were becoming more untenable with each new day.

"You are Diana Wilde, impoverished schoolfriend of Eleanor Forbes-Smythe," he'd told her when they came here. "That is how everybody must know you. Trust nobody with the truth." He'd looked at her sternly. "Nobody," he repeated, enunciating each syllable meaningfully. He hadn't even told Ella, although he said he trusted her, and she'd opened her home as Diana's sanctuary.

But the position he'd put her in wasn't sustainable. Keeping the pretense of being someone else had been easy on the journey from Norfolk to London. That had been just two days, in company with people she barely shared basic conversation with, and whom she would never meet again.

It wasn't too onerous to keep up the falsehood with

most people in Rotherton, either. Ladies such as Mrs. Bell and Mrs. Potter accepted Diana's story at face value, and they hardly spoke to her anyway. They weren't interested in her—although, she thought cynically, that would probably change if they discovered who she truly was.

Other people in the area were kinder, more accepting of the persona she presented to them, but they, too, had not become deep enough friends to warrant taking them into her confidence. Especially since she knew the slightest whisper of gossip would spread like fire over a river of lamp oil, and would, inevitably, get back to the men she hid from.

But Ella wasn't a gossip. She had welcomed Diana without question, put herself in danger for her, and had then coped with the effects of that danger without demur. Ella hadn't blamed Diana for the injuries to Terrence or Tom Coachman; hadn't demanded Diana leave, as many would have done. She'd upended her household to keep Diana safe. She deserved the truth.

Which is what Diana wanted to tell Fremont in this letter.

One other person needed to know, but Diana thought it would be harder to persuade Fremont of that. Even though, arguably, it was more important that Tristan know the truth than that Ella did. He was investigating the attacks on Diana, trying to protect her and ensure the villains did not succeed in taking her. She was withholding evidence vital to his success, and that was not fair. If he knew who she was, and what had happened in London, he would be much more able to hunt down the criminals. Which would, in turn, make her safer.

That was, of course, the only reason she wished to

tell Tristan the truth. So he could help her and keep her safe. It had nothing to do with the kisses they'd shared, or what had happened on the chaise longue in the sitting room. It was just that he needed to know the truth.

And if he knew? What then? Would Tristan look at her differently? Think differently about her? If he did, would that be a good thing? Or a bad?

Diana hadn't met many men, socially. She'd been familiar with Papa's associates, of course, and had met them in social settings, but that had been for the good of his businesses. She'd acted as hostess to those people at dinners designed to increase his success and his wealth— smiled and made conversation with them, then charmed their wives while Papa did his deals over the brandy. Some of those men, though not many, had been single, but they'd always been circumspect, their interest not in her but in their wallets and how much her father could thicken their contents.

She'd also met a few people away from business settings across the world. In every colonial community there were women who gushed about how *wonderful* it was to meet her, and how she looked *divine*, and they *must* know the name of her modiste. There were men who rushed to scribble their names on her dance card, and who waxed lyrical about her eyes "like the flawless sky on a summer day," apparently, her hair "a shining golden halo," her beauty, her grace, her elegance—all of which inspired the most awful poetry a woman could be subjected to. Diana had often wondered, wryly, what they would say if they saw her at the start of each day, her hair like a bird's nest and her cheeks bearing the marks of the creases in her sheets.

The one thing they all failed to mention when they

heaped their praises upon her was the one thing she knew to be her most important asset of all, where they were concerned. Her money. Without it, she knew she'd be nothing to them. Diana Villiers might be beautiful, irresistible, Botticelli's Venus. She had a feeling that Diana Wilde would be ordinary, a wallflower, and unworthy of any attention at all.

But Tristan had paid attention to Diana Wilde. He'd made her feel as if she mattered, as if he saw *her*, *sans argent*, and still found her beautiful.

She didn't want that to change. Though, inevitably, it would. How could it not? Her dowry alone was twenty thousand pounds, and her inherited bank balance was many times that. To say nothing of the ships, properties, and other investments she now owned. Nobody, no matter how unmercenary they generally were, could ignore all of that.

The trouble was, she had feelings for Tristan, and she thought he had feelings for her. Feelings she must not encourage until he knew the truth. Before she could tell him the truth, she must speak to Fremont. She'd promised to do nothing without his permission, after all.

Fremont had made no secret of his lack of trust in Tristan. He'd been decidedly cool toward him when they met in Rotherton's home. Which meant the chances were he would refuse to allow her to confide in the man.

So what was the point of even asking him?

With a frustrated growl, she threw down the quill and walked away from the escritoire. She paced the room, her hands clutched in front of her waist, elbows in tight to her sides, lips pressed together and brow furrowed. It was a conundrum.

"I will say nothing for now," she decided. "Not to

Tristan, and not to Ella. Not until I've spoken to Fremont." Though it went against every grain of honesty within her.

This subterfuge was wearing, on both the body and the soul. "No wonder Fremont always looks so serious," she muttered. "His secrets must weigh him down indeed!"

She threw herself into a chair near the fireplace, leaned back into it in a most unladylike pose, and resolved to write to Fremont in a vague, nonspecific way. If she asked him to come, she could explain what she wanted to his head and, perhaps, more easily persuade him to her way of thinking. Having decided that, she rang the bell. A cup of tea should soothe her nerves and chase away her feelings of restlessness.

The door opened far too quickly for it to be somebody summoned by her ring. Ella's butler, Carlton, entered the room and bowed to her.

"Pardon me, Miss Wilde. Lord Leonard is here. Are you at home to him?"

Was she at home to Tristan Leonard? Did the sun rise in the east? She sat up straighter in her chair and struggled to keep her smile from being too broad, too revealing.

"Yes, Carlton." To her own ears, her voice sounded more high pitched than it should, her words too fast. She cleared her throat and tried again. Slower. An octave lower. "Yes. I am at home." That was much better. "I just rang for tea."

"Very good, ma'am."

A moment later, Tristan came into the room. She stood and curtsied in answer to his bow, then sat so that he could. He seemed nervous, uncertain. He sat on the front edge of the chair, which, she thought, could not be comfortable at all.

"Good day to you, Miss Wilde," he said.

"Good day, my lord."

A moment of silence, before he added, "You are well?"

"Very well, my lord. And you?"

He nodded. "In fine fettle."

There was another hesitation. He was clearly anxious, and that made Diana anxious, too. Had something happened? Had her attackers tried to find her again? She didn't think he was here to say he'd arrested them. He would not be uneasy about telling her that.

"Miss Forbes-Smythe? She is well?" he asked, eventually.

"She, too, was in fine fettle when I saw her this morning at breakfast."

Diana smiled and hoped to put him at ease. Whatever he'd come to tell her, however bad the news, it didn't do for him to be so on edge. "She is out," she continued, "visiting tenants, I believe. She said something about refurbishing cottages and discovering which repairs should be done first. She made some of them sound quite urgent."

That had puzzled Diana. From all she'd seen, Ella kept her property in good order. There might be minor repairs needed, but Diana couldn't think there would be anything dire.

"Good." His response was as surprising as Ella's stated intention had been. *Good?* What was good? That Ella had gone out, or that there were repairs to be done?

The maid brought in the tea tray and put it close to Diana. Neither she nor Tristan spoke until the girl had gone, carefully leaving the door ajar. Tristan looked over at it, a pained expression on his face. Whatever he had to say, then, needed privacy, and he didn't want the servants listening. Not that Diana thought Ella's servants would listen. They were better trained than that. And really, there was nothing to be done about it. An unmarried woman shouldn't be alone in a room with a single gentleman with the door closed. She'd probably scandalized the entire household last week, when she was closeted in the sitting room with him. They clearly weren't going to let it happen again.

"Tea?" she asked.

"Thank you. I—er—I—hoped to ask you a question." He glanced at the door again. So did she. "Forgive me," he murmured. "It's not something I've ever asked before." He looked into the fireplace, as if he could not meet her eyes. "I'm certain my…circumstances are well known. You are probably as aware of them as anybody else, but suffice it to say, I am—well, I'm not a rich man. I'm not broke, as such, but I am—not well off."

His gaze flickered at her, then away again. His eyes were shadowed with shame. Diana held herself rigid, trying to stop her inner fidgets, brought on by his words. She wished he would stop. She didn't need him to lay his soul bare in this way.

"Truth is, Miss Wilde," he continued, "I have but one property left in my possession, and that is let. I have little other income." He swallowed, hard, then seemed to gather his pride as he looked squarely at her. "I work for Lord Rotherton because I cannot afford not to."

Diana poured the tea, more to be able to look away from him than for the beverage itself.

"However," he went on, "I am not in debt. I cleared all the debts my late brother incurred, when I inherited." He swallowed, hard. "I—realize I am not very eloquent, but what I'm trying to say, Miss Wilde, is that, although we do not live in the lap of luxury, my family will always be able to rest assured in the knowledge that I can take care of them. My wife could expect always to have food on her table and good shoes on her feet. Her clothes may not ever come from the most prestigious modistes, but they would be of a quality that befitted her station. Any children of mine would be cared for properly and, in the case of daughters, I would hope to provide a modest dowry by the time they were of age to need it."

Oh, no! This could not be what she thought it was. He could not be about to make her an offer! Not now, when she could not accept him. He didn't know who she was, or what she was. She could not betroth herself to him until he did know.

But oh! how she wanted to accept. She wanted to say yes. *Yes, and yes, and yes!* Because his words, awkward and stilted as they were, were the push she'd needed to examine how she felt.

And how did she feel? Quite simply, she loved him. She loved Tristan Leonard.

She'd liked him before, when he'd been a charming gentleman, treating her as a lady when many of their neighbors were disdainful of her. His determination to protect her—and the whole area for that matter—from the villains who terrorized them, had deepened that liking of him. And, she could not deny, the things he'd done to her in the sitting room had created within her a craving for him, a constant yearning that bordered on obsession.

But she'd finally known for certain that she loved him when he prefaced what must surely be an offer of marriage with a list of his shortcomings and difficulties. The honor that had compelled him to do that, to make sure she knew exactly what sort of a bargain she'd be getting should she say yes, told her everything she needed to know about him.

Fremont was wrong. Tristan Leonard was not someone to be wary of trusting. He was chivalrous, and courageous, and true. A man she could love.

A man whose offer she could, and would, accept.

Just as soon as she'd told him who she truly was.

She wondered, briefly, how he'd take the news. Would he be shocked? Stunned and stupefied? Most men would be pleased, wouldn't they? Relieved that they and their families need never worry about finances again?

But Tristan was a proud man. He might not like the idea that his wife's money had saved him from penury. A man with his sense of honor might even be put off by the truth.

"What I'm trying to say, Miss Wilde," he said now, "is that, I would deem it the greatest honor of my life if you consented to be my wife."

Time. She needed time. Time to sort through the arguments going back and forth in her head. Before she could answer him, she needed to think. To talk to Fremont. She needed…

Before she could finish the thought, much less answer him, the door swished open and Ella stood in the space it left. Her hair was less than perfect, hanging down over one shoulder where she'd obviously lost her pins. Her hat sat at a strange angle, looking as if it would tumble at any second, the weight of the ostentatious feathers making it list to one side. Her color was high, her eyes too bright, and she brandished her riding crop like a weapon, ready for battle.

"Diana," she said, breathlessly. "Are you all right?"

****

Tristan bristled. What did Ella mean, was Diana all right? Did she think he would do her friend harm? True, she'd walked in on them the other day and it must have been obvious to her what they'd been doing. That time, her voice, calling along the corridor, had given them time to sit up and put a decent distance between them. Diana had pulled down her skirts and tidied her bodice, but she could do nothing to hide the way her hair fell wantonly down her back, or the high color in her cheeks, and the swell of her well-kissed lips.

Ella had said nothing. She'd looked askance at him, then talked about something else, although what that was Tristan could not have said if his life depended upon it. She kept up her cheery banter while Diana's color returned to normal and her demeanor calmed. Meanwhile, Tristan sat in an armchair, silently conjugating as many Latin verbs as he could remember until his own body settled, and his breeches lost their painful tightness.

When he made to leave, Ella had taken him aside. He'd tensed, expecting a dressing down. But all she said was, "Don't break her heart. She doesn't deserve that."

But now, when he was in the brightly lit morning room, sitting a good six feet from Diana, and with the door open as propriety demanded, Ella was concerned for Diana's welfare? What did she think he could have done in here? With a maid coming in with tea, and Carlton no doubt hovering, listening to every word, ready to intercede if he tried anything he shouldn't? Tristan didn't know whether to be flattered at Ella's opinion of his capabilities, or insulted that she thought he might hurt her friend.

Before he could say anything to that effect, though, Ella put her hand to her chest and breathed out in relief. "Oh, thank goodness you're here, Lord Leonard. If I'd known that, I would not have raced neck-or-nothing to get back here."

The absurd thought came that yes, she probably would have. Tristan had seen her drive. She went everywhere at the gallop.

Then he registered the rest of what she'd said. She hadn't known he was here with Diana. Was glad that he was. He frowned. "What has happened?"

"There was a man," Ella said. "A horrid little man. Well, I say little. He wasn't, actually. He was quite tall. Almost as tall as you. But there was something about him. Something I didn't like. And he was…lurking. Watching."

"Watching what? You?"

"The house. He was quite some distance from it, but he was definitely watching it."

All business now, Tristan strode to the window to look outside. The gardeners were standing to attention near to one another, each of them armed with something that could cause damage if it came into sharp and heavy contact with a person: shovels, rakes, an axe. The footmen were in the distance, searching near where the park became woodland.

"You won't see anything. He wasn't that close, and he ran when Steven challenged him."

"Steven?"

"One of my footmen. He's a big, burly chap; you wouldn't want to tangle with him. That's why I took him with me when I went— He started toward the man. He was going to ask him what he was doing, and warn him off, but the man turned tail and fled into the woods. But the way he was watching the house, I thought, what if he's not alone? What if he's supposed to be a—a—lookout or whatever they call it? So I came back. I thought Diana might need my help."

What did she think she could have done to help Diana? Ella was no more than five foot three inches tall, and she was as slight as she was petite. Even if she put all her weight behind it, any blow she aimed would not cause much damage to a man, especially one used to hard knocks.

"I hope you weren't thinking of taking unnecessary risks," he said.

"Of course not!" Ella looked appalled at the idea. But just as he relaxed, happy that she was sensible after all, she robbed him of his peace of mind again. "Any risk to me wouldn't have been unnecessary, would it? Not if my friend was being assaulted."

God save him from pedantic females. Tristan's headache began to rebuild. His neck was tense. He longed to roll his shoulders.

"The pair of you should come into the village proper for a few days," he decided. "There are spare rooms at the vicarage—"

"Certainly not!" Ella was outraged.

At the same time, Diana said, "We cannot put you to so much trouble."

"You cannot stay here," he argued.

"We dashed well can," answered Ella. "This is my

home. I'll not be driven from it by an upstart like that man."

"You're too far away," reasoned Tristan. "By the time I know there is cause for alarm and get my men here to help you, it could be far too late."

"I don't need your militia. I have five footmen and two dozen gardeners, and—"

"You thought someone had got past them today."

"A momentary panic. If I'd thought, I would have known nobody had breached the house."

"Yet." He didn't want to frighten these ladies, but he suspected it was the only way to get them to agree. They weren't safe here. Whoever was after Diana was determined and tenacious. It was only a matter of time until they reached her. Tristan would die before he let that happen.

"No place is completely impregnable," he told them. "No perimeter cannot be breached if the enemy wants it badly enough. Sooner or later, those men will get past your guards."

"They'd get past yours, as well," Ella pointed out.

He couldn't deny that. But, "the vicarage is smaller than Amberley, so its perimeter is easier to secure. My men have been trained. Plus, being in the village, there'll be others nearby who can also come to your aid, and quickly. I can guard you, and keep Cassie safe, without splitting my force. In fact, I would welcome your men as reinforcements."

There was a little more argument, a little more back and forth, but his logic had taken the heat from Ella's opposition. She was proud, he knew that, and she wanted to think her home was safe. But she was also worried about Diana. She would do nothing to put her friend further into harm's way. If that meant a temporary evacuation, so be it.

As for Diana, she was clearly just as worried for Ella as Ella was for her. Tristan could see the guilt etched on her face, and he knew what she thought—if she hadn't been here, Ella wouldn't be in danger. He wanted to tell her that was balderdash. For, while it was true that Diana's presence had drawn those men to Amberley this time, it was also true that the gang had been operating in this area for months, targeting everybody. They would have come after Ella, her people and her property sooner or later, Diana or no Diana.

At last, the ladies agreed to come to the vicarage. While they packed whatever they thought essential for a few days away, Tristan went out to Ella's men. As he'd suspected, they'd been unable to find the intruder. He'd disappeared, said one gardener, like morning mist on a hot day.

He explained the new arrangement, and organized a group to come with them now, supplying a guard for the ladies. The rest would secure the house and follow behind.

"We'll keep 'em safe," said one. "We'll give them blackguards the fight of their lives."

Tristan nodded. "And we will win," he vowed.

Chapter Seventeen

Tristan left Cassie to welcome Ella and Diana into the vicarage while he packed his own things and took them to the coachman's room above the stables. That took care of propriety over sleeping arrangements.

What had he been thinking? Having Diana so near to him for so much of the time...while they would not be sleeping under the same roof, their paths would cross frequently. He must still take his meals in the house, and do his work in the study, and access his bath, for he drew the line at washing under the pump in the kitchen yard. They would constantly be thrust together closely.

Then again, what else could he have done? The ladies had not been safe at Amberley. An army of gardeners and footmen could, and would, deter the common burglar, but it would not deter for long a determined gang, street-hard and vicious and willing to kill to get their way. The man Ella had seen today had not breached the defenses, but the more Tristan thought on it, the more he surmised he'd never intended to. He thought the villain had been on a recce, surveying the lay of the land, summing up his opposition, to better plan a successful assault.

No. The ladies could not stay there.

Nor could they go anywhere else in the neighborhood. To ask someone else to take them in would be to put that host in danger, too. He wouldn't play so fast and loose with the denizens of Rotherton like that. The vicarage, then, had been his only choice.

It was true what he'd said, too. He could guard the vicarage far more easily than he could guard Amberley. The perimeter was smaller, and not surrounded by woodland that might hide a hundred marauding miscreants. He had a band of volunteers, augmented by Ella's people. He had a better chance of keeping Diana safe here.

All of them. Of course he meant a better chance of keeping *all of them* safe. Not just Diana. Although, he couldn't deny, she was uppermost in his thoughts. Hers was the face that came when he closed his eyes, hers the anxious look as she blamed herself for the mess her friend was in. He longed to wipe that anxiety from her brow, tell her it was not her fault. It was the fault, entirely, of the blackguards who pursued her so relentlessly. It mattered not why they pursued her. Whatever she'd done to provoke those men, it was not her fault they'd embroiled others in their attempt at retribution.

He found it harder and harder to believe she'd done anything to warrant such retaliation from them anyway. The Diana he'd come to know was not vindictive or dishonest. She was caring and kind and thoughtful. Not the sort of woman to have behaved in any way that would bring these villains after her.

Perhaps she had knowledge of the men, knowledge they didn't want her to share? That didn't ring true either. They had to know she was here under the protection of Lord Fremont, and that meant she'd shared whatever she knew with him, making silencing her a moot point.

What if she didn't just *know* something about the

men? What if she'd *witnessed* something? What if Diana had witnessed a heinous crime and Fremont had brought her here to keep her safe until she could give her statement in court?

That threw everything else into disarray. She might not be a schoolfriend of Ella's after all. Which would explain why she looked several years younger than Ella. It explained her wariness, her unwillingness to share, too.

She hadn't answered him this morning when he'd proposed to her. True, any woman might want to think on her answer to such a momentous question. It was also true that Ella had interrupted them at what could have been a crucial moment. But not before Diana had bitten her lip, before her eyes had clouded with emotions he could not decipher.

Diana Wilde was a good woman. He knew it, instinctively. She wouldn't want to entrap a man who did not fully possess the facts about her. Facts she may have been told not to divulge. Whatever she knew, whatever she'd witnessed, it must be important. As must be the perpetrator of whatever crime had been committed. The men attacking her now were of the lower orders— fishermen, smugglers, Rookery bullies—but somebody directed them from behind the scenes.

Milton Percival, perhaps? From what Tristan knew, the man was powerful and growing more so. But he wasn't the only wrongdoer in England, and Tristan was hard put to think of him and Diana being close enough for her to witness anything that would damage him. And it had to be damaging, or there would not be so much effort put into attacking her.

Perhaps it wasn't Percival at all. The man was a

useful scapegoat, the perennial bogeyman to scare everybody. But others were as bad. Worse. Percival didn't hide his crimes or his past behind a veneer of respectability. Others did. They graced the drawing rooms of Mayfair, smiling and charming dowagers and debutantes alike, while in secret committing acts that would sicken and appall even the most jaded of men.

Tristan was now certain of four things. Firstly, Miss Diana Wilde was terrified of someone who intended her harm. Secondly, that someone was capable of hurting her, and was in a position that allowed them to keep trying. Thirdly, until that person was stopped, Diana would not be safe, and until she was safe, she could not move forward with her life.

On a purely selfish note, that included giving him an answer to his offer. If she answered him now, while the threat hung over her, she must say no. He knew enough about her to know that. Before he could press her for an answer, then, he needed to learn her secret, and eliminate the threat that secret engendered.

Which brought him to his fourth point. Fremont. Fremont knew what was behind all of this. Fremont could help Tristan put an end to it and see her safe. If he would.

Tristan would write to him now. He would explain the growing threat and ask for his help. If they joined forces, perhaps they could protect the woman Tristan had come to love.

Leaving his things on the bed of the coachman's quarters, he went to his study to write the letter.

He'd just sanded and sealed his missive to Fremont when there was a knock on the study door and Sergeant Busby peered in. "Got a moment, sir?"

Tristan's heart sank. *What else could go wrong today?* He gestured that Busby should enter. "What can I do for you, Sergeant?"

A wide grin split the sergeant's face. He looked like a little boy who'd found a stash of toffees. "It's what I can do for you, sir," he said. "For the militia." Tristan frowned, puzzled, and the sergeant went on, "specifically, armaments. I've managed to procure muskets. Twenty of them. With balls and gunpowder, too. With your permission, I'd like to start the men to training with them as soon as maybe."

"Muskets?" That was not what Tristan had expected the sergeant to say. Where on earth had he found twenty muskets? Together with ammunition? It wasn't the sort of thing one found abandoned in the hedgerows. Which probably meant… "Do I want to know, Busby?"

Busby gave what could only be described as a sheepish grin. "Probably not, sir."

Tristan closed his eyes. The headache that had been building for the last three hours throbbed. His sergeant had stolen twenty muskets. He didn't see Captain Allenby tolerating that. The man was likely on his way here now, with a contingent of men, hell-bent on arresting the sergeant and whichever men he'd taken with him on his pilfering exercise. Tristan, too, he shouldn't wonder.

"Allenby will likely see us swing for this, Sergeant." His mind was whirling, trying to think of ways to return the firearms to the garrison's armory without being caught. Although he would dearly love to arm his men against the smuggling gang, he wouldn't do it at the price of hanging any of them.

"What Captain Allenby don't know, don't hurt

him."

"You think the armorer is not going to report the theft of twenty muskets, plus ammunition? He'd swing, himself, for that."

Busby's grin broadened. "Didn't get them from the armory. Didn't get them from the garrison at all. They was evidence. In a trial. About two years ago, they was meant to go out to France to arm the Bonapartistes, but the cargo was seized and the geezer what paid for the guns was arrested. The guns was locked up, to be used in the court case. But before he could be tried, the man died, and the evidence has just sat in the stores ever since, completely forgotten. My cousin, he keeps the inventory for the stores, and when we set up the militia, he made it possible for us to, er, borrow the guns. Long as he gets 'em back when the battle's done, he's happy."

"What if someone comes looking for them before the 'battle is done'?"

"They haven't in two years, sir. But if they do, he'll stall while we put them back."

The sergeant's blasé attitude made Tristan think this wasn't the first time things had been "borrowed."

"Things go missing all the time, sir," confirmed Busby, as if he'd heard Tristan's thoughts. "Evidence gets destroyed, or sent to the wrong place, put in the wrong warehouse… It'll take them months to even try to track these guns." He sighed heavily. "We can't go up against those cutthroats with a few cudgels, a couple of pistols, and a rusty musket."

Tristan nodded, more in resignation than outright agreement. "Very well. See to the training. And Sergeant? If there should be repercussions, you acted on my orders."

Busby raised an eyebrow, but simply said, "Yes, sir," gave a salute, and left the study.

When Busby was gone, Tristan picked up his letter to Fremont and took it to the Golden Goose. With luck, it would be with the viscount tomorrow.

On the High Street, he saw soldiers moving from door to door, asking questions of the servants who answered, before going inside the houses. Most people let them in and the exchanges remained polite. One man tried to assert his right to refuse, and was roughly pushed aside.

Tristan's blood ran cold. Were they searching for the missing muskets already? What would happen when they reached the vicarage? Part of him wanted to race back and warn Busby, but that would draw attention to him. He would just have to pray that the sergeant had not left anything where it might easily be found. He didn't believe Busby was that stupid, but if the man felt safe, he might become complacent.

"He's not in there, sir," said a soldier as he and his mates came out of the house next to the apothecary's. The corporal nodded.

"Didn't think he would be. Talk about a wild goose chase." The corporal sighed. "Carry on." The soldiers moved along the street. The corporal bobbed his head at Tristan in acknowledgment. Tristan nodded back, his breathing a little easier. The soldier had said "he," not "they." They were looking for a person, not for guns.

Briefly, he wondered who that person might be. Since he'd not been apprised of the search, it must be a military matter—a soldier who'd deserted perhaps? He must have taken the regimental silver with him to warrant this sort of search.

Still pondering the issue, Tristan went into the Golden Goose to hand in his post. Seth Fayers stood at the bar, talking to Lieutenant Paisley. He shook his head at a question Paisley had obviously just asked.

"As I said, I haven't seen him. Haven't seen any of them. But they're not stupid. They're not going to waltz in here and ask for a pint of ale and a plate of stew, are they?"

"They'll be long gone," offered Susie. She wiped a table with a rag, then wiped down each of the chairs around it before moving to the next one. "Hopping on a ship to the Americas, if they've got any sense at all."

Paisley grimaced at Susie's words. Which meant he either did not agree with her or he already had men searching all the outbound ships within his jurisdiction. There would be many to search, what with ports such as Hastings, Brighton, Winchelsea and Deal, Newhaven, Seaford and Shoreham all in close proximity.

"They could be headed for London," supplied the innkeeper's wife. She stood near the kitchen door, hands on her ample hips as she listened to the exchange. "You'll never find them there."

"I dunno." Seth stroked his chin, his meaty fingers rasping over the day's growth of beard. "Rumor is, they didn't run of their own free will. Which means they were forced. Maybe you should be looking for the wrong 'uns that forced them." Seth saw Tristan then and grinned broadly. "Good day to you, my lord, what can I get for you?" His whole demeanor changed, and he was once again the consummate landlord, all hail-fellow-well-met. Tristan handed over his letter, paid the postage, then turned to Paisley, who looked frustrated, to say the least.

"How do you today, Lieutenant?"

Paisley looked from Seth to the women, then turned to Tristan. "Might I have a word, my lord?"

He led the way out of the pub and along the street. As they walked, he spoke, keeping his voice low as if he didn't wish to be overheard.

"There have been two developments within the last day, my lord. One has quickly become common knowledge." He grimaced. "That's not a surprise. If you send soldiers to search door to door, everybody soon knows your business."

"You would have handled it differently?" asked Tristan, keeping his own voice equally low. Mayhap the inferred confidentiality was because of Paisley's implied criticism of his superior officer.

Paisley shrugged. "I don't see things in stark black and white, my lord. As I am sure you can attest, once one has a few years' experience under one's military belt, shades of grey, cream, and beige bleed into the picture."

"So, Seth was right? Your miscreants didn't run of their own free will?"

Paisley pulled a face. "Potentially not. And, of course, if that is the case, a more circumspect chase might have had benefits. The men involved could have been persuaded to turn on their masters, and we could have cut the head from the snake, rather than toying with its tail. As it is, we have every man out searching, in the wrong places, and with orders to shoot on sight." He deepened his voice and mimicked his captain. "They're obviously desperate men, and ruthless. If they weren't guilty, they would not have run. Shoot them like the rats they are, and save us the hangman's fee."

That did sound like the captain. The man was not only inexperienced but, apparently, something of a martinet, to boot. Tristan had met several such officers. They advanced because of birth and connections, not through merit. Often, while they themselves remained unscathed, the men under their command died by the dozens.

"What did your fugitives do to warrant Captain Allenby's anger and have him send so many men after them?" Perhaps these men had taken the regimental silver, after all.

Paisley looked at him, surprised. "You don't know? I thought you would have been informed. You are the ranking civilian authority in Rotherton. Sorry, my lord. I should not have assumed…" He sighed, heavily. "There was a jailbreak at Haywards Heath. Sometime after midnight, a group of men attacked the prison, and opened some of the cells. Releasing prisoners is rather cocking a snook at our authority, is it not? Allenby cannot, and will not, be seen to tolerate that."

A strange feeling of foreboding swept through Tristan. He had the impression he already knew the answer to his next question. "Who, exactly, escaped?"

"Every last one of the men we arrested for smuggling in the last month. All those waiting to be tried at the next Assizes."

The bad feeling increased. "Every one of them?" Tristan thought of John Carter, how he'd seemed a reluctant smuggler, at best. Tristan had planned to write to the judge on the man's behalf, and to ask David to do the same. But if Carter had broken out of prison, nobody short of Prinny himself could hope to find him leniency.

"Every last one of them," confirmed Paisley. "Though, as Seth said, there is evidence they might not have gone willingly. A witness, a woman who was…er…visiting, said the prisoners were marched out at gunpoint. Of course, none of the male prisoners left corroborated her story. They saw and heard nothing."

"But the woman said they were forced to leave?"

"She did. Alas, the captain does not believe her."

"What about the guards? What do they say?"

"Funny thing, that. It seems something occurred at the other side of the prison. I'm not too clear on what it was, but it needed all the guards to deal with it, leaving nobody anywhere near the cells in question."

"Convenient."

They reached the Assembly Rooms and turned off the High Street onto the path that ran beside the building. Behind it, there were large, flat lawns, surrounding a bandstand at the center. The lawns were edged with colorful flowerbeds and, around the periphery, trees in myriad greens, together with rhododendron bushes. Paisley looked around at the pretty scene but Tristan didn't think he noted it.

"I fear they intend to use the freed prisoners to distract us, so we cannot come to your aid when they attack you, in retaliation for your routing of them at the Goose the other day." The lieutenant smiled. "We heard about it. Good for you. As long as you're aware there will be consequences."

"We shall endeavor to be prepared for them." *Thank God for Sergeant Busby's muskets.* "The jailbreak seems to be common knowledge, though. You said there'd been a second development. One that is less well known?"

"Aye, my lord." Paisley looked around, as if he searched for eavesdroppers. Nobody else was in the gardens. "The men who attacked your sister and her friends after the Assembly?"

Tristan stiffened. If he got his hands on any of those louts—

"They're dead."

Paisley's words took a moment to sink in past the rage that built within Tristan every time he thought of that night. That none of the ladies had been hurt was a blessing, but he was well aware it was no thanks to him. He and the other men who should have been nearby to protect them had been further along the street, oblivious to the danger. If they had been the helpless females most men thought them, the attack would have been successful, the ladies hurt, or worse, before any of the men were aware. It was chastening.

But… "Dead?" He could hardly credit that. He'd thought they would be difficult to track down, given that Ella had not recognized them, which meant they were not local men. He hadn't expected them to die. Not before their trial, anyway.

"Did your men shoot them?" If so, had it been in an incriminating standoff that pointed to their guilt, or the result of information received? What proof was there that these were the men?

"Not us. We didn't find them. There are times when I doubt we could find our arses with our hands. No, they fetched up on the tide this morning. They washed along the river and ended up near Lewes."

The River Ouse, which ran through the market town of Lewes and down to the sea at Newhaven, was tidal. If the bodies had turned up there, they'd likely been dumped into the sea, but not too far from land. Which suggested no ships had been involved. A ship's crew would have offloaded them farther out, where there was less chance of them being discovered.

"You're certain these were the men?"

"They fit the description the ladies gave." Paisley sniffed, his face wrinkled with his distaste. "Their throats were cut. I'd say whoever hired them did not appreciate failure."

"Possibly." Tristan had seen enough of the world to suspect that some criminals would deal harshly with underlings who had served their purpose, whether they failed in their tasks or not. Slitting a man's throat was cheaper than paying him, if you were unlikely to need him again. And it had the bonus that he could never talk about you, either. "What did Captain Allenby say?"

"He called it a falling-out among thieves, pronounced the ladies of the area safe from future molestation, and said it was a closed case."

Tristan shook his head. The man was an idiot. "Now what?"

"I'm not convinced the ladies no longer need protection," said Paisley.

"They will get it. The Rotherton militia will see to that."

"As to the other matter," Paisley said as they finished their tour of the gardens and returned to the path back to the High Street, and the higher probability of being heard, "I don't like the idea of unnecessary bloodshed." He looked, meaningfully, at Tristan. "I would never condone any action that went against my explicit orders, of course. But, if a civilian authority were to keep those men who escaped alive and well until they could receive a fair trial, and maybe even persuade them to turn King's Evidence, well, that would not break my heart."

Tristan studied him for a long moment before he

nodded.

"Thank you for helping me search the Assembly Gardens, my lord," said the lieutenant, a little louder. "If you or your people see or hear anything, you know where we are to be found." He gave a polite bow and strode away, back to his men.

Chapter Eighteen

Diana couldn't sleep. It wasn't the bed. That was beautifully crafted, its ropes sturdy, with no creak to them at all, while the mattress was perfect: soft enough to cocoon a body, yet firm enough that one did not sink into it. It was more than conducive to a comfortable night's sleep.

The room she'd been given was fine, too. The chamber was at the back of the house, its windows facing southeast, which meant it would get the morning sun, bright enough to cheer and warm the place, but not so it would be in the harsh direct path of the light.

The walls were painted, the bottom half a dusty rose pink, which set off the lighter pink of the rugs and curtains, and the satin quilt on the bed. Above the dado rail, the walls were a warm cream, as was the ceiling.

As well as the bed, the room contained an armoire, where she had hung the four dresses she'd brought with her, all grey and drab, and the cause of many of Ella's most pained expressions. The armoire matched a dressing table with a small mirror fixed to its top, and a modest chest of drawers, into which she had packed her small clothes, fichus, shawls and gloves. A writing desk was under the window, a small chair beside it, while a stool sat in front of the dressing table, its cushioned top matching the rose curtains, and an armchair, also upholstered in rose, was set before the narrow fireplace.

She got out of bed, crossed to the window and sat on the wide sill, staring out into the night. The garden was bathed in soft lemon moonlight, which made the grass of the lawn shine silver, while the terrace was a white grey, and the outbuildings, including the stable where Tristan slept, were nothing more than silhouettes, dark, flat shapes against the not-quite-so-dark sky. There were thousands of stars, some shining a strong and steady white, while others blinked like myopic old ladies, and still others shimmered coquettishly. Some gathered in clusters, as if indulging in celestial gossip. The ones nearest to the moon were almost obscured, their lights swallowed, heavenly wallflowers.

Movement in the garden caught her eye. Heart pounding, breath caught in her throat, she peered down, then breathed a sigh of relief. Two of Tristan's volunteers paced from the shadows at either side of the garden, and met in the middle of the grass. Both had muskets sloped over their shoulders, and they stood to attention, backs straight, heads held high, their pride in their positions unmistakable. Their presence heartened her.

The men exchanged a brief word, then turned in perfect choreography and marched back the way they'd come until they were swallowed up into the shadows once more.

For a moment, Diana rested her head against the windowpane, relishing the cold glass against her warm forehead. Then she straightened. This would not do. She could not spend the night lollygagging by the window, counting off the seconds before the sentries met in the middle of the lawn again. Not only had she been brought up to believe every moment was precious and wasting time one of the worst things a person could do, but she would be useless when morning came. She'd be tired, irascible, unable to function at a time when she might need to function well, and quickly. But, at the same time, there was no use going back to bed, if all she would do would be to toss and turn and still not sleep.

"I wonder if there is any of that cordial left that we had at dinner," she mused. The drink had been refreshing and satisfying, and the more she thought of it now, the more she craved it. So, tying her wrapper tight and pushing her feet into her slippers, she sneaked from her room and headed to the kitchens. She stayed to the sides of the corridors and stairs, since experience taught that the boards tended to creak less there than in the middle. The moonbeams filtering in through the quarterlight above the front door gave enough light to see her way.

As she walked along the corridor toward the kitchens, a door opened, shedding the amber light of a lamp onto her. Diana jumped and gave a tiny squeal of alarm.

"Miss Wilde," whispered Tristan.

She put her hand to her throat, and felt the flutter of her pulse, too fast, too unsteady. Her breath was shallow and unformed, and a tremble went through her, making her stomach tumble and her legs feel weak.

"I'm sorry," he said. "I didn't mean to startle you."

"No, no," she argued. "It's your home. I am the interloper."

"Never."

His eyes were dark in the shadows, so she could see no hint of his thoughts or feelings within them. The planes of his face seemed sharper, too, all angles and edges. His hair was tousled, as if he'd run his hands through it more than a few times tonight, and he had shed his coat and cravat. His waistcoat was unbuttoned and his shirt open at the neck, displaying a vee of skin. She wondered if the skin under his shirt was as tanned as his face, or was it, like her skin, pale, untouched by the sun?

The thought of the sun touching her skin made her think of other things that had touched it. His fingers. His lips. Her mouth dried and the breath that had been so shallow suddenly refused to come at all. Her heart beat so hard and fast she thought it would jump right out of her chest.

Suddenly, everything seemed sharper. Clearer. She could smell his cologne, along with the lamp oil and the polish coating the furniture. She tasted the nervousness within her, felt the cool night air on her heated face. Within the room a clock sounded, each tick loud and sonorous.

"May I help you with anything?" he asked. His voice was low, with a slight rasp she'd never noticed before. His shirt sleeves were rolled back to his elbows, revealing strong forearms that were as tanned as his long fingers. His gaze drifted from her eyes to her lips, and back again.

He had spoken. She was certain he had spoken. It took her a moment to piece together what he'd said. Oh, yes. He'd asked if he could help her.

"I was just…" She pointed vaguely to the kitchen. "I couldn't sleep. I thought a glass of cordial might help."

Tristan nodded. "Good idea. I need to get a drink for myself. Mind if I come with you?"

He picked up the oil lamp and came out of the room. From the book-lined wall, she assumed it was either a library or a study. The small smudges of ink on his fingers suggested he'd been writing. A study, then.

"You…" The word seemed to catch on the jagged-edged dryness in her throat. She swallowed, then tried again. "You're working late." As if it was her business when he tackled his paperwork. He was likely catching up, having lost time during the day. What with Lord Rotherton's ledgers and his own, training the volunteer militia, keeping the peace until Rotherton returned, and dealing with whatever emergencies cropped up, he had more than enough to do. But today, he'd also spent hours helping Ella and herself. He'd moved them into the vicarage and readied well-appointed rooms for them, no mean feat in a household with few servants. He had then moved his own things into the coachman's quarters where, presumably, he'd also had to prepare the room for his use. No wonder he was working into the night.

"I apologize," she said. She sensed rather than saw him stiffen at her words.

"For what?" he asked. He pushed the kitchen door open and held it for her to go through. "If you apologize, it must be for something." His voice was soft and low, little more than a whisper, though it filled the cavernous kitchen and made the air around her sing, the way it did before a thunderstorm. "If it was for commenting on my work, there's no need. To be working at this hour is unusual, and deserves comment." He grinned. "Truth is, Miss Wilde, I couldn't sleep either. I relied on the ledgers to make me drowsy. As you can see, it didn't work."

"I was apologizing because you were working so late," she answered. Her blush burned her cheeks. She hoped he couldn't see their high color. "We have put you out dreadfully."

"Not at all."

"How can you say so? We took up your time in the working day—"

"I willingly gave it."

"You had work to do, and we took you from it…"

He shook his head, a small smile playing on his shadowed face. "I would willingly stop whatever else I was doing to come to your aid." His gaze lingered on her lips. They tingled under his attention. Her own gaze softened, relaxing her jaw. Her breaths were in that strange place, neither one thing or another, too fast, yet too slow, heavy and deep, yet shallow, too. Her lips parted, slightly. The tip of her tongue darted out, licking at them, barely moistening them.

Tristan stared at them as if they had hypnotized him. He swallowed. His Adam's apple moved up and down in his throat. His eyes were totally focused on her.

She swallowed also. Her breasts rose and fell, stroking against the thin cotton of her night rail, chafing against it. The place between her legs was suddenly hot and heavy, wet and aching with need. Every nerve reached out, touching the surface of her skin. It felt like a thousand sparkles flowed through her, searching for release. She shivered.

"You're cold," he whispered. She opened her mouth to deny it, but his arms came around her, warm and strong and firm, and she said nothing. She could not. His touch, innocent and protective, had robbed her of the power of speech. All she could do was lean into him, let him hold her against himself. His shirt was soft against her cheek, the cotton warm with the heat of him. Below his solid chest, his heartbeat was fast, growing faster. She smelled the starch and soap embedded in his shirt fibers, and that indefinable scent that was only him. The kitchen fire was banked, just a few embers glowing red amidst the black coal and grey ash. Nearby, the metal of the oven clicked as it cooled and settled. A sink for washing glasses sat beneath the window, its wooden basin creaking rhythmically. An unlit candle sat in the middle of a huge table that had seen quite a few years of use, if the scars and pits on its surface were anything to go by.

Gently, making no noise at all, Tristan set his lamp on the table, and his second arm came around her, to hold her even tighter, even closer. She looked up at him at the very instant he looked down. They were so close, she could see the individual whiskers on his chin, the flicker of his pulse, the slight movement of his Adam's apple. His eyes were shadowed, but she knew instinctively that they watched her, intently.

He swallowed. His lips pressed together for a moment. He leaned closer. Slowly, she closed her eyes and tilted her head, offering herself to him.

The first kiss was gentle. His lips were warm, cushioning hers. It felt sweet, cherishing. Safe. Diana did not want safe. Not here. Not now. Not with him.

She parted her own lips, just a little, in invitation. It was enough. The tip of his tongue touched the inside of her mouth, a soft caress she felt all the way to her toes. She opened wider. His tongue entered fully, touched hers, withdrew, touched again, a little more.

Diana groaned. She couldn't help it. Could not have stopped it to save her life. Her breasts ached with heavy need. Tiny flames danced on skin that was too tight, too…containing. Her pulse beat an unsteady tattoo.

She pressed closer, wanting the feel of him. His arousal was hard against her stomach, and a feeling of triumph again surged through her that she'd done that to him. Her legs trembled, and the place between them grew hot. Hot, and wet, and needing…she could not say what. She didn't have the words.

He deepened the kiss, and his hand cupped her breast, his fingertips brushing the tip of her nipple. She gasped at the sensation and arched her back, pushing herself into his palm, encouraging his fingers, wanting them to stroke, to press, to feel. He rolled the nipple gently between his finger and his thumb. It grew, stood up, seeking more. She whimpered. He pressed harder.

His lips left hers, and nipped and feathered along her jaw to her ear. His teeth grazed her earlobe and sense flew from her. She no longer knew, nor cared, where they were. Nothing else existed. Just him and his clever mouth, and the torment of it, while his hands did indescribable, beautiful things to her body.

And then, he pulled back. Pulled away. Not sharply, not in confusion and shame because somebody was coming. He pulled back slowly, reluctantly. Because he felt he must.

Diana did not agree. She wrapped her arms around him, holding him to her, and kissed his jawline. It was warm and firm, the new beard growth against her lips a surprising mix of rough and smooth, hard and soft. She felt it on her skin, a beautiful sharp scratching, satisfying, yet leaving her wanting more.

Tristan groaned. It was no more than a whisper. "Diana," he murmured. "We cannot—"

"Don't stop," she answered, and she kissed him again. His skin tasted of the night air, mixed with that musky maleness that was him alone.

"I cannot do this to you—"

"Don't. Stop." It was not a plea. It was a command.

"You don't know what you are asking." His voice was strained, as if it was an effort to speak.

"Show me."

"Diana—"

"Show me. Please." She pushed her fingers into his hair, the silky strands cool to the touch.

"We're in the kitchen. Anyone might…" he stuttered, as if he had trouble forming a sentence. Which was good, because she could barely articulate, either.

"I want…" Diana could not say what she wanted. She could only show him. She wrapped her fingers into his hair and held on, as if her life depended on it, kissing and nipping at his skin, and pressing her aching breasts against his chest, seeking relief in the feel of him.

"So do I," he whispered. "But not here…not…"

Without conscious thought to guide them, her next words said exactly what she wanted. "Take me to bed, Tristan."

He stilled. His hands stopped caressing her, his lips stopped their exquisite torture of her ear and jaw. For a moment, she wondered if she'd gone too far, asked too much.

She'd been honest. No games. No coy pretense. It was what she wanted, and she'd asked for it. Was that so wrong? Did he now think her a wanton? A hussy? Would he turn away?

Tristan pulled back, just a little. Not enough to dislodge her fingers from his hair. Enough that he could study her with his shadowed eyes. She could not tell what he was thinking.

"Do you know what you ask?"

Diana bit her bottom lip. Did she know what she asked? She thought she did. She knew a little about the mechanics of the act, and she knew it could be pleasurable. She had learned that from listening to the wives of Papa's associates. She knew, too, that once it was done, it could never be undone. A woman, once touched in that way, was marked by it for life.

More than all of that, though, she knew this was something she needed. Something as necessary to her as breathing. Something she had to have, or she would…well, she wouldn't die, that was a tad dramatic. Even in the intensity of the moment, she knew that. She would not die.

But she felt as if she might.

"I know," she answered him.

There was a strange look about him, as if he fought a war within himself. A war he was losing.

"What you ask…" He swallowed. This was costing him. She could tell that from the tension of his muscles, the firmness of his jaw, his quick, short breaths. For a brief, horrible moment, she thought he would reject her.

Perhaps she would die, after all.

"What you ask," he repeated, "there's no going back. If I take you to bed…"

She nodded. "I know."

"Are you certain?" He swallowed again. "I will understand if…you don't have to do this."

"I want to." Indeed, she had never wanted anything so much in her life.

He watched her for a moment more, then lifted her into his arms and carried her from the kitchen.

Chapter Nineteen

Tristan carried Diana through the hall and up the stairs. She was light in his arms, much lighter than he would expect a grown woman to be. Her arms were around him, her fingers playing with the hair at his neck. He'd never thought of that as an erogenous zone before, but her touch, the way her fingertips grazed his skin, the gentle movement of his hair that made his scalp shiver...she was likely to drive him mad.

He should go. Set her down, tell her goodnight and beat a hasty retreat before anything disastrous happened. Anything *more* disastrous. He'd already gone further than a gentleman should, and fallen over the edge of respectability. Now, he stared into the abyss of complete and utter ruin. If he jumped, there would be no climbing back.

Then again, did he want to climb back? Did he want to walk away from this beautiful, wonderful woman, deny himself the pleasure of being with her, of claiming her for himself, once and for all? The answer to that was a most emphatic no.

He'd asked her to marry him. In all honor and honesty, he'd laid out his stall, told her what marriage to him would mean, what he could—and more importantly, could *not*—provide. Was this her answer?

It had to be. For once they had done this, once he'd made her fully his, there would be no other choice. He would marry her. She had to know that.

He'd been prepared to walk away. Still would, if she demanded it, though it might well kill him to do so. If she changed her mind, he'd let her go. And spend the rest of the night soaking in the stone cold waters of the horse trough.

God, he hoped she didn't change her mind.

They reached her bedchamber. He hesitated. Diana did not. She reached down and turned the handle, opening the door. Tristan stepped inside, pushing the door closed behind him.

He tried to move slowly across the dark room. Despite his every effort, his boot heels were inordinately loud on the bare wood floor. With every step, he thought they would be caught—either Cassie or Ella, or both, would investigate the noise coming from Diana's room. That nobody else within the house seemed to stir was a great relief to him.

At the bed, he lowered her to the mattress, so softly and carefully she might have been made of Dresden china. He sat beside her, his weight making the mattress dip, so that she leaned toward him a little, then wrapped his arms around her, and kissed her again. She tasted of tea and the sugary biscuits Cassie had served after dinner, together with her own mint toothpowder. The lavender scent of her filled the air.

Without breaking the kiss, he caressed her. His hand found her breast once again, and cupped its generous roundness through the thin cotton of her night rail. Her nipple pebbled, and she gave the tiniest whimper, pushing closer, begging him to touch her more.

Tristan was happy to oblige. Still kneading her breast, he used his other hand to pull at the drawstring tie at her neckline. The modest, sensible nightgown slipped from her shoulders and he pushed it down, exposing her throat, her arms, and finally, her breasts.

They were perfect. So perfect. For a long moment, all he could do was stare at them. They were full and beautifully shaped, their dark areola begging for his touch. He stroked his hand softly across the tips. She shivered and arched her back, granting him fuller access. His breeches tightened, his thighs hardened, and his stomach swooped even as his heart sped up until it seemed like one continuous beat.

He kissed her again. His tongue dipped into her mouth and danced with hers. She wrapped her arms around his shoulders, pushing herself closer, her breasts deeper, harder into his hands.

When he broke the kiss, she mewled her displeasure. Triumph surged through him. The mewl became a sigh as he feathered kisses over her jaw, nipped her neck, the soft space between throat and shoulder. His whiskers rasped against her smooth skin, and he tried to go slower, but it wouldn't matter. Her skin was so soft, his beard stubble was bound to mark her, if only for a few hours.

She ran her hands over his back, his shoulders, his hair. Every sweep heightened his desire. His breaths were short and sharp, his nerves so close to his skin that her touch threatened to shatter him, to break him into a thousand pieces he would never put together again.

His lips closed over her nipple. She gasped. He drew it further into his mouth, rolling it over his tongue, savoring the taste of it, the feel of it. She clutched at his hair, holding him there. He smiled against her skin.

Inch by agonizing inch, he moved her back until she lay on the bed, him beside her. Even fully clothed as he was, he felt her searing him, branding him.

Her breaths were shallow, ragged. He pushed the night rail down farther, his lips following it, kissing her ribs, her stomach, her belly. She moaned, her body writhing under his touch.

"I want to see you," she whispered. "I want…"

Tristan did not need telling twice. He sat up, pulled off his shirt and tossed it to the floor, then toed off his boots. His breeches and small clothes followed them, until he stood before her, naked. Diana looked at him, really looked at him, as if she was committing every inch of him to memory. Her gaze made him harder, more tense, more…everything. He was on fire, and she hadn't touched him yet. He didn't know how much more he could take.

****

Diana had never felt like this. Her heart beat so fast she thought it would burst, and every nerve within her tautened. Flames licked at her skin as his kisses pushed her nearer to insanity. Her limbs moved of their own volition, restless and wanting—she didn't know what. Between her legs was hot and wet, aching deliciously. She wanted to squirm and tense. She wanted to lie relaxed and still. She wanted him to touch her *there*. She wanted to touch *him*.

When he took off his shirt, she'd simply stared at him. Dressed, he looked strong and firm, with broad shoulders, wide chest, flat stomach and narrow waist. But without his clothes he was…magnificent. Those shoulders were sculpted to rival the statues she'd seen in Greece—muscular, smooth, strong. His chest held a smattering of dark hair that spread from just below his throat, around his flat nipples, then down, narrowing to a thin line over his stomach.

He removed his breeches and she bit her bottom lip, half in wonder, half in trepidation. She knew what was supposed to happen between a man and a woman, knew what she wanted to happen. But he was so big! Surely her body could never accommodate *that*! Because, unlike his shoulders, that part of him was *nothing* like the Greek statues.

Feeling more than a little discommoded, she moved her gaze and stared instead at his thighs. That felt no safer. His legs were well shaped, muscles honed, the short, dark hair that covered them somehow accentuating his masculinity. He lay down beside her again, his mouth on her mouth, hot and heavy and heavenly. His hands touched her breasts, her stomach, her belly, and his lips followed them.

He touched her ankle, his fingers circling it, caressing it, sending a jolt of electricity through her. She wanted him to let go. To stay there forever. Her hips writhed, and the hot wetness between her legs increased.

His hand moved slowly up from her ankle. He pushed up the hem of her night rail and stroked her calf. Her skin tingled. He caressed the back of her knee. She jumped. He grinned against her skin and moved his fingers over her knee again. Diana groaned. It was torture. Terrible, wonderful torture. Her hips bucked. She couldn't breathe.

Tristan stroked his way up the length of her thigh. The cotton of her night rail whispered against her skin, making her want...more. Her legs trembled. Goosebumps made every hair stand to attention.

And then, he reached her center. He touched her there, maddeningly gentle. His fingers stroked her, and her legs parted, inviting him in. He touched the nub of nerves at her opening, bringing her higher, higher. Her hips bucked and her legs shook, and her back arched as she tried to offer herself to him and escape him, all at the same moment.

Something built within her. She could feel it growing. She panted, hardly able to catch her breath. Without stopping the movement of his clever fingers, Tristan moved back up and kissed her mouth.

She bucked and writhed and screamed into his kiss as the dam broke, and feelings she had never known flooded through her. Her body moved on its own, her breathing labored. She saw stars. One final thrust into his hand, and she fell over the cliff edge.

He gathered her in his arms. His kisses now were gentler, more chaste. The male part of him pressed into her thigh, and he moved slightly, as if he tried to hide it from her.

"You haven't..." she whispered, and she reached down to touch him. He jumped, and his breath hissed, and he pulled away from her. "Did I hurt you?"

"No, darling," he whispered. "But if you touch me, this will be over before it has even started."

Diana nodded, though she wasn't entirely sure she understood. "What do I do now?"

"I will show you. If you're sure. We can...we can stop." The look on his face begged her not to stop, but, she made no doubt, if she said so, he would. "At present," he murmured, "you are still a maiden. I am..." he swallowed, hard, "gentleman enough..."

"No." She put her finger to his lips to silence him. "Don't stop."

His smile was relieved. "You are certain?"

She nodded. "Make love to me, Tristan."

"Yes, ma'am."

His hand travelled back over her again, stroking her skin, stoking the fire within her. This time, Diana tried to touch him, to give him the same pleasure he was giving her. She smoothed her hands over his shoulders and arms, felt the play of his muscles, before stroking her fingertips across the wide plane of his chest, his muscles hard under his warm skin. She reached his nipples and played with them as he had hers. He gasped. His nipple grew, as if it sought her touch, and she rubbed it softly between finger and thumb.

Tristan groaned. Then, so did Diana as she felt his finger move across her most private place, stroking her there, before his finger slipped inside. Her heart beat painfully against her ribs now, and her breaths came out in rasps. She moaned again.

He withdrew his finger, then pushed into her again. She felt his hand inside her, gently stretching her, readying her. The sensation of rising above the earth grew within her once more. She soared again, then shattered.

Tristan covered her body with his, his manhood at her seam, nudging at her. Her legs parted, allowing him closer. He rested the top half of his body on his elbows, keeping his weight off her as slowly, slowly, he pushed himself into her.

There was a sharp, burning pain. She cried out and he stopped. He held her close, whispering in her ear, "I'm sorry. It will pass. It's just the first time. I'm sorry."

She swallowed, and nodded.

For a long time they stayed still, holding one another. The pain subsided, and she relaxed.

When she was ready, he pushed in. Withdrew. Pushed in again, a little farther, a little harder, slowly at first, then faster, faster. The feelings rose within her again. This time, when she tumbled, so did he.

****

Diana woke as the dawn light showed grey through the window. Outside, the first birds sang, and a soft breeze swished the leaves of the trees at the edge of the garden. In the house, there was no sound at all. It took a moment to remember that Tristan and Cassie lived frugally, employing one live-in manservant, and a cook who came in daily from the village.

Thinking of Tristan brought back last night and she turned from the window to the side of the bed where he had slept.

It was empty. The sheets were cold, indicating he'd left some time ago, though the pillow still held the indentation where he'd lain his head. His clothes were gone, too, of course. Except for that pillow, and the slight soreness between her legs, there was no sign he'd ever been here.

But he had. He'd been here, and he'd given her the most wonderful experience of her life. She could still feel his hands on her, the warmth of his body next to hers, the fullness of him inside her. The pillow smelled of him— bergamot, and sandalwood, and him. She licked her lips and tasted his kiss. For a moment, all was wonderful.

Her eyes widened as the ramifications fully hit her. They had made love. Or, at least, they'd had sex. She wasn't entirely sure it counted as love. Even though he'd asked her to marry him, he'd never actually professed any finer feelings for her. She hoped, of course. But hope was all she had.

Then again, why else would he ask a woman to marry him when he believed her to be impoverished, possessing no dowry to save him and his estate?

The answer came to her in a flash of inspiration. Because his circumstances were so dire, his pockets so empty and his estate so meager, Tristan's choices were limited. A baron was the lowest ranking member of the nobility. Any father with the funds Tristan needed to set things to rights would be angling after an earl, at the least. Yet most women, on becoming a baroness, would expect a standard of living that included maids and a line of credit he could not afford.

But Tristan must marry. He must have an heir to his title, even if the title was all the poor little boy would ever inherit.

Was that why he'd asked Diana to marry him? Because he thought she was not accustomed to the trappings of wealth, and happy to settle for a make-do-and-mend lifestyle?

At least he wasn't pursuing her for her money, she thought with a wry grin. That grin faded as she decided that being pursued for practicality was no better. If the man did not love her, the marriage was doomed. Especially since she knew, without a shadow of a doubt, that she loved him. Sooner or later, that meant he would break her heart. Diana would rather remain a spinster than be hurt like that.

A spinster, but no longer a maid. Last night, she had gifted Tristan Leonard with her virginity. Made free with that which, according to everything she'd ever been told, should only be given to her husband.

She didn't blame Tristan. He hadn't seduced her. If anything, she seduced him. And she'd wanted all that happened. He'd offered her every opportunity to change her mind, to stop before it was too late. She hadn't wanted to stop. Even now, in the cold light of dawn, she felt no regret.

No regret, perhaps. But that did not mean there was no cause for worry, for the reckless acts she did not regret might very well have consequences. Tristan had spilled his seed inside her. She might, even now, be carrying his child. And while she did not object to becoming a mother, *per se*, having it happen now, at this time, was…complicated.

Diana had always assumed that, one day, she'd be a mother. Until now, though, the concept of her baby was very much an abstract one. In her imagination, she'd held a child in her arms, but she'd never seen its face, nor the face of its father. There'd been a shadow in the background of the picture, a mysterious gentleman smiling anonymously at her.

Now, though, she saw him clearly. And she saw the children: a boy with his father's face and mischievous smile. A girl with her blonde curls and his brown eyes.

Oh, Lord! The fond smile slipped as reality seeped in. She might, even now, be with child! Increasing, and unmarried. Ruined.

"It's worse than that," she whispered at the growing fingers of light coming through the window. Ruined, she could handle. Once the threat to her was lifted, it would be easy to slip away, have the babe and return to England as a "widow." It wasn't the threat of ruination that bothered her.

It was Tristan.

Tristan, who had asked her to marry him. In the most gentlemanlike manner, with honesty and respect…and absolutely no emotion that she could discern.

He would expect her to accept that offer now. And she would. If she could. If she could convince herself that he had feelings for her, feelings that went beyond mere lust, then she'd jump at the chance to be his wife.

But...before she could accept his offer, she needed to tell him the truth. Who she was, what she was. And why she was here, in Rotherton.

Would knowing those things change his mind?

Diana knew he would not be put off by knowing why she'd come here in the first place. Tristan was no coward. He would not run from the likes of the Hicks brothers, nor even the menacing power of Milton Percival. If anything, he would draw nearer, wanting to protect her. He would do all he could to stop them, even to the point of putting his own life on the line.

Which was the last thing Diana wanted him to do.

Not that he would listen to her. He would do what he felt he had to do, and sweep away her objections. Papa had been the same. And look where it had got him. A lump filled her throat as she thought of her father and all he'd tried to do to protect her. Protections she had circumvented in her determination to get her own way, until...

Fremont said it was not her fault. That Percival and his bullies would have killed Papa anyway. Perhaps he was right. It didn't make her feel better. They'd killed him that day because they saw her. And that, to her mind, made her responsible.

She did not want to be responsible for the death of Tristan Leonard, too.

That was, however, only one of the secrets she carried. Tristan had proposed to Diana Wilde, impoverished spinster. That was the woman he had chosen. The woman he'd offered for. The woman he'd bedded. How would he feel to know his choice was not what he had believed?

Many men would be thrilled to find themselves betrothed to Diana Villiers, heiress. They would be in alt to know how wealthy she was. But Tristan...

He would be hurt. Humiliated. He would think himself a kept man.

She had to tell him. As soon as she possibly could.

Of course, the ideal time to tell him would have been before he'd bedded her, for now he might feel duty bound to keep his offer open. In which case, it would be up to her to save them both from a lifetime of misery.

Diana would tell him everything. She would watch him closely and try to gauge his reaction. If she saw anything that made her think he regretted his offer, she would refuse him, and release him.

Even if it broke her heart.

She'd spent more than an hour deliberating. Noises downstairs told her the cook had arrived. She could smell gammon cooking, and fresh bread, and her stomach rumbled. Quickly, she washed her face and hands, dressed herself, and tidied her hair into a neat chignon, then headed down to what she hoped would be a hearty breakfast.

Almost at the bottom of the stairs, she heard the raised voices. The cook cried something that sounded like, "Mercy on all of us," and someone, she thought it might be Mr. Fielding, said he was certain it would be all right. Others added words she did not catch, and Tristan and Ella appealed for calm.

Alarmed, she pushed open the kitchen door and

found a scene of chaos and panic. The cook stood at the stove, spatula in hand, although she seemed to have forgotten the gammon, which was now burning in the pan. Ella took the pan and dragged it from the heat, which probably saved the house from burning down. Tristan stood beside the table, flanked by Mr. Fielding, Mr. Corby, the local builder, and several members of the volunteer militia. A group of men faced them, their expressions a mixture of anger, fear and distress. Diana did not recognize all of them, but she knew Mr. Bell and Mr. Potter, as well as the apothecary and one or two of the others.

"What's happening?" she asked.

"We're to be murdered in our beds!" cried the cook.

"Of course we aren't!" Angrily, Ella snatched the spatula from her. For one awful moment, Diana thought she would strike the woman with it. Instead, she threw it onto the table, where it clattered against the crockery the cook had laid out ready to serve breakfast on.

"We're ready to fight," said Sergeant Busby, who stood near Tristan, one hand on the butt of the pistol tucked at his waist.

"You might be," said Mr. Potter. "I am not. I'm no fighter. And I don't want my wife and daughter put in danger, just to save him!" He gestured at Tristan. A murmur of agreement went through the group.

Diana felt the blood drain from her face. *To save Tristan? What on earth did he mean?*

"If I thought it would help any of you," said Tristan, his voice calm and in control, "I would go now and offer myself. But you must know that would not be the end of it."

"On the contrary," said Mr. Fielding, "it would only

be the beginning."

Diana swallowed, though her mouth was dry. "What has happened?" The words were squeezed out, reluctant.

Mr. Potter turned to her. His face was pale and unshaven, as if he'd left home in a great hurry, and she saw fear in his eyes.

"His militia," he said, "has stirred up a veritable hornet's nest. I knew there'd be consequences. As soon as I heard what they'd done, I said there'd be consequences."

"He showed they can be beaten," argued Mr. Corby. "We can do it again."

"He had the element of surprise. We no longer have that. Those men are killers." The men behind Mr. Potter nodded agreement.

"It's you they want," said Mr. Bell.

"This time," said Mr. Corby.

"Somebody tell me! What is happening?"

As one, everybody turned to Diana. All faces were grim. For a few seconds, nobody spoke.

Then Ella said, "It's the man from London. The one who's leading the smuggling gang."

"Hicks," supplied one of the men, and Diana's blood ran cold. "Mickey Hicks," he continued. "Nasty piece of work. He wants the militia disbanded and Lord Leonard here delivered to him. He's given us till six o'clock on Saturday. Then he's going to burn Rotherton and kill every man, woman and child in the place."

Chapter Twenty

Tristan had known there would be consequences for what he and his volunteers had done at the Golden Goose. He had impressed that onto each man who joined him, warned them the gang might—would—seek revenge, and they should be vigilant. Men who would terrorize ordinary people to enrich themselves would not want to give up that lucrative and easy method of income, not if they could help it. They certainly wouldn't want Rotherton's stand to set a precedent, encouraging other villages to rebel as well.

His mistake had been assuming that the gang would come after him and his men, and would leave alone people who hadn't been involved. He should have known better.

Now, the people of Rotherton were afraid for themselves and their families. With good cause. And they blamed him.

His militia volunteers had stayed in post, willing to continue the fight. If they'd deserted him today, he made no doubt, he would already be trussed up like a side of pork, being led to his fate. No amount of reasoning would have prevented his neighbors from taking him to their tormentors.

He was grateful too, for the other men who stood at his side, Fielding, and Corby. As a clergyman, Fielding had the perfect excuse to remain apart, refusing to involve himself in the fray. Of course, the smugglers had involved him, inasmuch as the note bearing the demand had been tied around a rock and hurled through the window of St Bartholomew's Church, which Fielding led. Even so, he could have simply passed the message and retreated to the relative safety of the Curate's Cottage in nearby Crompton Hadlow. Many a cleric would have done just that.

As for Corby—Tristan didn't really know the man. Tristan hadn't exchanged more than a dozen words with the builder in his life before today. Yet here he was, at Tristan's side, fending off his neighbors and doing what he could to help.

The mood of those neighbors was ugly, and growing uglier by the second. At any moment it could turn physical. People could get hurt, although he'd do all he could to make sure it didn't come to that. His biggest fear, should things become violent, was that there were three women in the line of fire: The almost hysterical cook, Ella, and Diana.

Of the three, Diana was in the most danger. Ella and the cook were by the stove, with several militia men between them and the villagers. And if that line of protection didn't hold, they were near enough to the pantry to run inside it and barricade themselves in. But Diana...

Diana was between the two groups. Directly in the battle zone. He glanced at her, willing her to retreat, to get out of the way.

Of course, she didn't. She looked from one group of men to the other, listening as they argued. Her forehead creased and her eyes narrowed, and her lips pressed into a thin line.

After a moment, she nodded, as if she had debated with herself, and come to a conclusion she was in complete agreement over. She looked up and their gazes met. The resolution in her beautiful blue eyes unnerved him. What did she plan to do? He prayed it was nothing reckless.

She mouthed something, but he couldn't hear what she said over the raised voices all around him. Menace filled the air, stifling the kitchen. The press of people seemed to force out the light, so that much of the room was in shadow, many of the men little more than rowdy silhouettes.

Whatever she'd said, she said it again, more forcefully. Then she turned to the men who faced him and shouted, "Gentlemen! Please!" Her voice was stronger than he had thought, the voice of someone used to giving orders and having them obeyed. There was a confidence, a resoluteness about her that made everybody take notice. Her back straightened and she seemed to grow two inches taller, her chin defiantly raised, cheeks pink, eyes glittering with determination.

"Gentlemen," she called out again. The noise faltered and died as, one by one, the men stopped arguing and turned to face her.

"I have just one thing to remind you of, gentlemen," she said, once the room was still. Her voice was soft, yet it carried, as strong and clear as any orator he'd ever heard. "One word," she continued. "A word you may have heard in your history lessons. A word you'd do well to reflect upon now." She paused and swept her gaze across their faces. "That word is Danegeld."

Behind Tristan, Ella said, "Exactly." Corby and Fielding nodded agreement. Mr. Potter frowned, thoughtful, and Mr. Bell looked ashamed. The apothecary seemed to squirm. Other men looked at one another, some guiltily, others perplexed.

Then, one man, a laborer by his dress, asked, "What's Day geld?"

Tristan was unsurprised that he didn't know. Men of his status might have received basic instruction in reading and writing, but they would not have spent time on lessons like history.

Diana explained. "Danegeld. When the Saxons ruled England, they were plagued by raids from the Danes. Ships full of warriors would come, kill the people, burn the towns, and carry off slaves and livestock. Some towns paid them to go away and leave them in peace. The money handed over was called Danegeld.

"But..." She held up her hand to stop the murmur. "The trouble with Danegeld is, you have to keep paying it. The marauders came back for more. You paid again, or you suffered."

"What's that got to do with this?" asked the laborer.

Mr. Bell turned to look at him, and at the others around him. "We'll be paying, just like Danegeld," he said. "If we give in to the gang's demands, they'll come back for more. And next time, Lord Leonard and his men won't be here to help." He crossed and stood next to Jonathan Corby.

"You give in to bullies once," said the apothecary, "you give in for life."

Others agreed. One by one, they moved from the group, until there were only three men left, their faces dismayed as they realized they'd lost.

Tristan began to breathe more easily. He'd been

truthful when he said he would hand himself over if that would solve the problem, but he'd be damned if he'd die for no reason.

Now they knew the risks, and that trouble was imminent, perhaps more of these men would join his volunteers. In two days, he couldn't train them to army standard, but he could teach them some basic skills.

And right now, he needed every man he could get.

"They'll burn our houses," argued one of the three remaining men.

"We'll rebuild them," answered Corby.

"They'll kill our families," said Mr. Potter. "With the best will in the world, Leonard, you cannot guard every corner of the village. You don't have the manpower."

That unnerved some of the others. They looked at Tristan, uncertain. He opened his mouth to counter Potter's argument, though he had no idea what he would say. Diana bit her lip, anxiously. He wanted to assure her all would be well, that he'd protect her. He needed to take her in his arms and hold her close.

Good God, man, get your priorities in order!

"We don't have to guard every corner of the village," said Mr. Fielding. Everyone turned to him, so he went on. "We know when they're coming. They've been kind enough to warn us in advance. I say we make use of that. Two hours beforehand, every man, woman and child should gather at St. Bartholomew's. It's a sturdy building, designed to withstand the attacks of the world. The women and children, and the elderly and the infirm can take refuge inside, while we defend it. Far easier to do that than to try and save individual houses. As Mr. Corby said, we can rebuild our homes. We cannot rebuild people."

The last resistance crumbled as the three remaining men agreed to the plan. Ella announced that the ladies could help with preparations. They would collect for children, sick people and any injured men, plus cushions, because the church pews were hard enough to sit on for one hour on Sundays, and nobody could tolerate them for as long as the fight might take. On a more serious note, she asked the apothecary to collect together medicines, tinctures and salves.

As each man was assigned a task, he hurried away, until the only people left were Ella and Diana, Tristan, Busby, and the cook.

"I'm glad that's over," said the cook, slumping onto the table, dramatically. "I thought they was going to murder us all in our beds."

Ella rolled her eyes. "We should see what we've got to make bandages with," she said. "Come, Diana."

Tristan watched them go. For a moment, he wished he could follow. He wanted to talk to Diana, hold her, reassure her that all would be well, even though he could not say such things with any certainty. He and his men would do their best, of course, but there were so many things against them. They only had twenty muskets. They would be given to the men who shot best, and hopefully they'd be of use. But each musket held only one ball at a time. An elite Rifleman in the army could load, shoot, and reload his musket three times a minute. The men under Tristan's command were not elite Riflemen. He didn't think most of them could load, shoot, and reload more than one round every three minutes.

They were farmers and laborers. Eager and willing,

yes, but they'd be facing seasoned fighters. Possibly even killers.

"I don't suppose we can rely on Captain Allenby's men to come to our aid," muttered Busby, keeping his voice quiet so he didn't frighten the cook again.

Tristan shook his head, then led Busby to his study, where they could be more private. "No, we can't rely on them," he said, once they were there. "Allenby's too busy chasing fugitives to help us." He thought for a moment. "I want you to take our best shots and practice increasing their speed and accuracy. Tell Smith to put the other men through their paces. We have two days to turn them into soldiers."

****

Ella, Cassie, and Diana spent the next few hours searching the vicarage for anything that might be useful in a field hospital. They'd found a quantity of willow bark, which could be brewed into a pain-reducing tea, plus some wych elm powder, labeled a "superior substitute for laudanum," and a box of ground yarrow leaves, which could be made into a poultice. They instructed Ella's servants to carry barrels into the church and fill them with water, and found blankets, pillows, and cushions to be taken there, as well.

Now, they were looking for material from which they might make bandages. They'd used a couple of the more threadbare sheets but knew they might need more.

"We may have multiple injuries on our hands, once the battle commences," Ella said. "These villains are a nasty lot."

Diana agreed. The smugglers would aim to kill or maim as many people as possible. Men, women, even children would be in their sights. A few strips of sheeting would never do.

What she did *not* agree to was the plan Ella and Cassie came up with next. Ella decided she had a home full of sheets and bath sheets, and more cotton petticoats than she could wear in a lifetime. These, she said, would give an ample supply of bandages.

In itself, the plan wasn't too bad. They could, Diana thought, send men who would bring the things here. However, Ella did not propose to send men. She and Cassie decided they would go themselves.

"The men are too busy preparing for their roles," said Ella.

" Ella's right," said Cassie. "Perhaps a couple could be spared to accompany us, but I doubt we could take more than that. They're needed here."

"Besides, they wouldn't know which things to bring. Only I can decide that." Ella nodded, agreeing with herself. "And while we're gone, Diana, you can see what else we can use from the pantry."

Diana was not fooled. What Ella meant was, Diana could not accompany them on their dash to Amberley. Diana knew she was the target of the attacks they'd suffered, and it was safer and more sensible for her to remain within the vicarage. Even so, it rankled that she'd been rendered useless at a time when everyone must play their part. In just two days, the men of Rotherton, led by Tristan, would fight, and the women of the village would tend their wounds, if necessary. Meanwhile, she...

She could fight. Not hand-to-hand combat, of course, and not firing muskets. But she did have some skills.

"Can you bring your bows and some arrows when you return?" she asked.

"My bows and arrows?" Ella was taken aback, but Cassie clapped her hands, pleased.

"Capital idea, Miss Wilde," she announced. "Are you a good shot? Tristan always tells everyone I'm as good as he is."

"I can shoot tolerably well," nodded Diana. "I usually hit my target."

"There's a world of difference between hitting the gold and aiming at a man," warned Ella.

"A man who will kill us, or worse, if he's not stopped," countered Diana. "If I keep that in mind, it will be easy to hit him, if only in the arm or leg. Enough to stop him in his tracks."

"Bows and arrows it is," said Ella, though she still seemed skeptical.

Three hours later, Ella and Cassie returned, but things were unexpectedly different. Whereas they'd had two footmen to escort them to Amberley, they now had four. Diana stood at the kitchen door and watched their approach with surprise. She'd thought all of Ella's footmen, and most of her gardeners, had decamped to the vicarage already.

Ella and Cassie alighted, and the original two footmen took the cart to the stables while the other two escorted the ladies inside. As they came nearer, Diana saw they were not of the usual standard expected in Ella's household. Their uniforms were ill fitting, and they were unkempt. Both could do with a shave. They looked around, furtively, before entering the kitchen.

"Where's the cook?" whispered Ella, urgently.

"She's gone home for the day."

"She makes the day's meals, and then she leaves," explained Cassie.

"Good." Ella's smile was relieved. "Her cooking is good, but she's the biggest gossip in Sussex. And we do not want gossip at this juncture."

"We don't?" Diana castigated herself for the stupid question. Of course they didn't want gossip. Who ever did? But what made "this juncture" more gossip averse than any other time?

"Is Tristan in his study?" asked Cassie, her voice, like Ella's, pitched low. Secretive.

Diana shrugged. She was now completely confused. "I believe so," she answered. "Why?"

"Miss Forbes-Smythe," said one of the footmen. "I don't think—"

"It'll be all right, John. Lord Leonard's a fair man. And I shall speak up for you. Not only that, but when he hears what you have to say, he'll see you as a good man, and act accordingly."

"I vouch for my brother," said Cassie. "He will listen."

John exchanged looks with the second ill-dressed footman. Both men nodded agreement and followed Ella into the main body of the house.

Intrigued, and a little bewildered, Diana followed.

They marched to the study, where Ella gave a sharp rap on the door with her knuckles. The call to enter had barely been made when she thrust open the door and led them inside.

Tristan looked up and let his gaze roam across the group, resting on each person for a moment. Not by so much as a flicker of an eye did he give away his thoughts. Apart from inviting the ladies to sit, he said nothing, either. Meanwhile, Diana could feel her nerves unravelling. She had no idea what was going on, and she could not be blamed for anything that had happened, but that didn't stop her feeling guilty.

Ella sat in a chair facing Tristan, her back ramrod straight, hands in her lap. She looked relaxed, though Diana knew enough of her by now to see the tension in the way she pressed her lips together, and the way she raised her chin, as if ready for the fight.

Cassie sat on one side of her. Her hands were clutched together in her lap, and her shoulders were raised. The two footmen were also clearly tense, and nervous.

Who were they? Whoever they were, they trusted Ella, though they were wary of Tristan and clearly unhappy to meet with him. Which must mean whatever they had to say to him was of vital importance and he was not going to like it.

A moment later, that was confirmed, when Ella said, "Lord Leonard, allow me to make known to you, Sebastian Thomas of Newhaven, and John Carter, a tenant on the Hadlow estate."

Chapter Twenty-One

Tristan was astounded. He'd recognized Carter the minute he entered, of course, but he couldn't believe the man would come here. He had to know Tristan was acting as the area's magistrate. And why the hell was he in Ella's livery?

"I promised them you would hear them and treat them fairly," Ella said.

He wanted to rail at the blasted woman. At all three of the wretched minxes. What did they think they were about? These were wanted men. Not only were they almost certainly guilty of smuggling, but they'd compounded their guilt by escaping from the jail. Anyone might hand them in for a hefty reward. They could be shot on sight and no questions asked. And a person caught harboring them...this was a serious matter.

Not only that, but how had they come to be here in the first place?

Had they sought Ella out? Ella was known to be sympathetic to their plight. She'd advocated for them and supported Carter's mother. But to get to Ella at the vicarage, they must have run the gauntlet of the men guarding the house. He didn't believe they could have done that.

They were wearing Ella's livery. All of which, taken together, meant...

"You've been to Amberley?" He tried to keep the anger from his voice. It wouldn't do to lose his temper before he had all the facts.

"A fleeting trip. We needed some things." Ella waved a dismissive hand.

"A foolhardy trip," he argued. "Miss Wilde's attackers are determined. The road to Amberley, though short, would have provided ample opportunity for them to try again."

"Diana didn't come," said Cassie. She sat back and stopped speaking when he glared at her. On the other side of Ella, Diana blushed a deep crimson.

"To be fair, Diana didn't want us to go, either," said Ella.

Tristan blinked, hard. "Well. I suppose that's something. One of you has more sense than God gave to a goose feather."

Ella sniffed at his scathing remark. "It's a good thing we did go," she said. "Had we not, we could never have heard the nefarious plans the smugglers have, not simply for Rotherton but for the regular militia, as well." She leaned toward Tristan. "You need to listen to these men," she said. "They're good men, and their information is useful."

He sighed heavily, closed his eyes, rested his elbow on the desk and pinched the bridge of his nose between his thumb and forefinger. This woman, aided and abetted by his sister, would likely be the death of him. His one consolation was, Diana was not part of whatever they'd done.

"Go on," he said wearily. He opened his eyes in time to see Ella nod at Carter. The man, clearly frightened, uncertain what Tristan would do, nevertheless took a step forward. "I'm not going to arrest you," Tristan promised. At present, two reluctant smugglers who'd escaped their prison cell were the least of his concerns.

"My lord," said Carter, "it's like this. We was taken from Haywards Heath and marched off to the Pevensey Levels, where we was held in a barn. We didn't get a say in it. They took us, willing or not."

"So I've heard. They took you to the barn. Then what?"

"They held us there. About fifteen of us. More of us than them that was guarding, but they'd got guns."

"Shot one man for saying he wouldn't do anything for them no more," said Sebastian. "Keeps you in line when you know that can happen."

"Yet you escaped?"

Sebastian nodded. "Once we realized we was going to die anyway. It takes the threat out of it when you've got nothing to lose."

"They were planning what they'd do this coming Saturday," said Carter. "We overheard."

Tristan stiffened. "Saturday?" Had the gang members discussed how they would attack? Such intelligence would be worth its weight in gold.

"Aye, my lord. Saturday. They're planning to come here on Saturday. Finish you off. But that's only half the job. They're going to try and destroy the regular militia at the same time. Get rid of a threat to them and make sure you've got no reinforcements."

"It's them coves what's come down from London that planned it," added Sebastian. "That Mickey Hicks, he's a killer. But it's his brother you got to watch for. He's got it, up here." He tapped his temple.

"He come up with this plan," said Carter. "We heard

257

the guards discussing it, wondering if it was too bold. Said it was a pity we—the prisoners, that is—would all have to die, because now they'd have to recruit more men to replace us."

Tristan looked from one man to the other, then glanced at the ladies. Cassie worried him. He could see in her eyes that she was having the time of her life. To her, it was as if she'd been transported to the pages of those novels she enjoyed so much, the ones full of villains and heroes and derring-do. Ella also listened avidly, although she didn't seem quite so eager to be part of it, thank goodness. Diana watched, her face a mixture of shock and anxiety.

"They're going to bring in three ships on Saturday night," continued Carter. "They'll force the men from the barn to unload them onto the beach."

At the same time they would attack Rotherton? That didn't seem feasible. "A sham run?" Tristan guessed. Something to attract the regulars, occupying them while the smugglers were elsewhere.

"No. A real run. They'll make sure the militia know of it. That captain at Winchelsea, he'll hear it's the biggest run in years. Dozens of men. Won't be able to help himself. He'll come running, with most of his men behind him."

"Why would they want the militia there, when they have three ships loaded with cargo?" That didn't make sense. The smugglers would lose a fortune.

"The men on the beach will be landing the cargo and bringing it up, ready to send it out. The militia will come down, thinking they've cornered them. At which point, the gang will attack the militia from where they've been hiding, behind the beach. The militia will be trapped, unable to get away. Easy pickings. There'll be no prisoners taken, no quarter given. And at the end of it, everybody on that beach, militia or runner, will be dead."

Diana gasped. Her eyes were wide and her face pale. "Diabolical," she murmured.

"Meanwhile," said Tristan, thinking aloud, "the main body of the gang will be here, attacking us."

"Another Senlac," agreed Ella. Cassie frowned, clearly not recognizing the reference, and Ella explained. "Senlac. A corruption of the French, Sang Lac. Meaning lake of blood. It's what they called the area where the battle of Hastings happened. Where Battle Abbey is now."

Lake of blood. Tristan stared down at the paperwork spread across his desk. It had seemed so simple. Take on the bullies, let them know the people of Rotherton would not bow to them. He'd known they might seek revenge against him and his volunteers. He hadn't expected them to be so vicious as to go for the whole place, nor so audacious as to include the well-trained regular militia in their destructive plans.

"It's that London bloke," said Sebastian, bitterly. "He plans things better than Wellington."

"Mick Hicks?" asked Ella.

"Nah," said Carter. "Mickey Hicks is all brawn and bile. He'll kill you soon as look at you, but he couldn't plan his way to the door of an empty room. His brother, though…Simon… he's got the nous."

"It doesn't matter who planned it," said Tristan. "Miss Wilde is right. It's diabolical. The regulars must be warned. I cannot stand by and watch them march to their slaughter. Never fear, gentlemen," he held up his hand to steady Sebastian and Carter, who both looked horrified. "I will not divulge the source of my intelligence."

It wouldn't help if he did. Allenby would declare any information from wanted men a Banbury tale, and demand those men be arrested. In fact, Tristan wasn't certain Allenby would treat information from him any less derisively. But he had to try. And, whatever the captain might say, all of them owed these men a debt. Tristan would not let it go unpaid.

"If you seek out Sergeant Busby now, he'll arrange for you to have a good meal, a bath, and some better-fitting clothes. After that, you may choose. If you leave the area, no one shall know from me in which direction you travelled. Or, you can choose to stand and fight with us. If you do, after the battle, I will do what I can to see your charges dismissed."

He hoped they would stand. Lord knew, he needed as many men as he could get, and men with their spirit were worth their weight in gold. But he would conscript nobody, and these men had earned the choice. *Their actions today may well save lives.*

The two men left the room. Once they'd gone, Tristan glared at the ladies. "Are you completely devoid of good sense?" he hissed. "I am certain I said you should stay here, within the vicarage, for your safety."

Ella pouted. "Diana did stay here," she said, as if that made it all right.

Tristan clenched his jaw and held on to his temper. It had but one thread left.

"She was the one most in danger," reasoned Ella. "We thought—"

"You thought wrong! Diana is not the only one in danger! All of you have been attacked," he held up a hand to stop her protest, "whether you were the primary targets or not. Those men know that you're friends with Miss Wilde. You are a means of getting to her when all other methods fail. Do you not think they would have taken you to force her hand? Or mine?"

Ella scoffed. "You credit them with far more intelligence than they have. The men who attacked us are—"

"Dead, Miss Forbes-Smythe. All three of them are dead."

Diana put her hands to her mouth, in horror. Cassie sat up straighter, her shock plain.

"Dead?" asked Ella. She looked uneasy.

"Dead," he confirmed. "Murdered, because they failed." He didn't know that for a fact, of course, but it was a safe bet, and it wouldn't hurt these ladies to believe it. They needed to know the nature of the men who threatened them. "Which will increase the incentive on those who come after them, do you not think? Besides, it isn't the men who come for you who need the intelligence. It's those who instruct them. And we've already established they are very good at planning their actions."

Ella lowered her eyes and looked contrite. "I'm sorry," she said.

Tristan sighed. What more could he say? "I need to go to the barracks and warn Allenby." He dared not entrust the information in a letter. Those could be intercepted. "I will have your word that none of you will leave the vicarage until I return, and then only with my knowledge beforehand."

Each of them solemnly pledged that she would stay.

"When will you be back?" asked Cassie.

"Tomorrow, I should think." He rose from his seat. "Just…stay out of trouble. Please."

He left the room. If he hurried, he might get to the barracks before nightfall. He certainly didn't fancy being abroad once it grew dark.

****

As he expected, Tristan got short shrift from Captain Allenby.

"Where *do* you get your information, Lord Leonard?" he sneered. "An attack? On my men? You have to know, I have over a hundred men at my command."

"Estimates suggest they can call on five hundred."

"Balderdash! You are far too credulous, sir! I've come upon this gang at various times, and I cannot say I have ever seen more than twenty. But of course, they would exaggerate their numbers. It suits their purposes."

Tristan pursed his lips and struggled not to make a scathing reply. This officer was like so many he'd encountered during his own time in uniform, while the men under him were lions, strong, brave, and true. And doomed to die because of the idiot commanding them.

"Captain—" he began.

Allenby cut him off. "It also suits their purpose to have you come to me with this cock-and-bull story. If I believed you, I might be tempted not to go to the cove and, therefore, they'd have a clear run." He chuckled. It wasn't a pleasant sound. "If they think I will not take the chance to crush their organization—and taking this much from them in one fell swoop would certainly help in doing that—they are mistaken. And before you say it, I am aware of what happened at Rotherfield jail. I know they retrieved their goods from there. They won't find it so easy to do the same again here."

Tristan wanted to shake the man until his teeth rattled. His hubris was beyond belief. He was ignoring intelligence brought to him by what should be regarded as a credible source. Tristan was tempted to throw up his hands and walk away, leaving him to his fate. Unfortunately, that would also send a lot of good men marching to certain death. He could not do that.

He opened his mouth to speak again, but Captain Allenby beat him to it.

"I'm surprised at you, Leonard. I would never have taken you for a gull. You have to know this is a ruse. It's what they want you to believe." Allenby's eyes narrowed. "Or do you already know that? It is, after all, to your advantage if I don't send my men after the smugglers at Fairlight Cove on Saturday, is it not?"

What?

"I'm aware of the threat made against Rotherton and, perhaps more importantly, against your person. It would benefit you if I did not risk this ambush you seem to think will happen at Fairlight, but if instead I sent my men to help you ward off the attack…would it not?"

Tristan stilled. An icy anger spread through him. He glared at Allenby. "Are you calling me a coward, Captain?" His voice was low and even.

A second went by. Another. Then Allenby sighed. "No, my lord. That was not my intention. I…apologize."

Tristan glowered at him for a moment longer. Then he said a curt, "Good day, sir," turned on his heel, and left the office.

How dare he? How dare that man imply that Tristan's warning was self-serving? That he would deliberately encourage a captain of the militia to neglect his sworn duty so that he might come to his aid instead? The very thought was beyond the pale. Had not Allenby apologized immediately, Tristan would have been compelled to call him out for it. Might still do so, if the captain ever repeated the slur.

He'd ridden the thirty miles to Winchelsea as fast as he could without killing himself or his horses, stopping to change mounts at the most respectable inns he could find along the way. It had taken more than three hours. Immediately upon his arrival, he'd sought out the captain, and given his warning. Only to be sneered at and, most likely, ignored.

"As if I don't have better things to do," he muttered as he made for the barracks gate. He'd find a room at the town's inn, then set out for Rotherton with the dawn.

He was almost at the gate when somebody called his name. He looked over his shoulder to see Lieutenant Paisley coming toward him.

"Lieutenant," said Tristan, and was shocked at the mix of weariness and bitter anger in his voice. He cleared his throat and tamped down his temper. Paisley had done nothing to deserve his ire. The man was not responsible for his superior officer's stupidity.

"Lord Leonard, might I have a word?" Paisley led Tristan aside and spoke to him in a low tone that was unlikely to be overheard. "Captain Allenby's adjutant came to me. He…the door was ajar, and he sits beside it. He did not overhear on purpose." He looked around, as if to make sure they were not being watched. "He told me of your warning. I thank you for it, and will do what I can to ensure the safety of the men."

Tristan nodded. "Then my trip has not been in vain."

"Do you return to Rotherton tonight?"

"I should." Lord knew, he had much to do in Rotherton if all was to be ready for the threatened attack. "But riding alone at night would be folly. I hope to get a room at the New Inn, and set out at dawn."

"I'm just about to take a patrol out," said Paisley. "We will head across country looking for tubmen, and our search might well take us all the way to Rotherton. I'd be glad for the company of another man proficient with both gun and blade, if you'd care to accompany us."

Tristan smiled. "I'll find my horse," he said.

Chapter Twenty-Two

Cassie and Ella had almost finished their breakfasts when Diana joined them on Friday morning. She immediately felt guilty about being the last one to rise, although it was only a little after nine, so she hadn't completely slept the morning away.

She would probably have been awake earlier if she hadn't spent half the night tossing and turning, her mind whirling. There was so much to think about at present, so much happening around her, and in the dead of night those things had melted together, creating one gigantic tangle that could not be unraveled.

For one thing, the Hicks brothers were in the area, and she couldn't think that was coincidence. Yes, they were involved with the smuggling gang that was terrorizing Rotherton, but she did not believe that was why they had come. They had, somehow, followed her trail, then seen an opportunity to profit here. Which meant, in a roundabout way, she was to blame for the increased sufferings of her neighbors.

She could tell herself she was not responsible until the cows came home. That the bullying of local people by the smugglers had been going on for longer than either she or the Hickses had been here. It didn't help. Diana may not have brought the village to the attention of the gang in the first place, but she was the reason the brothers were here. The reason the violence had escalated.

The letter threatening the village, the volunteer militia, and Tristan himself was from Mickey Hicks. Without him to lead them, the gang might not have had the audacity to do such a thing. Hicks had done so, and she was absolutely sure he would carry it out.

Thoughts of Tristan gave her another thing to worry over. He had ridden to the militia's barracks at Winchelsea, to warn them about the ambush being laid for them. She prayed he made it safely there. She knew he planned to stay overnight rather than risk traveling alone after dark. He was expected home around midday. Then he'd make himself busy with preparations for the attack on Saturday.

There was little she could do to help, but she couldn't just cower in the corner while others protected her. She'd done that before, and Papa and Addams had died. This time, she determined, she *would* play her part.

Ella had brought the bows and arrows, as Diana had asked. Diana and Cassie would spend today practicing, brushing the cobwebs from their skills. Then, on Saturday, they would climb the church tower so they could fire down on the marauders. It wasn't something she looked forward to. She might not hit anyone. But she had to try.

On top of all these things, there was a constant feeling of guilt that she'd lied to Tristan about who she was. She hadn't trusted him with her secrets. It did no good to tell herself she'd acted on Fremont's advice. Diana had a brain; she could think for herself. She should have trusted him, and told him the truth. The longer she left it, the worse it would be.

The first fingers of light smudged the darkness when

she finally resolved to tell him. Today. Not the best timing, perhaps, but it could not be put off anymore. She had to tell him everything.

The decision made her feel easier, and she had slept, then paid the price with a late morning.

"Good day to you." Ella grinned. "Did you sleep well?"

Diana's face heated with her blush. "I'm sorry I'm so late down."

"No matter. We have no pressing appointments."

"Not since Tristan put us under house arrest," grumbled Cassie.

Diana went to the sideboard and helped herself to food. "We have much to do, though."

Ella wiggled her hand in a yes-and-no answer. "Much of it is done. We'll collect the last few things we need from the vicarage attics, and then it's simply a case of getting it all to the church, and ready."

"I'll join you when I've finished eating," promised Diana. She poured herself a cup of tea.

"Right, then. Upstairs," said Ella to Cassie. "We can have it done before your brother gets home." Chatting amiably about what they were looking for, the two left the room.

Diana had almost finished her breakfast when the door opened again. She looked up and was surprised to see Lord Rotherton. His clothes were travel-stained and his hair windswept. He looked around the room, then smiled.

"Good. You are by yourself," he said, and came fully into the room. "May I sit?"

"Please do. Would you like breakfast? I think Tris—er, Lord Leonard's man is around. I can ask him for a fresh pot of tea."

"No. I don't have time for that. And neither, I'm afraid, do you, Miss Villiers."

She gasped at his use of her real name.

He smiled. "Fremont told me who you were. He has charged me with taking you to safety."

That was not what she'd expected, or wanted, to hear. "Safety, my lord?" Safety was an illusion, a distorted image of reality, like the reflections in the strange mirrors at a fair. "Lord Fremont brought me here for my safety."

"But they've tracked you, have they not? I am told Percival's men are here, and with the imminent attack on Rotherton by—"

"Mr. Percival's men are everywhere, my lord, or so I'm told. His reach is very long. And as for the expected attack, I'm not the only person in danger."

"That is true. But you're the only one here with a fortune to tempt a saint to sin. If Milton Percival were to get his hands on you, and through you, your fortune, there'd be no stopping him. Your ships alone would make him too powerful to be contained. We cannot allow him to find you…"

Diana put her elbows on the table and covered her face with her hands. "This will never stop," she murmured. "I will never be safe."

"That's why I'm here, Miss Villiers. One of your ships, *The Lady Diana*, docked two days ago. After she unloaded her cargo, her captain was given orders to sail around the coast to Pevensey. We will meet him there and get you on board. He will then sail for—"

"No!" She glared at him. "No. I will not go."

"Miss Villiers—"

269

Diana shook her head. Enough! This man Percival had taken too much from her already. She'd lost her father, and Addams. She'd been exiled to Rotherton, where she'd been forced to lie to people she cared for. She'd even lost her own identity and been forced to pretend she was somebody else.

All in vain.

"Mr. Percival found me here. He will find me anywhere. He is a very determined man."

"If you are not in the country—"

"He cannot bribe sailors? He cannot arrange to have me taken from the ship once your back is turned? As you see, my lord, I have thought of all the possibilities. When pitted against his determination, my ship is no safer than this vicarage."

"Please, Miss Villiers—"

"I have run, and I have hidden. I have cowered, frightened of shadows, while he escapes justice for his crimes. Well, no more. I am in Rotherton, and here, in Rotherton, I will stay. Here, at least, I am surrounded by people I trust."

"But is that trust reciprocated? Miss Villiers." The words were angry, dripping with bitter sarcasm. Both Diana and Rotherton turned to see Tristan, his hair wet from the bath he'd obviously taken, his clothes clean, his jaw newly shaved. His eyes sparked with venomous fury as he glared at her.

****

"Tristan—Lord Leonard. I hadn't realized you were home."

"That is obvious." Tristan struggled to keep his tone even when he wanted to shout and rail at her, yell and howl until the anger and humiliation building within him dissipated. He felt bloated with it, until he could barely move, until there was no room within him for breath, or thought, or feeling.

She'd lied to him. Oh, he knew she'd been hiding something, running from something, but he'd thought it was something reasonable—running away from an abusive father perhaps, or an unwanted marriage. He'd even suspected she might be embroiled in the crime world that was layered beneath London's respectable streets. The one thing he'd never expected, not for a moment, was that she was a runaway heiress. To the Villiers fortune, no less!

Tristan had heard of Charles Villiers. Who hadn't? The man was renowned for his business acumen, his ability to take small opportunities and turn them into astounding successes. He had interests in every moneymaking scheme imaginable: shipping, banking, coal mines, gold mines, manufactories, and Lord knew what else.

Vaguely, he remembered talk of the man's daughter, his only child. There was speculation in the *ton* that there was something wrong with her, since she'd never been seen in London Society and her father kept her with him on his incessant travels. He'd heard Lancelot, and others, wonder if she was dicked in the nob, or worse, at least as far as those men were concerned, ugly as sin. Tristan could attest to the fact that she was neither.

What she was…was a liar. A spoiled minx who had played him for a fool. And what a fool he'd turned out to be. He'd laid it all out for her, told her everything about his circumstances, how she would be a lady in name, but not in the glittering trappings she might expect. She'd heard him, and she'd never said a word.

How she must have laughed at his sincere regrets that he couldn't buy her jewels and finery. Had she mocked his heartfelt proposal, sneered at his audacity in approaching her?

She hadn't answered his proposal. Hadn't told him "no" in any straightforward and honest way. Was that because she enjoyed playing with his emotions?

More likely, it was because she needed his protection and was worried he'd withdraw it if she refused him. Which served to show how little she knew him. If she thought him so petty, so dishonorable as to turn his back on a lady in peril, then she didn't know him at all.

"Leonard…" David stood and faced Tristan, while the lying minx simply sat there, her eyes wide in her too-pale face. She looked stricken. As well she might. Nobody was ever happy to be caught.

She wasn't the only betrayer here, though, was she? He'd thought David his friend.

"You might have told me," he said, addressing the earl. "You left me to manage the area in your absence. I deserved to know of…of potential problems and risks to people's safety."

"Tristan…" she began. He glared at her and she closed her lips on whatever she'd been about to say.

"Only found out myself last night," said David. "Fremont told—"

"Damn Fremont!" The words burst from him and released some of that het-up, inflated feeling in his chest. "He has the gall to question *my* integrity, *my* honor? The man is dishonor walking! He lies and schemes and manipulates without remorse, and then says *I'm* not to be trusted?"

"It's his job," said David, lamely.

"You went along with it. Both of you."

"I did no such thing!" Anger flashed in David's eyes. "I defended you to him. And I didn't lie to you. I didn't know until last night that Miss Villiers—"

"Miss Villiers. Miss Wilde. Whatever you care to call yourself, madam." His eyes burned and he felt a tremble at his lower lip, which he covered by clenching his teeth together. She would not know how his heart broke. He would not give her that satisfaction. His anger? Oh, yes. He'd give her that. But no more than that.

"You know me. Regardless of anything Fremont may have said, you know *me*. For God's sake, I asked you to marry me. Without a dowry, without…Lord, I'm a fool." Another thought occurred then, and he closed his eyes on the pain of it. "Does Ella know? Was she laughing at me as well?"

"Nobody was laughing at you," she said as she got to her feet. "And no, she doesn't know. Nobody knew. Only Lord Fremont, and myself, and now you and Lord Rotherton." A lone tear escaped her brimming eye and slid down her cheek. "I wanted to tell you. Had made up my mind to tell you—"

"Don't." He held up his hand to silence her. He didn't want platitudes and lies now. They would not make him feel better.

"Tristan…"

He couldn't stay here. Could not allow the pain inside him to show. Not to her. Not now. She'd humiliated him enough. He would give her no more.

"I have a church to reinforce." With that, he turned tail and fled his own dining room.

****

Diana sat and covered her face with her hands. Her eyes were hot and full, her cheeks wet, and there was a boulder of granite blocking her throat. Her heart hurt. It was not an ache but a sharp pain, as if somebody had stabbed her over and over again.

"Miss Villiers?" Rotherton's voice was soft, sympathetic.

She sniffed and wiped away the tears on her cheek. He handed her his handkerchief, and she dabbed at her eyes, blotting them.

"He asked you to marry him?"

Diana nodded. She didn't dare speak. Not until she'd wrestled her emotions back under control.

"He loves you."

She shrugged her shoulders. He had. Until she'd killed his love with her lies. Why hadn't she told him? All those times she'd thought about it, dithered over it, second-guessed herself. If she'd only told him...

It was easy to blame Fremont. To say the viscount had forbidden her to tell anyone lest she compromise her safety. There'd been sense in that advice. Of course there had. One did not stay alive and hidden by broadcasting one's identity to all and sundry. But Tristan wasn't all and sundry. He was the man she loved. The man who'd loved her. She could have told him. He was right about that. Right that he'd deserved to know.

"He did," she said, in answer to Rotherton's assertion. The lump in her throat made the words sound hollow.

Rotherton smiled. "Does," he insisted. "You can't hurt a man that badly if he doesn't love you." He stared at the teapot, lost in thought for a moment. Then he shook himself and smiled sadly. "And if he loves you, truly loves you, this will not destroy it."

"It looked rather destroyed from here." The last word cracked and her bottom lip trembled and she worked hard to push it all down again.

"He has a lot on his plate. This was a shock. Give him time." Rotherton sighed. "You're not going to get on that ship, are you?"

She shook her head.

"Don't do anything foolish."

"I won't."

Rotherton gave her a polite bow. "I'll go and see if he needs my help. If he'll talk to me, of course." He grinned, clearly trying to lighten the moment. "I've never been given the cut direct by one of my tenants before. First time for everything, I suppose."

Then he left, and Diana was alone with her heartbreak.

****

She did not see Tristan for the rest of the day. He busied himself at the church, and with his men, and did not arrive for dinner.

The evening meal was a somber affair. Everyone at the table—Cassie, Ella, Diana, and Rotherton—knew that by this time tomorrow, there might be no vicarage in which to sit. No village. Nothing. In fact, any or all of them might well be dead.

Nobody spoke their fears out loud, of course, but they hung like a pall of darkness over them. Once or twice, someone tried to spark up a lighthearted conversation: an anecdote here, a remembered witticism there. Everybody laughed where they were supposed to laugh, but the sounds were brittle, like shattering glass, and the conversation soon dried up again.

Surreptitiously, Diana glanced at the empty seat at the head of the table. Tristan had sent his apologies to Cassie, told her he was busy with last-minute preparations and would dine with his men. Diana wondered what last-minute preparations required his presence. According to Rotherton, who'd been down to the church to see if he could be of help, there was nothing left to do now until the battle started.

"All is ready," he said. "Everyone knows their orders. St. Bartholomew's Church is likely better protected than the Tower of London. Leonard knows how to defend his ground, I assure you. And," he added, trying to lighten the mood, "if any of the villains should sneak past him, I daresay God will have a thunderbolt or two to throw at them. With, of course, perfect aim."

"I'd sooner not test His willingness to intervene," answered Ella, acerbically.

Nor would I. Silently, though, Diana prayed that He would intervene, by keeping Tristan safe. Not just Tristan, she hastened to add. Everybody who risked their lives to keep the people of Rotherton out of the gang's clutches. And if Tristan's name came up more often than most in her prayers, what was the wonder of it? She knew him better than any of the others. Of course she would worry about him more.

Dinner was followed by a deliberately lively evening of music, cards, and conversation in the drawing room. Then Rotherton went to the church to see if they needed an extra sentry, while the three ladies went to bed.

On Saturday, after nuncheon, members of the militia escorted the ladies into the church and helped them settle before they went to the other houses in the village to fetch the people. The apothecary had brought a lot of potions and salves, and had spent the last two days securing them in a corner of the church, ready for use if they were needed. Seth Fayers had brought a couple of barrels of ale, and had had to promise he would not allow the defenders to drink before the job was done. He'd also promised there would be no free drinks for anybody, at any time. That had made Ella laugh.

"I cannot believe anybody seriously thinks that a threat to our safety," she said. "If Seth Fayers starts handing out free drinks, we will know our troubles run much deeper than a few strutting smugglers."

Diana caught sight of Tristan when she arrived at the church. He was directing operations by the vestry, consulting with Rotherton and Mr. Fielding, before leaving two volunteers, both no more than young boys, to guard the tiny room, which had a door that led out into the graveyard. Diana surmised that was Tristan's way of keeping the boys safe. If the attackers got through that door to them, it would mean there'd been a catastrophic breach in the wall of defenders outside.

He turned around and looked straight at her. Their eyes met. In his, she saw a maelstrom of emotions: hurt, betrayal, anger, shame. She wanted to go to him, to talk to him, tell him she was sorry for lying to him, even by omission. She hated the way he looked at her now.

She took a step forward. His top lip seemed to curl and he turned and walked away, effectively cutting her. Tears threatened and her cheeks burned with humiliation. Rotherton had said Tristan loved her. It certainly didn't seem like it today.

Blinking rapidly to dispel the tears, Diana grabbed the bow and a quiver full of arrows and headed up the narrow spiral of worn stone steps that led to the top of the church's bell tower. From there, she and Cassie hoped to shoot down into their attackers. Even if neither of them actually hit anybody, the arrows coming at them might give the smugglers pause and allow the defenders the upper hand.

By ten minutes to six, the church was filled with people. Children ran up and down the aisles, or played hand-clapping games near the altar. Miss Thompson, Caroline Potter's governess-companion, had gathered the smallest children and was reading them stories. They sat, spellbound, at her feet.

The adults were, of course, far more tense. Mrs. Potter and Mrs. Bell sat in a corner, whispering, then looking around in disdain at other women, who sat in the pews, talking, comforting those with husbands and sons among the defenders. John Carter and Sebastian Thomas were stationed at one of the lead-paned windows on the side of the church. They had each removed a pane of glass from its place, ready to push their musket muzzles through when the moment came. Young boys stood behind them with a second musket each, ready to hand them over and reload the first guns while Carter and Sebastian sniped.

Tristan didn't know what she and Cassie planned. Cassie had said it might be better to ask for forgiveness when all was finished rather than permission beforehand, which they both knew he would not grant.

"Your brother doesn't seem a very forgiving man," Diana had pointed out.

Cassie frowned at that. Of course, she didn't know what had happened yesterday. She'd been in the attic with Ella and probably wasn't even aware that Tristan and Rotherton had been in the house.

"He doesn't hold a grudge," she said, now. "He'll probably scold us, then forget about it."

Where you're concerned, maybe. Cassie was his sister. He'd be exasperated. Angry, even. But he would forgive her. When it came to Diana, she wasn't sure the same would apply.

At five minutes to six, a hush descended. All the chatter that had carried up from below ceased. Even the children's games stopped. The atmosphere grew heavy, pressing down on them. Cassie stood at one of the narrow, glassless windows in the tower, and looked across at Diana, standing at the other window, opposite her. Between them, bell ropes hung, thick and still and steady. The dust of ages settled on every surface, making the place smell, a sweet musty perfume that tickled Diana's nose, and scratched her throat.

Four minutes to six. Pigeons cooed goodnights in the trees beyond the churchyard. Other birds chirped. The sounds of a normal, country evening. It made the tension within the church seem tighter. Diana felt that if she moved her hand, she could pluck that tightness and make it sing.

Three minutes. Nothing moved on Rotherton High Street, as far as she could see. The shops were in darkness, the houses too. Not a cart or a horse or a donkey was in sight. She peered down. Men were dotted about the church's perimeter. Others were hidden behind larger gravestones, and sarcophagi.

Two minutes. A fox barked. A rooster answered. The sounds were incongruous on the tense evening. Diana took several deep breaths to calm her jumpy nerves. Cassie picked up her first arrow, ready to put it in place. Diana did the same. Her hand trembled. She closed her eyes and tried to banish her fears.

One minute to go. Her mouth was dry and her throat tight, and her heart raced, eighteen to the dozen. She sent up a last-minute prayer that God would see them through this.

Six o'clock. Diana heard the whirr of the church clock, and the heavy clunk as the minute hand moved. Above her, hidden by the wooden ceiling, cogs turned, squeaking and clunking their way through their motions. A deep throated chime sounded six times.

For a moment, nothing moved. No sound came. Even the birds had fallen silent. Diana's skin prickled. Goosebumps formed on her arms, and shivers ran the length of her spine.

Then, from along the High Street came a dull thud, followed by another, then another. It took Diana a moment to realize what she heard.

Doors being kicked in. Houses entered. Then shouts. Curses.

A voice yelled, "This way, lads. Let's get 'em!"

More shouts. A bloodcurdling war cry.

Silhouetted men came marching down the High Street.

The battle of St. Bartholomew's had begun.

Chapter Twenty-Three

Tristan stood at the church porch with David to one side, a volunteer to the other. The man was about twenty, the freshness of youth still in his face, his beard no more than fluff on his chin, but he held his musket steady, as determined and courageous as any seasoned soldier. David held a pistol at his side, and he'd strapped his sword belt around his waist.

In his head, Tristan did a calculation of what he had. Twenty-five men, counting Carter and Sebastian, and the two boys in the vestry. If either of them was more than thirteen, he'd be amazed. But they were willing to stand, and he needed every man he could get.

As far as Tristan knew, David had no military experience, but he had the calm demeanor of a man who knew what was coming, and what he must do. He had a brace of pistols, his sword, and a knife in his boot, and assured Tristan he knew how to use them all.

Busby stood at one corner of the church, watchful, waiting. Now and then, he murmured, "Easy, lads. Easy. Not yet."

The rest of the men were in position, some encircling the church, others ready to ambush the attackers from behind headstones and graves. There were snipers at the church windows, too. He'd thought about putting a sniper in the bell tower but decided against it. He wasn't sure any of his men were good enough to fire accurately from there, and he needed everyone to be as effective as they could be.

Along the High Street, he heard shouts. Curses carried on the still, evening air. Doors were kicked open. Someone shouted a war cry. It was a frightening sound. The young man beside him fidgeted. He wiped his hands down the sides of his tunic, one at a time.

"It's just a man, shouting," Tristan whispered. "I've heard more terrifying sounds when you men try to sing."

The volunteer straightened, his nervousness under control once more.

"Here they come," said David. Tristan looked along the High Street, and saw the men, silhouetted against the early evening sky. At first, it was a seething mass, no individual standing out. Then men ran from the rear, bringing flaming torches, giving them into eager hands.

The torches showed detail. About seventy men, marching together, their heavy boots ringing on the dry-packed road. Most of them were stripped to the waist, their skin coated with the orange torchlight, making them gleam. Many had tattoos. Some showed off vicious scars that told, at a glance, their experience in battle and their willingness to fight. As an intimidation tactic, it was brilliant. Some of his men, as yet untried and unbloodied, would find the sight terrifying. Hell, Tristan found it frightening, and he'd been at Waterloo.

At the front were two men who had not stripped down. One was short and stocky and crudely dressed, the other tall, slender and dapper. The Hicks brothers. Both carried pistols and knives.

Beside the brothers was the long-haired man who'd chased Diana in the woods. He was stripped, displaying an impressive chest and thick, muscular arms. He held a cutlass.

The gang sped up. The man beside Tristan turned aside and cast up his accounts, then wiped his mouth with the back of his hand, and took his position again.

Busby murmured, "Steady, boys. Wait for it."

Tristan took a deep breath. His body was tense, legs restless, ready to run, arms itching to swing his blade at the first man who came close enough. David cocked his pistol.

With a yell, the smugglers raised their weapons high—knives, swords, cudgels and pistols brandished proudly. The Hicks brothers stepped aside, and their men swarmed the churchyard. Some ran through the lych-gate and up the path. Others scrambled over the wall.

Busby shouted, "Fire!" A volley of shots filled the air with noise and smoke, and the smell of gunpowder and burnt cotton wadding.

Four smugglers went down. Two were clearly dead. The other two soon would be. The gang had obviously not expected armed resistance, because the volley made them hesitate. They seemed confused.

The shooters stepped back to reload. A second line of men stepped forward and took aim. Busby shouted, "Fire!" again. A second volley left more smugglers writhing in agony.

Some gang members took shelter behind headstones, and encountered Tristan's hidden men. Hand-to-hand skirmishes broke out. The long-haired man yelled, "Up and at 'em, lads!" He fired his gun. The ball wedged into the brickwork, a few inches above Tristan's head. Instinctively, he flinched as tiny chips of stone rained on him. Other guns sounded, some fired by his men, others by the smugglers.

An arrow hit the ground at the long-haired man's feet. He took a step back, startled. No more than Tristan was. He wasn't aware his men had bows and arrows. He looked up, and saw a second arrow fly from the bell tower. He frowned. Who was up there? Not that it mattered. They'd bought his men precious seconds.

A man screamed. Tristan took his attention from the bell tower back to the fight, and saw a smuggler, face twisted in agony, an arrow protruding from his shoulder. He scrambled to take cover behind a headstone, only to encounter one of Tristan's men, who raised his cudgel and brought it down hard on the smuggler's head. The smuggler fell, senseless.

The two forces converged. There was no more time for loading and firing guns. Now, it would be hand-to-hand combat. He raced into the fray, sword drawn.

The long-haired man stepped into his path. He moved his tongue in and out of his mouth rapidly, taunting Tristan, before he lunged forward, bringing his cutlass down in a deep arc that would have sliced Tristan in two, had he not parried the blow. The swords clashed. Vibrations from the blow rolled along Tristan's arms, hurting his wrists and his shoulders. The man grinned, disengaged, and moved around Tristan as if looking for a weak point.

Again, the man sliced. Again, Tristan parried. They parted, lunged, parried, circled. Tristan was the better swordsman; more experienced and better trained. But his opponent was bigger, stronger, and determined, which made up for his lack of finesse.

Smoke from myriad gunshots hovered in the air, misting the battlefield and cutting visibility. The bitter stench of gunpowder filled his nostrils, mixing with the coppery taste of blood to raise his hackles and spur him on. He heard the shouts of the fighters, the screams of the wounded, the sound of metal against metal as his sword clashed with the smuggler's cutlass. He knew he yelled, because his throat hurt, but he did not hear himself, did not know his words.

The man pulled his cutlass back for another blow. Tristan slipped past his defenses, and ran him through. The man looked surprised. Then he fell back, toppled over a headstone, and lay still, head at an awkward angle, feet still caught on the grave.

Tristan did not savor his victory. Did not rejoice at the loss of life. He put the man from his mind and took on a new opponent. And after that, another. And then, another.

****

Diana and Cassie stood at the windows in the bell tower, arrows nocked, but they couldn't fire. Diana had managed to loose just two arrows before the opposing forces came together, making it impossible to shoot again. She had no idea how Cassie had fared on the other side. Her view was of the rear of the church, where little seemed to be happening.

"I've nothing to fire at yet," grumbled Cassie, as if she'd read Diana's thoughts. She looked over her shoulder at Diana. "Did you hit anything?"

"A smuggler," replied Diana. She peered through the window, trying to make sense of the scene below. It was a chaos of bodies, joining, parting, grappling with each other, circling, wrestling. Always moving, no rhyme or reason to it, like ants near their nest entrance. "I wounded him," she continued. "Took him out of the fight." Her voice was devoid of all emotion, as if she

285

recounted the tale of something that had happened to somebody else. Which was the way it felt. Distant. Detached.

Shouts and cries came to her, though she didn't hear individual words. Knives glinted in the final rays of the setting sun. Discarded torches burned on graves, their flames now friendly and calm. At least ten men, all smugglers, lay still. She wondered if the man she'd shot was among them. Part of her hoped he was, for then he would pose no further threat to Tristan. The other part of her prayed he was not. She didn't know if she could live with having actually killed a man.

Two smugglers broke from the melee and ran for the lych-gate. She watched them, glad to take her eyes from the battle. They ran through the gate, onto the High Street, where the Hicks brothers stood in the gathering gloom.

Mickey Hicks shouted at the fleeing smugglers. They said something to him, then started along the High Street. Mickey aimed his gun. He fired, and one went down. His friend turned, saw his fallen mate, glanced back at Mickey, then ran. Diana watched in horror as Mickey grabbed Simon's pistol, took aim and fired. The second man stumbled, almost righted himself, took three more steps, fell and lay still.

Calmly, Mickey handed Simon's gun back to him and both reloaded. Then, without saying a word, they moved through the lych-gate and into the churchyard. They didn't join the fight, though. Instead, they made their way through the shadows, skirting the action, to the back of the church. Three smugglers followed them.

"They're looking for a way inside," murmured Diana. With most, if not all, of Tristan's men engaged in the battle at the front, the rear was vulnerable. An image came to her of the vestry, its outside door guarded by two boys. If there were no defenders outside that door, or if those defenders succumbed, the boys would be easy pickings.

There was nothing Diana could do up here. But perhaps she could help the boys. She couldn't do much, she knew that, but it might be enough to see this attack fail.

Quickly, she shoved two arrows into the pocket of her skirt. With the one in her hand, that might be enough. She doubted she'd need more. If she failed to stop them with three arrows, she'd probably be dead anyway.

"Make every shot count," she told Cassie, and she left the bell tower. The arrows weighed her pocket down, their tips poking through the frayed seam at its bottom, their fletches keeping them from falling through completely. The shafts bounced uncomfortably against her leg as she hurried downstairs.

She reached the vestry at the same moment the outer door's jamb splintered. Another hefty kick or two and that door would open. Frantically, she looked around. There was furniture that could be put in front of the door, heavy enough perhaps to hold it, but there was no time to move it. The boys looked terrified, but they pointed their pistols at the door, steady in their duty.

Another kick. The wood around the door fractured. Diana stood, her arrow nocked, ready.

The door rocked. One more kick and it burst open. A smuggler came through. The first boy fired and the man fell. Behind him, the other smugglers scrambled to the side, out of the line of fire. The second boy held his aim, as did Diana, while the first boy tried to reload.

Shock had him trembling so much, he could hardly manage it.

A smuggler fired into the room, then ducked from sight again. His ball caught the first boy in the upper arm. The boy scrambled behind an ancient lectern. The smuggler peered around the door again. The second boy fired. Missed. The boy hid behind the vestment cupboard, breathing heavily, trying, and failing, to reload.

Diana ignored them. She aimed her bow at the door. Took a deep breath in, forcing her mind to be calm, her body to be still.

A second passed.

Then another.

Simon Hicks came through the door. He looked around, took in the scene and grinned. He clearly thought one woman and two boys were no threat. His eyes locked with the boy behind the lectern, and he brought his pistol up, taking aim.

He was going to shoot him! Even though the boy was injured, no further threat, Simon was going to kill him.

There was no time to think. If she hesitated, the boy would die.

The vestry faded away. The noise of the battle disappeared. There was just her, Simon, and the boy he meant to kill.

In a strange, slow motion, she let loose her arrow. It flew through the air, straight and true. Simon pulled back the hammer on his pistol. The boy closed his eyes.

The arrow found its mark. Dead center.

Simon looked shocked, as if this outcome was inconceivable. His pistol fired, but the arrow's hit had knocked his aim, and the ball buried itself in the lectern.

There wasn't much blood. Just a neat and tidy smattering of it where the arrow had penetrated. Simon corkscrewed to the ground and landed in a heap. He looked as if he was praying, kneeling, head bowed forward, forehead to the floor.

Diana reached into her pocket and pulled at the fletch of a second arrow. The tip caught on the frayed seam, and it took a second to pull it clear. She didn't have time to position it before the second smuggler came in. She discarded the bow and brought the arrow down like a dagger. He jumped back, but he wasn't quick enough. It slashed his torso, ripping the skin in a long line from just below his left shoulder to above his right hip. Blood oozed from the wound. He hissed in pain, and put his hand over his chest, pressing down as if he could stop the bleeding.

The second boy fired again. The injured smuggler staggered back, the ball in his thigh. His leg crumpled and he went down, his face twisted in agony.

Mickey Hicks entered. He saw Simon kneeling on the floor, and he kicked him. Simon fell to the side, and lay still. Mickey gave an almighty roar, a mix of rage and grief, then fired his gun blindly. He missed the boy, who hid behind the cupboard once more.

Diana raised her arrow again, but she no longer had the element of surprise, and Mickey was quicker. He grabbed her wrist, wrenched the arrow from her fist, and threw it down, then dragged her out the door and into the churchyard. She stumbled and pulled back, trying to free herself, but he was too strong. All she could do was run after him, and hope to keep her balance. If she fell, she knew he would drag her.

The last smuggler followed. They raced across the churchyard to the rear wall. Behind her, she heard a soft whistling noise, and a dull thud. The smuggler grunted and stumbled. She glanced back to see him lying prone, one of Cassie's arrows protruding from his back.

Mickey's pace did not falter. He left his man where he fell, unlamented, already forgotten, as he dragged Diana on, weaving through the headstones until they came to the wall and the wrought iron gate in its narrow opening. It wasn't locked, used as it was for parishioners from the Hadlow and Amberley estates to access the church without going all the way into the village, saving them nearly a mile of their journey.

She wished it were locked, wished it would trap Mickey here, and give time for her rescue.

He opened the gate. Diana pulled back, trying to dig her heels in. It didn't help. He was so much stronger than she was. He turned to her and grinned, grimly.

With her free hand, she clawed at him. She aimed for his eyes, but missed, and her nails scraped his cheek. Three angry scratches oozed blood. With a shout of pain, he hit her, hard. Her cheek stung, and her eyes watered and lost focus. Her ear rang and, for a moment, coherent thought was impossible. Flashes, like fireworks, burst before her.

"Bitch!" he muttered, and dragged her along the lane on the far side of the wall.

"You're abandoning your men," she said, partly because the fact that he'd done that was abhorrent. What happened to honor among thieves? But also, she hoped somebody would hear them, and come to her aid.

"They're not my men," he sneered. "Bunch of bleedin' nodcocks. Call themselves a fighting force?

Couldn't fight a kid in a bleedin' cradle."

He started forward again. Diana pulled back. "Let. Me. Go!" His grip on her wrist tightened. "They'll look for me," she tried. "They'll chase you, block the roads to stop you. You can't run fast enough to get away. Not with me in tow."

"Who's running?" he answered. He veered off the road into the thick woodland. "We'll hide till they give up. A few days and they'll think we've escaped. Then we can."

The sounds of the battle faded as he pulled her on. Twigs snapped under her feet, and bramble suckers snagged at her clothes. She stepped in a puddle. The water splashed, going over the top of her half boot and seeping down to her foot.

A fox barked, sharp and jarring on the night air. Then a rooster crowed.

Diana frowned, confused. A rooster? At night? That couldn't be right.

Mickey didn't seem to notice. "You're worth a pretty penny, you are," he said. "Those stupid... They won't mess this up."

She pulled back. His fingers slipped on her wrist, then squeezed, tighter. It burned her skin. He slapped her again. "Do as you're told," he hissed. "Just be thankful you're worth more alive than dead. Even after you killed my brother." Under his breath, he uttered a string of obscenities.

They left the wood and crossed an unkempt, overgrown park to a large house. Completely in darkness, it had an air of neglect about it, an atmosphere of emptiness, and she knew immediately where she was. Hadlow Hall.

"Found this place weeks ago," he muttered. "Nothing worth stealing. But I knew it'd come in handy." He pulled her up lime-spotted steps onto a terrace of uneven flagstones, weeds growing in the cracks between them. With his elbow, he punched out a pane on one of the French doors. She heard the glass tinkle against the wood floor on the other side.

He put his hand through the hole he'd made, twisted something, and the door opened.

Shards of glass crunched under their feet. Then her heels clacked loudly over the wooden floor of the sparsely furnished dining room, along a tile-floored corridor, and upstairs. A few paintings adorned the walls, but there were far more squares where the wall hangings were brighter, betraying where other pictures had once hung. A layer of dust coated everything.

Upstairs, he took her to a large chamber. Again, it was neglected and sparsely furnished: a bed with no sheets or blankets, a nightstand, a dressing table, and a garderobe. The wall hangings were peeling, and there was a musty, damp smell to the place.

Mickey thrust her forward, and she sprawled across the bed. The arrow in her skirt pressed into her thigh, and she struggled not to show the pain, as she scrambled up to the headboard and sat, fists clenched, ready to defend herself.

He scoffed. "Don't flatter yourself, sweetheart. I ain't touching you. Not worth it. He wouldn't pay much for my leavings, would he?" He walked to the door, turned the key in the lock, then pocketed it, before checking the doors to left and right. They were both locked.

"Make yourself comfortable, Princess," he said.

"We'll be here till they stop searching."

Or until you turn your back. She lowered her hand to her side, and felt the reassuring weight of the arrow against her leg. *Please, turn your back.*

Chapter Twenty-Four

The battle lasted just over an hour. By the time it ended, twenty smugglers lay dead, and thirty more had been arrested, most of them injured. They would be held in the church crypt until the militia could come and take them. The others had fled, but Tristan doubted they'd get far. The gang's power had been broken today. There was still a substantial number of them out there, but today had shown they could not force the people to their will. The reign of terror was over.

By some miracle, not one of Tristan's men had been killed, though four had been injured. Tristan himself had a gash in his side, which would need tending once everything else was done. For now, though, his main concern was the jittery feeling in the night air, a feeling he knew all too well. This was the most dangerous moment of any battle: the aftermath, when men were elated, fired up, looking for trouble anywhere they could find it.

Sergeant Busby's experience made him worth his weight in gold. He gathered the men now, and found tasks to keep them occupied until they'd had a chance to calm down. Tristan began to breathe a little easier. Perhaps all would be well.

No sooner had the thought gone through his head than he heard his name called. He turned, sharply, and saw his sister running to him, a bow in her hand.

"It was you?" he demanded. Part of him was proud of her spirit, proud she'd taken part in the fight to save their village from thugs and bullies. At the same time, he wanted to shout at her for putting herself in danger.

"What?" She looked down at the bow and grimaced. "Oh. Yes. And—no." She dismissed the topic with a shake of her head. "Tristan, he's taken Diana."

For a moment, he stared at her blankly, unable to make sense of what she'd said. Who had taken Diana? Where?

David came to them. He'd heard what Cassie said. As had most of the men, all of whom stopped what they were doing and stared at her. Many straightened their shoulders and checked their weapons, ready for another fight.

"Who's taken Diana?" asked David. He shared a glance with Tristan, which showed he was as worried about this as Tristan was. They were, so far as he knew, the only two people present who knew her true identity.

"I don't know," said Cassie. "A man. He grabbed her and took her. I shot the man who was with him, but I couldn't...not without..." She ended on a distressed huff, her hand at her throat, eyes brimming with tears.

"Show me." Tristan pushed down his panic and forced himself to be the cool, calm officer he needed to be. He took Cassie's arm and walked her back into the church. David followed. A couple of the men made to come with them, but Busby put a stop to that.

"Not so fast, boys," the sergeant said. "If Lord Leonard needs us, he'll call for us. Meanwhile, we've got this mess to clean up." He pointed to the churchyard, littered with bodies, injured men, broken headstones, and the other detritus of the battle.

Some of the men grumbled, but they went about their tasks.

Cassie led Tristan and David through the church, where women cared for children, comforted their neighbors, and tended injuries. Two smugglers sat, their wounds bandaged, guards watching them warily. The smugglers looked defeated, no threat, but nobody was taking chances. Ella directed operations as other women tidied the church, helped the apothecary administer medicines, and set things to rights.

They passed the hustle and bustle and followed Cassie along the south aisle. The flagstones were uneven, worn down. On the wall were several plaques dedicated to the memory of noteworthy parishioners.

At the far end of the aisle, they went through the doorway into the vestry. There was a sight to make Tristan's blood run cold. While he and his men had skirmished at the front of the church, this door had been breached. It hung off its hinges, the jamb broken, unable to hold it closed. Three men lay in the middle of the floor, clearly dead. Two were bare-chested. Based on the amount of blood around the legs of one, Tristan surmised his femoral artery had been severed. Beside him, the third man, Simon Hicks, was curled on his side, an arrow embedded in his chest. The tiny amount of blood told Tristan the arrow had pierced Simon's heart, killing him instantly.

He looked for the boys he'd set to guard the vestry, thinking this would be the safest place to deploy them. How wrong could he be? What had happened to the men he'd stationed outside the door? Had they left their posts to join the fight? If they had, he'd have their guts for garters.

A shiver of fear went through him when he did not immediately see the boys. It was followed by a relief so great it almost felled him when he found them behind the lectern. One boy was trying to bandage his friend's arm. The wound, from what Tristan could see, was superficial. It would hurt like the devil, but it wouldn't threaten his life. He sent up a silent prayer of thanks.

"What happened here?" asked David. The uninjured boy scrambled to his feet.

"We had a bit of a dust-up, my lord," he said. "The gentlemen wanted to come in. We disagreed."

David grinned at the lad's sanguinity. Tristan might have smiled too, if he weren't so anxious about Diana.

"What about Miss…" He hesitated. He'd been going to say Miss Wilde. But she wasn't Miss Wilde, was she? He didn't know what to call her.

"The lady came to help us," said the injured boy. "She saved my life when she shot him." He pointed at Hicks. "He was going to shoot me. She stopped him."

Tristan closed his eyes, pained to think Diana had been in the middle of all this.

"Where is she now?" he asked, though he dreaded the answer.

"They took her," said the injured boy.

"I couldn't reload fast enough to stop them," said the second boy. Tears of shame shone on his cheeks.

"You did your best, lad," said David. "Where did they go?"

"Through the back gate," said Cassie. "I shot one, but I couldn't get a sight on the other. And then, it was too late." Her voice cracked. Her bottom lip trembled and she reached for Tristan. He embraced her, wincing a little as she pressed against his injured side. Then he let her go and spoke to David.

"Can you take charge here?"

David shook his head. "Your sergeant is more than capable. And Fielding will help, won't you?" Tristan turned to the door leading to the church and saw the curate, surveying the scene, his face impassive.

Fielding nodded. "You two find her," he said. "Do you need any more help?"

"If we do, we'll send for it," said David. He and Tristan checked their pistols were loaded and headed for the outer door. Cassie called out for them to be careful. Mr. Fielding told her and the boys to come into the church.

The two men made their way across the churchyard, through the gate, and out into the lane. The road was hard, so there'd be no easy trail to follow, especially at night. Tristan looked to right, then left. "Which way do you suppose?" he asked.

A shudder ran through him. He assumed the man who'd taken Diana was Mickey Hicks. An educated guess, because he was nowhere else to be found, though his brother lay dead in the church, and they had seemed to come as a pair. On top of which, the other attackers would not want their escapes hampered by a kidnapped woman. Only Hicks knew her value.

"It has to be Hicks," he murmured.

"I agree," said David. "How well does he know the area? Could he have transport waiting?"

The thought that the villain may already be on his way out of the area was almost too much to bear. "We have to find her." His words were no more than whispers, squeezed past the lump of terror threatening to choke him.

He couldn't be too late. He had to save her. He didn't care who she was. She could be a poor relation, or as rich as Croesus, or the queen of England. All that mattered was her safety. She needed to be safe. Safe and well. Away from men who would hurt her. Including him.

For he had hurt her. With his temper and his petulance, his lack of understanding for all she'd been through. He'd been unreasonable in his anger, and he'd turned away from her. Now, if he didn't find her in time, if anything terrible befell her, he'd never forgive himself.

"Should we split up? You go one way, I go the other?" he asked.

David grimaced, but before he could voice his opposition, a rooster crowed. Tristan frowned, perplexed. What rooster crowed after dark?

David, however, grinned. "Ned?" he called, softly.

Leaves rustled and Ned Fellowes came from the undergrowth. He jumped the narrow ditch and landed, soundlessly, on the road.

"Did you see the lady being taken?" David asked, without preamble.

Ned mimed someone being held by the wrist, struggling to break free. Tristan closed his eyes in a profound relief. She was alive, and it sounded as if she was unhurt.

"Where did he take her, Ned?"

The boy pointed at the wood behind him, then made a variety of sounds that accurately portrayed somebody running through woodland—breaking twigs, rustling leaves, splashing water. Tristan's hopes rose. If they'd run through the woods, Hicks hadn't had a vehicle waiting for him. He'd have to access one, which would take him time, especially with a struggling victim in tow.

"Can you take us to them?" David asked Ned. Ned nodded and turned back to the wood.

"If that blackguard has harmed a hair on her head…" Tristan whispered, as they followed the boy into the trees.

David looked back at him. Even in the dark woods, Tristan saw the speculation in his gaze. Then the earl's lips twitched into a knowing smile, and he followed the nimble boy.

They came out of the woods into an overgrown park. Tall grass waved on the night breeze. A small herd of deer moved stealthily through the grass, heading for the wood. Beyond the park, stood an imposing building, completely in darkness.

"Hadlow Hall," whispered David. "Good place to hide. Nobody lives here."

"There's no place he'll hide if he's hurt her," vowed Tristan. He peered at the house, hoping to see some movement.

"David watched him for a moment. "You love her," he said.

It wasn't a question, but Tristan nodded anyway, and braced himself. He knew David would object, tell him not to be so stupid. A woman like Diana Villiers was not for the likes of him, an almost bankrupt baron with a tarnished family reputation.

"Well, we'd better go and get her back, then, so you can tell her," said David, and he followed Ned through the park. Astounded, it took Tristan a few seconds to pull himself together enough to follow.

Ned led them around the house, onto the terrace, and to an open door with a broken windowpane.

"At least we know roughly where he is," said David, his voice so low Tristan barely caught his words. "Do you have any clue whereabouts in there...? Ned?" He sighed in frustration. Ned was already halfway across the park, running toward the trees. "It's just you and me, then," David went on. "Let's see what we can find."

They split up inside the house, with David taking the rooms on the left and Tristan going to the right. They agreed to meet at the foot of the stairs in fifteen minutes, unless one of them found anything. Then, a shout would bring the other running.

Tristan started in the drawing room at the front of the house. He checked under the dust sheets covering the furniture, and behind the tattered, cobweb-covered curtains at the window. He even looked into the dark cavern of the fireplace. Finding nothing, he backed out of the hearth. Cold metal touched the back of his neck, and he heard the unmistakable sound of a pistol being cocked.

****

Diana sat on the bed, her back against the headboard, her knees bent so they hid what her hand was doing as she carefully, slowly, maneuvered the arrow back up from where it had fallen through the frayed seam of her pocket. Inch by excruciating inch, she pulled it up. The tip caught on the material and she had to tug, which made her dress move. She covered it by fidgeting a little, as if trying to get comfortable on the musty mattress.

Finally, the whole arrow was in her pocket, ready to be pulled out at the opportune moment. She moved it slightly, putting it so the tip was no longer lined up with the hole in the seam, then sat, praying the moment would come when she could use it.

She didn't want to kill him. She'd hated killing his brother, although it had been necessary. He would have shot the boy had she not stopped him. But having to do something was not the same as accepting it. The day she could shrug off the idea of killing a man was the day she'd be no better than the Hicks brothers.

That day, she vowed, would never come.

Mickey walked from the window and paced to the door, then turned and paced back. He was little more than a silhouette in the moonlight, but she didn't need to see him to feel the tension rolling off him. He muttered to himself, obscenities and curses, some of which she'd never heard before, not even on Papa's ships. The language of sailors was often what Papa called "fruity," but none of them had ever used words like Mickey did.

He scratched his head, replaced his hat and paced the room again. This time, he stopped halfway and perched on the edge of the dressing table, arms folded over his chest. She felt, rather than saw, the glowering look he gave her. She stared back. She might be terrified, but she'd never give him the satisfaction of knowing it.

The silence between them stretched. Diana refused to break it. That, she knew instinctively, would give him the power.

Eventually, he was the one to speak. "You caused us so much trouble," he said. "Led us on a right merry chase, you did."

She did not acknowledge him. Just sat as still as she could, face impassive, fingers around the arrow shaft in her pocket.

"Went all the way up to Norfolk, we did. Nearly got caught there. Quite a guard your auntie's got."

Good. Diana still said nothing aloud, still kept her

face as blank as she could.

"We'd still be there now, if Sam Kydd hadn't sent a message to say he'd seen you. Said he'd had to look twice. Hardly recognized you."

Diana didn't know anybody called Sam Kydd.

Mickey laughed. "Don't suppose you know him," he said, as if he'd read her mind. "But he knew you. He'd seen you, see? Coming down to your dad's office on the Wharf. That was before he got turned off, of course. Said he was thieving." The laugh was cruel. "Knowing Sam, he probably was. Course, he wasn't Sam then. Had to change his name and move away to get work. Shaved his beard, grew his hair…imagine his delight when he saw you. When he realized he could get his revenge on you and your dad."

The long-haired man! It had to be. No wonder he'd stared at her. He'd probably seen her countless times at the docks, knew her face as well as anyone's.

She hadn't thought of that as a possible source of danger. Diana hadn't been known to the *ton*, because she'd never been in London during the Season, so both she and Fremont had deemed it a safe bet that nobody from that world would recognize her. Papa's ships were all at sea, so the sailors wouldn't be there to betray her, either, and the other business interests were all far enough away that they were no threat. She'd never thought that a stevedore would remember her, and then find himself in exactly the place she'd chosen to hide.

"Course, he's dead now, so he won't be getting his revenge after all. Not that he'll see, anyway. On the bright side, we don't have to pay him. He won't need money where he's gone." He laughed again, clearly delighted at having saved his coin.

Her legs were uncomfortable from having been in one position for so long, and her bottom was growing numb, but she didn't dare move. If she did, he might see the arrow and she'd lose what little chance of escape she had.

"You didn't have to kill my brother." Mickey wiped his hand over the tip of his nose. "I ought to kill you. An eye for an eye, and all that. Fitting, really. That's in the Bible, and you killed him in a church. If the boss didn't want you so bad, I'd kill you now."

The boss. Milton Percival. The monster in a thousand nightmares.

"Whatever he's paying you," she said, "I'll double it. Let me go."

"You must think I was born last Tuesday," he sneered. "I wouldn't live long enough to spend anything you gave me."

"What if I gave my word not to go to the authorities until after you'd got away?"

He threw back his head and laughed heartily. "I ain't scared of no authorities. Been dodging them since I was six years old. But there's no money, no riches, what can get me far enough from *him*. His reach is long, and he never forgets a slight. If I betrayed him, I'd be signing my own death warrant."

"You take me to him, you'll be signing mine." She was under no illusions about that. As soon as he'd married her and laid claim to her fortune, her life wouldn't be worth a farthing.

Mickey shrugged, nonchalantly. "Better yours than mine."

He stood straight and paced the room again. Diana sat on the bed and bided her time.

****

In the drawing room, Tristan froze, the gun at his nape sending chills through him. He couldn't conceive of how Mickey had sneaked up on him. The thug didn't seem the stealthy type, yet he'd heard nothing. Not a footfall. Not a creak of a floorboard.

"Keep your hands where I can see them," said a voice behind him. Not Mickey. Educated, more upper class. Who was it? Why was he here? How did he fit in to what was happening?

"I think there's been a mistake," Tristan said, playing for time.

"My thoughts exactly." David's sardonic words were accompanied by the cocking of another pistol. The barrel of the man's gun moved from Tristan's neck and he turned to see his assailant, hands raised, allowing David to take the pistol from him.

"Who are you? And why are you here?" asked David, in his no-nonsense magistrate's tone.

"I live here," said the man. "I have every right to apprehend burglars."

"Nobody lives here," argued David.

The man grinned, though there was no humor in it. "They do now." He turned his head to see David standing behind him, pistol at his back. "I am Hadlow," he said. "And I assume you're searching for the couple who broke in earlier."

David lowered his pistol and Tristan turned fully to face Hadlow. "Do you know where he took her?"

"I do. I'm sorry I wasn't in a position to intervene when they arrived. But now, I'm armed…" He gestured to the pistol David had taken from him and David handed it back. "…and at your disposal."

"I should warn you," said David. "the man we seek is dangerous."

Hadlow nodded. "I got that impression."

"Was she hurt?" asked Tristan. The thought of Diana at the mercy of that thug was almost more than he could bear.

"She didn't appear to be. I saw no evidence of it."

"Where are they?" asked David.

"Upstairs. In one of the bedchambers."

"Which one?" Tristan started forward, but David put his hand on his arm to hold him.

"We cannot go blundering in," he said. "Not if we don't want her killed."

Tristan closed his eyes, and pushed down the blind fury engulfing him. He'd spent the whole of his military career planning and carrying out raids against the enemy. He'd always been cool, calm, and detached. Qualities which seemed to have deserted him now.

"You're right. I'm sorry."

The three men discussed the situation. All the time, Tristan was aware that Diana was up there, in that bedchamber, enduring Lord knew what at Hicks' hands. He was fidgety, anxious to rescue her, to know she was safe. He wanted to hold her, to never let her go. He needed to beg for her forgiveness for the way he'd reacted when he discovered who she was.

As if that mattered! Miss Wilde or Miss Villiers. A penniless companion or one of the wealthiest women in England. Those things meant nothing. Whatever the outer trappings, inside she was the same Diana. The woman he loved.

The plan they came up with was deceptively simple. Hadlow and David would go into the rooms on either side of the one where Hicks held Diana. As stealthily as they could, they would unlock the doors between the rooms. Then, at the agreed moment, Tristan would kick in the door to the corridor and the others would rush in from the sides, taking the villain by surprise.

"We will, of course, repair the door for you, afterward," said David, whose plan this was.

Hadlow looked pointedly around the room they stood in. The wall hangings were torn, the curtains tattered, the paint on the window frames peeling, exposing the wood which looked soft and rotten. "Why bother?" he asked. It lightened the mood, momentarily reducing the tension.

They synchronized their timepieces.

A few minutes later, Tristan stood in the corridor outside the chamber. He checked his watch one last time before he put it into his fob pocket, then took a step back, braced his leg and gave a hefty kick to the door, just above the lock.

The door buckled, the jamb broken. A second kick and it flew open, and Tristan rushed in, pistol in hand. Hadlow and David came into the room from the side doors, their pistols also raised and ready. But the sight that greeted them turned Tristan's blood to ice.

Mickey stood, back to the wall, Diana in front of him. His arm curled around her neck, a knife tip less than an inch from her throat. She stood straight, head raised, as if she tried to distance herself from the blade. One hand was in the pocket of her gown.

What happened next was both a lightning fast blur and ponderously slow. Every move was clear and precise, seeming to last eternity. The shouted threats Mickey made, David's call for him to let her go and surrender, all sounded distorted, deep and off key, the words slow and slurred. Hadlow aimed, his feet apart to better control his shot. Tristan's gun was level, ready, but his heart beat so fast, he didn't know if he would hit anything he aimed for. His eyes met Diana's briefly. He tried to give her comfort in his look. He took comfort from hers.

Slowly, carefully, she pulled something from her pocket, her hand fisting around it. Only when she had it fully out, did he recognize it as an arrow. Mickey's attention was on the three men who faced him. He yelled that they should drop their guns or he'd kill her. His knife trembled and wavered, dangerously close to her creamy skin. Tristan didn't dare breathe.

Then, with all her might, Diana drove the arrow deep into Mickey's side. He roared in pain and jerked back, letting go of her for an instant. It was enough. Diana dropped to the floor and curled into a ball.

Mickey's face twisted with ugly rage. He raised his knife, ready to plunge it into her. Three shots fired, almost simultaneously. Three balls found their marks in Mickey's chest. He jerked, then fell back and slid down the wall, landing in a heap on the floor. There was a strange look on his face. Disappointment, as if he'd somehow been cheated. Then his head lolled forward, and he died.

Tristan pulled Diana away, wrapped her in his arms and held tightly.

Time returned to normal. Sound rushed back in, at the right pitch and tempo. The smell of gunpowder and smoke was sharp in the air.

Diana pushed against Tristan. He wanted to object, to hold her close to him forever.

"I—can't—breathe," she whispered.

Her words brought him to his senses. He loosened his grip and smiled at her, apologetic, yet not.

"I thought I'd lost you," he murmured.

Behind him, he heard David say to Hadlow, "Welcome to the area. It isn't always like this. Sometimes, it's actually quite exciting here."

Hadlow laughed. The tension broke.

For now, the battle was over.

Chapter Twenty-Five

By noon the next day, most of the mess had been cleared. The smugglers had been taken to Haywards Heath to await trial. Most would hang. Those who didn't would be transported. Tristan set his volunteers to repairing the church and graveyard. In a very short time, there'd be little to no indication that anything untoward had ever happened here.

Diana was asleep. She'd spent most of the night giving David her account of what happened, and David had now gone to Haywards Heath to question the prisoners. In his capacity as magistrate, he'd found John Carter and Sebastian Thomas not guilty of the charges levelled against them, then sternly warned them not to do again the things the law said they hadn't done this time. They both swore they wouldn't.

Ella and her people had returned to Amberley, the threat having been lifted. Cassie worried Tristan, though. She was too bright-eyed, too full of nervous energy. He prayed that a few months of peace and ordinary living would bring her back to her normal self.

He'd only just sat down to a nuncheon of bread, cheese and ham when the front door knocker sounded. Grimacing, he wondered who needed him now. His instructions had been clear to his men, and Busby was more than capable of overseeing them. His stomach rumbled a protest that he might have to forgo lunch.

A moment later, his manservant showed Fremont into the room. Inwardly, Tristan groaned. The viscount was the last man he needed to see. But, being polite, he asked him to sit and eat with him.

"You had quite the party last night, I hear," said Fremont, cutting a piece of bread for himself.

"It was a little lively," agreed Tristan. "I didn't realize you were in the area or I'd have invited you."

"I was at Winchelsea."

Tristan grimaced and wondered if the captain had led his men into an ambush despite the warning he'd been given.

"You will be pleased to know your warning was taken seriously," said Fremont, as if he'd heard Tristan's thoughts. "Allenby created an ambush of his own. Sent a patrol down to the beach, as they expected him to, but kept the larger body of his men back, waiting. When the villains showed themselves, they were caught between the two, with no escape. He killed or rounded up about thirty men, and collected the contraband from three ships, all without losing a single man of his own. He's cock-a-hoop about it."

"He should be."

"He's not a bad man. A little…overzealous at times, perhaps, but he'll learn. Don't judge him too harshly." Fremont smiled, ruefully. "Advice I should take myself, perhaps. That's why I came, really." He shrugged his shoulders. "When I make an error of judgment, I own to it. And my judgment of you was flawed. I based my opinion on what I knew of your brother. It was wrong of me, and I can only apologize. Profusely."

Tristan froze, the bread halfway to his mouth, and stared at Fremont. The viscount concentrated on cutting cheese.

A moment went by. Two.

Tristan sighed. "Lancelot was always a rogue when we were children," he admitted. "Nothing bad, or malicious. Just mischief. The man he became…"

"Forget that. Remember the boy," advised Fremont.

They sat for a minute in a silence which was almost companionable. The two might never be friends, but Tristan hoped the animosity between them would disappear. Then, just as he began to relax, Fremont made him tense again, when he said, "I understand you asked Miss Villiers to marry you."

Diana must have told him, for nobody else knew, as far as Tristan was aware. His shoulders stiffened, preparing for the attack that would surely come. Fremont would tell him he was a fool, unworthy, that Miss Villiers was not for the likes of him.

Then again, he hadn't actually offered for Miss Villiers, had he? The woman he'd wanted to marry had not been the obscenely wealthy heiress, had she?

So, "No," he answered Fremont. "I did not offer for Miss Villiers. I asked Miss Wilde."

Fremont grinned. He looked strangely satisfied. "You'll do," he said. "You will do."

He stood, saying he couldn't stay, he had other visits to make before he returned to London. He walked to the door, stopped, and looked back at Tristan. "Of course, if she married, Milton Percival would no longer be a threat to her. Her fortune, controlled as it would be by her husband, would no longer be within his grasp." He paused for a second, as if to let that thought sink in. "Ask her again." Then he left the room, closing the door quietly behind him.

Ask her again? How could he? He was a poor man, almost bankrupt. He had a title, yes, but nothing to go with it. If he married Diana Villiers, of course, that would no longer be true. He'd be a very rich man. Did that make him as bad as the fortune hunters of the *ton*? Money-hungry men who waxed lyrical about the attractions of heiresses they could barely stand to look at, but whose fortunes would save their ailing estates or, more likely, allow them to continue their gambling, vice-ridden forays into London? He couldn't be like them. He would not be like them.

Then again, he wasn't like them. Was he? He hadn't asked Diana Villiers to marry him. He had, as he'd told Fremont, asked Diana Wilde. That made all the difference.

As for Milton Percival…it didn't seem fair that, in order to save her fortune from him, Diana had to give it to somebody else. It was the law, he knew. Upon marriage a woman's assets became her husband's property. But being the law didn't make it right.

He was still pondering that two hours later, when he sat in his study, unable to concentrate on anything else. It was a conundrum, to be sure.

There was a tiny knock on the door, and Diana came in. She had about her the wide-eyed look of someone not long woken from a deep sleep. Her hair was pulled back into a neat chignon, and she wore another of the drab grey dresses of a poor companion. Although she looked lovely to him as she was, Tristan would like to see her discard those gowns, replacing them with the jewel-bright colors that would suit her far better. He supposed her finery was still wherever she'd lived before she'd had to take on her disguise.

He stood and rounded his desk to come closer to her. The urge to reach out, to touch her, to hold her in his arms, was overwhelming, and he fought to keep his hands at his sides as he asked, "How are you?"

"Well, thank you. No ill effects at all." She bit her lip and lowered her gaze. "I must…that is, I should…I apologize for not telling you the truth about me."

He shook his head. "No. Don't apologize. There's nothing for you to be sorry for."

"I lied to you," she insisted.

He waved her hand as if erasing her words. "You didn't inform me of the truth. Which is not the same thing. And you had good reason."

"I hurt you."

"No. I hurt myself, and it served me right. I behaved like a petulant child. I'm the one who's sorry."

"So…you don't hate me for it?"

She looked so uncertain, so delectably unsure of herself, and his heart went out to her. He stepped forward and took her in his arms. "I don't hate you," he whispered. "I couldn't." This was it. Now or never. Tell the truth and lay his heart on the line. "I love you, Diana. Whatever last name you choose to use. Whatever your lifestyle. Rich or poor. I love you."

She looked up, her eyes shining. A tentative smile played on her lips. "You love me? After everything?"

Tristan smiled. "Nothing could stop me loving you." She bit her lip. His knees almost gave out, threatening to fell him at the sight.

"Does that mean…does your offer still stand? I mean, I will understand if it doesn't, but—"

Hope made his heart stutter. "It does. I would love you to be my wife. But on one condition. We will have the marriage settlements drawn up so that your money is your money. Your businesses are your businesses. The rest of the world won't need to know that, but I do. I don't want your money. All I want is you."

Her smile broadened and she wrapped her arms around him. "I love you so very much, Tristan Leonard. And I want to be your wife." With that, she pulled him closer. Her embrace caught on the wound in his side, and he hissed in a breath at the pain. It had been treated and dressed, and he'd been assured it was superficial, but it hurt like the devil.

She narrowed her eyes, moved her arm away from it, and gave him a stern look. "Promise me, though. There will be no more battles."

He chuckled. "I promise."

"So do I." She reached up and he leaned down, and they kissed.

Author's Note

The battle in this story was inspired by the bravery of the people of Goudhurst, a village in Kent, England, about ten miles from my home.

In the 1740s, the whole of the South Coast of England, from East Kent to Dorset, was terrorized by a band of smugglers known as "the Hawkhurst gang." They were vicious, ruthless, and determined. There were about five hundred of them at their peak, and they thought nothing of killing those they felt had opposed them: customs men, soldiers, villagers who turned down the offer to work for them, a pub landlady who mocked them. Nobody was safe.

Goudhurst is very close to Hawkhurst, where the gang originated, and it suffered greatly. People started moving away, afraid to stay. It looked as if Goudhurst would become a ghost town.

But cometh the hour, cometh the man. William Sturt, a former army corporal, decided to stand up to them. In April 1747, he persuaded the villagers to form a militia, and they made it clear the gang was not welcome.

Enraged by this, and realizing that if they didn't stop it, other villages would follow suit, the gang, led by Thomas Kingsmill, sent a threat: they would burn the village and kill all the residents unless they disbanded the militia and handed Sturt over. Their hubris was such that they set an appointed time for these actions.

The people of Goudhurst gathered in the church for safety, and the militia defended it. Many of the attacking smugglers were bared to the waist, showing off tattoos and scars in a bid to frighten and intimidate the defenders. They thought it would be an easy victory. Nobody had successfully defied them before, and they didn't expect the people of Goudhurst to do it now.

In the first volley, Kingsmill's brother was killed, and several other smugglers were wounded. By the time the battle was over, three smugglers were dead, many were injured, and the rest had fled. None of the militia were killed.

Their power broken, the Hawkhurst gang faded into obscurity. The leaders were hanged, and others were transported.

William Sturt died in 1797, at the age of 79.

A word about the author…

Caitlyn Callery lives in Sussex, southern England, near the Regency towns of Brighton and Tunbridge Wells. She is passionate about writing and suffers withdrawal symptoms when she takes a few days away from her work.

Before becoming a full-time writer, she worked in banking, as a waitress, in the motor repair industry, in a call center, and for a charity. As part of this last job, she helped build a school in Kenya, and drove a vanload of wheelchairs from the UK to Morocco.

She also loves reading, knitting, walking by the sea, the theatre and spending time with her family.

CaitlynCallery.com

Thank you for purchasing
this publication of The Wild Rose Press, Inc.

For questions or more information
contact us at
info@thewildrosepress.com.

The Wild Rose Press, Inc.
www.thewildrosepress.com

www.ingramcontent.com/pod-product-compliance
Lightning Source LLC
Chambersburg PA
CBHW072059020726
47501CB00003B/644